"Read it, Irene."

"No, George. It's embarrassing. A man of y   ith a sex manual."

"I find i

"The an

"Page s

"I don't care about my pleasure, George."

"You should."

"Sex isn't parcel post, George. You don't have to deliver the goods every time."

Hot to Trot
John Lahr

A FAWCETT CREST BOOK

Fawcett Publications, Inc., Greenwich, Connecticut

A Fawcett Crest Book reprinted by arrangement with Alfred A. Knopf, Inc.

ACKNOWLEDGMENTS
Grateful acknowledgment is made to the following for permission to reprint previously published song lyrics:

Anne-Rachel Music Corporation (Aberbach Group): Lyrics from "Honeysuckle Rose" by Andy Razaf and Thomas "Fats" Waller. Copyright 1929 by Santly Bros., Inc. Copyright renewed 1956 and assigned to Anne-Rachel Music Corporation. Used by permission.

Chappel & Co., Inc.: Lyrics from "They Can't Take That Away From Me." Copyright © 1937 by Gershwin Publishing Corporation. Copyright renewed. Used by permission.

Frank Music Corp.: Lyrics from "Take Back Your Mink" by Frank Loesser. Copyright © 1950 by Frank Music Corp. Used by permission.

Screen Gems—Columbia Music, Inc.: Lyrics from "Will You Love Me Tomorrow" by Carole King and Gerry Goffin. Copyright © 1960, 1961 by Screen Gems—Columbia Music, Inc. Used by permission. All rights reserved.

Warner Bros. Music: Lyrics from "My Special Angel" words and music by Jim Duncan. Copyright © 1957 Viva Music, Inc. All rights reserved. Used by permission.

Hy Weiss: Lyrics from "We Belong Together" by Carr-Mitchell-Weiss. Copyright © by Car-Mitchell-Weiss. Used by permission. All rights reserved.

Williamson Music, Inc.: Lyrics from: "Happy Talk." Copyright © 1949 by Richard Rodgers and Oscar Hammerstein II. Used by permission.

To Karel and Betsy Reisz
    &
Steven M. L. Aronson
    &
once again to Anthea

With admiration and enduring affection

. . . I'd like to know that your love
Is love I can be sure of
So tell me now and I won't ask again
Will you still love me tomorrow?

—Carole King & Gerry Goffin

Hot to Trot

SAY that again, Sally? I'm sitting on my new water-bed. The phone got caught in the undertow."

"I said, 'George, will you sleep with me tonight?' "

"It's my birthday. Gave myself the day off. I've been lying here listening to Ella sing Gershwin."

"I'm cashing in some of my chips, George. I need you tonight."

The first time Irene and I walked down Palisades Road to John and Sally's for dinner, every shadow spooked us. We were strangers to country life, even the silence kept us awake at night. We knew nobody in Sneden's Landing until Dad told me to look up John Prescott, a bigwig at ABC he'd done business with. The Prescotts were the first entry in our datebook—May 3, 1965. I suppose Irene wouldn't remember, she's got a one-track mind.

"George? Are you listening? Jenny's coming home from Bard. I've got last-minute shopping. Yes or no?"

"I'm supposed to meet my mother at the Christian Science Reading Room. A lecture by the author of *God Calling*."

11

"They're rerunning your 'Evenings with the One and Only Rita Hayworth.' Tonight it's *You Were Never Lovelier* with Fred Astaire. We could watch it on my king-size Easy Rest with Magic Finger attachment."

"I get teary seeing Rita."

"Oh, honestly, George, you'd cry at card tricks."

"At 11:22 p.m., Sally, I'll be thirty-six. Do you realize when we met you, Irene and I didn't have kids? I can't remember a time without kids. Maybe I better take a raincheck."

"George, you wouldn't be making decisions at ABC if it weren't for me. I'm offering a little tit for tat."

My snapshots of Tandy and George, Jr., are blown up and mounted on the wall across from my bed. They're the first faces I see in the morning. They give the new apartment a sunny, playful feeling. Tandy's dressing up in front of Irene's wardrobe mirror. It was our favorite game. Tandy's poppet-pearl choker makes her look severe, but elegant. Let's face it, she's a mature eight.

George, Jr., is on the football field in his New York Jets T-shirt and the girdle of plastic strips they use for flag football. He should be pursuing the Bronco halfback, not yelling for the rest of the team to grab him. Even at six, he's got to learn to make that great second effort.

"We have a lot to talk about, George."

"Don't rush me, Sally. How are Irene and the kids?"

"That's one of the things I think you'll want to discuss. There's been a Bentley outside your garage for three days."

"Son of a bitch! Why didn't you call me?"

"I'm telling you now."

"The license plate wasn't FL-1, was it?"

"How would I know?"

"A navy blue car with a silver statuette of Mickey Mouse on the hood?"

"That's the car, George."

"Excuse me a minute."

As I stand up, the waterbed pitches and rolls behind me as if bodies were humping on it. Outside, a freighter glides past Gracie Mansion. Mothers in the park hold children the ages of Tandy and George, Jr., up to the railing. They wave at the boat.

My "Marcus Welby, M.D." punched the heart out of NBC's "Jeopardy." I pioneered "The Partridge Family," which went up against CBS's "The Andy Griffith Show" and cornholed it. I pushed Johnny Cash into prime time and the demographics showed ABC held all the Wednesday night aces. Cash was another Batman. I'm a media "weenie." I've got a winner's rep. Irene can't do this to me. Everything I've achieved has been for her.

My cock is hard. I pick up the phone. "That longhair needs a rap in the mouth. He's got Mafia connections—all rock stars do. How do you think they get their dope? If Irene doesn't obey his every wish, she could endanger the lives of our children. She's written me a birthday card. Signed and sealed on the dresser. The jealous bastard won't let her out of the house to mail it. This isn't the first time he's tampered with the U.S. mail. Two of my child support checks were returned with 'Keep your money' scrawled on the back in an unfamiliar hand. He's trying to buy Irene's affection. He's ruthless. That 'wrong number' I got two hours ago was probably Irene breathing. She's too terrified to speak. I warned him to stay away. His ass is grass!"

"You'll be here, then?"

"George Melish—the shit-kicker and city slicker."

"What time?"

"I'll see you when I see you."

"I'm counting on you, George."

"One thing, Sally."

"Hurry up, this call's costing a fortune."

"Do you love me?"

"George, this is Sally Prescott, 'La Presidente—La Grande Horizontale.' Love is a tennis score."

I ring up to cancel Mom. She says it doesn't matter about tonight. She says she's gotten used to being alone. She wishes me a happy birthday. "You were born under a lucky star, George. I hope you thank God."

I mix myself a quick V and V—Valium and vermouth. It does the trick.

The MG is my style: lean and mean. Sometimes I park it outside Friday's when I'm cruising for crumpet up First Avenue. I ask a passerby to sit in the driver's seat to see how I look.

I look tough.

The "Avenger" has everything. Hand-painted racing green chassis. AM-FM radio. Tape deck. Telephone. Police aerial. Fuel injection. On a sunny Saturday, I can sit with the top down for half an hour inhaling the smell of sweating leather from the bucket seats. After nine years of a station wagon and plastic seat covers, it's fun to sink into the saddle and ride solo.

The "Avenger's" engine hums as we pace the slowpokes going uptown on the West Side Highway. I turn up the car radio as loud as it will go. Let the old and good times roll!

You're mine
And we belong together
Yes, we belong together
For all eternity.

They're excavating our music. They're turning me and my generation into "golden oldies." I was wearing my blue madras Bermuda shorts the first night I heard Robert and Johnny sing that song. I can still feel the deep Atlantic Beach sand in my black knee socks as I chugalugged a Ballantine. Bonni Dubermann, my date, applauded coyly. By firelight, the Clearasil patches were completely hidden on her face. She looked beautiful.

A few weeks after the news of my separation hit the columns, I got a call from Angie. He'd just given up his photography studio to take a big job at BBD&O. He asked me over to play poker with some of the executives. After four years, it was nice to see him again. Angie spun some of the old sounds. "We Belong Together" was one of them.

"Melish, baby, the Four F's are forever," Angie said, taking the cellophane off the plate of roast beef sandwiches. "Find 'em. Feel 'em. Fuck 'em. Forget 'em." Angie could always make me laugh. And he was right.

Straddling the divider lines across the George Washington Bridge, I buzz north along the Palisades, whipping around the curves so that my tires squeal on the asphalt. The "Avenger" knows every bend in the road to Sneden's Landing; it's the perfect vehicle for these search and destroy missions. I've blitzed our house many times since Irene got the injunction against me. I didn't say I'd slit the Big Bopper's throat, that's lawyer's double-talk. I said I'd slit his tires. And I did.

I walk down the street now, thinking, "I could fuck you and you and you." I look the foxes in the eye. They stare back. The sap is running. The salmon in me is going upstream. I must give off a sense of experience—an odor, a musk. I wonder if they can sniff out the ten years of marriage, the hefty five-figure salary, the sexual athlete underneath this three-piece herringbone tweed. They don't know me. They may think they know me, but they don't. Irene didn't. My mystery is catfish-deep in my Ivy League soul.

I look polite. I was brought up properly. I went to Miss Harris' Dancing Class and was made a Bachelor of Foxtrot. I'm the only executive at ABC with an MA Oxon.

I was raised in the tradition of gentlemen. Not any more, lady. All these years of living my prep school motto: "The other fellow first." Forget it, jim. I'm going to kick ass. 1974 is not too late. Maybe I'll date black for a few years, one of those high-toned spades with long legs and crow-black hair and light blue eye shadow. A few heads would turn at "21." Kids don't think anything of it anymore. I can remember when just the thought gave me a hard-on. Maybe I'll try boys. That's cool, too.

Irene doesn't know shit from Shinola. Why shouldn't I go out to the old homestead? I've got a date down the road, sweetheart. I'm the birthday boy.

> *Georgie cuts the cake,*
> *Georgie cuts the cake,*
> *Hi-ho, the dairy-o*
> *Georgie cuts the cake.*

Mom holds the mocha cake with my name and the number "9" iced on it up to my face. She hushes the other boys quiet. "Wish for something big, George."

I blow out the candles. My friends applaud.

Mother puts her hand on my shoulder. Her charm bracelet jangles. "What did you wish for, darling?"

"To go fishing this summer."

Mom lights another candle. "Try again."

I puff and then look up at her smiling face. "I asked to be a doctor."

"Good boy."

It's my house. It's my wife. I built and paid for them both. I should knock on the door. I should demand a hearing. If I have to stay out of my house, where does FL-1, alias Fat Lip, alias Fucking Lothario, code name Pussyface, get off trespassing on private property? I told Irene when I found out, "Take the house. I won't stand in your way." She took it. Six months ago, *Better Homes and Gardens* ran a two-page spread about it. FL was lounging on the sofa in the background, as inconspicuous as a Pole at a wedding. The bitch didn't even have the decency to use her married name. We're not divorced, yet.

The next day I bought the "Avenger."

My lawyer tells me he's negotiating "liberal visiting privileges." It's my home, not a hospital. She said she'd keep the house for the kids' sake. What about me?

Before I was suspended from the League of Legitimate Parents, I saw Tandy and George, Jr., once every one hundred and thirty-six hours. A car delivered them at ten on Saturday and picked them up at six Sunday night. Not a word—never even a note—from their mother. Irene was glad to pack them off so she could fuck herself blind with that scrawny pothead. The woman's as promiscuous as a pigeon.

Rolling on my waterbed is not the same as Irene's squeaky four-poster. I remember after Tandy was born, we'd lie with her between us. We were all nude. The room smelled of starch and summer sun. I'd watch them both—mother and daughter—breathing in unison. Tandy reclined like a woman—one knee raised, the other sprawled languidly against mine. At five months, I knew she'd be a stunner: that lovely, bulging ribbon of fat where her breasts would be; those delicate, touching fingernails which someday would be buffed and polished like her mother's. Even the little slit between her legs was fetching. Tandy slept in perfect peace. Her pudgy hands stretched out—palms up—on our chests.

A month ago, on our last weekend together, Tandy called me George. That's because her mother calls me George.

Irene used to call me Pooper.

Tandy used to call me Dadda.

"You'll find Sneden's Landing a great place to raise kids," Sally says, handing me the croutons for the pea soup.

The Prescotts' daughter pushes open the pantry door and passes through the dining room carrying a cup of cocoa on a small tray. " 'Night, Mom. 'Night, Dad."

"Jenny, meet the Melishes. His father's the man who produced your favorite film."

"Run Riot?"

"That's my father."

Jenny grins, peeking at me from underneath her bangs. She's got Prescott's deep-set brown eyes and Sally's lanky torso. Jenny looks down at her bare feet and the flannel pajamas already too high above her ankles. "Are you from around here?"

"We just moved in. Stop by some afternoon."

"Got any children?"

"Not yet," Irene smiles.

"Have more than one," Jenny says and continues out of the room. "Nice to meet you," she adds without turning around.

We concentrate on the soup. Finally, Sally looks up. "Twelve's a difficult age."

"You think she'd like to go on a movie set? Dad's just starting *Crazy Sunday*."

"She'd love it," Sally says, touching my hand. "So would I."

"I like kids, but I'm scared of having them. The noise. The mess. The bother."

"It's too late to worry," Irene says, glancing sternly at me.

"When you think of how long kids have to put up with our quirks," Prescott says, "I think we can put up with theirs for a few years."

Irene laughs. "I must remember that. It's a nice thought."

"He's great on theory, dear," Sally says.

"I was an only child, too. Things get better once you get into college."

"Where'd you go?" Sally asks.

"Yale."

"So did John."

At the Landing, I park the car by the water. I take the scenic foothpath which winds uphill a half mile past Jerome Robbins' shack and Katharine Cornell's old house to the Hancocks' garden. In the corner of the garden is the treehouse—my home away from home. From here, I can see straight across the road and into our bedroom.

Except for his hookah and the poster of His Highness looking like Jesus Christ with the words SPIRIT IN THE FLESH scrawled around his head like a halo and POSITIVE ENERGY over each bicep—nothing's changed. The velvet hangings (Irene called it a whore's boudoir— how right she was!), the canopy, the marble bathroom with sunken tub and waterspouts the shape of fishheads, the Chippendale breakfront with my first editions of Dickens, the kids' pictures above the bed. It's just as I left it.

In the summer, we'd leave the window open and watch the moon rise over this oak tree. We'd keep each other awake and make love in the glow. Moonlight love, she told me, is lucky love.

Nine-forty-five by my Benrus. Irene still keeps to her old schedule (the woman's a robot). The children should be bathed and in bed. She's kneeled down with them and said the Lord's Prayer. I wonder if I'm still in their "God Blesses." Soon, she'll be taking off her makeup.

"How do I look, George?" Irene says, opening the bedroom door and parading her black velvet cocktail dress. She holds her skirt with one hand and her tennis bag with the other.

" 'Now awful Beauty puts on all its charm.' "

"Too much makeup?"

"Painted means tainted."

"It's too much, is it?"

"Compared to the first time I saw you at the Merton Commem. Ball, this is positively Quaker."

"Some people thought me dramatic, actually."

"Gold lamé boots? A serpent bracelet halfway up your arm? That's not dramatic, that's Hollywood."

"I don't like being teased." Irene sits on the windowsill and looks down at the sundial in the Fellows' Garden. "When I was little I wrote plays for myself. I acted the King and the Queen. I stood on the steps to the Great Parlor and made my nanny listen. Sometimes I let her play a slave. I'm a tragic figure."

"The Lorelei of London."

"What's that supposed to mean?"

"The first female to stalk me in my university rooms. A temptress on virgin territory."

"Sorry about dinner tonight," Irene says, putting on her coat. "You should've rung me earlier."

"I called Wednesday."

"That's too late for the weekend. I try to keep busy."

"What about tennis next week? This time we'll go to dinner. I'll stroll you around Oxford. Maybe I'll pitch a little American woo."

Irene takes out her datebook. "I can do Wednesday or Thursday."

"Can't do the weekdays. Exams coming up. How's the weekend?"

"I'm afraid I'm booked up."

"One of your Etonians? Change it."

"That's just not on, George."

"Do you like me or not?"

"Of course I like you. But one's got to have many beaux to one's string. Thursday'd be super."

"Studying."

"At Oxford, term time is for socializing. The vacs are for study."

"See this picture, Irene? That's my Mom and Dad. This picture was taken at the Academy Awards. Dad has three. More than any other independent producer in America."

"Hollywood's so terribly vulgar."

"There's nothing cheap about Dad's fame, Irene. Sometimes fame's quick, but it's never easy. America's no island. It's a continent with a hundred and eighty million people. Dad works hard to stay up there. It's not power in any ordinary sense."

"It's all Cadillacs and sunglasses and big cigars. All that waste. It's sick-making."

"It's something knowing you're in other people's minds. Even if Dad died tomorrow, the idea of Sol Melish would be preserved in his films. Think of the medieval frescos with the gold halos around the saints. Fame's like that. After these exams, I'm finished with my education. I don't want to waste a minute. I want light around me."

"You expect so much."

"What's wrong with that?"

"Dreaming always gets me into trouble. I stop myself. If you don't dream, you're not disappointed."

I slip my hand behind Irene's ears, into her auburn hair. I lift it slowly. Her hair dangles to each side in well-combed clumps like a spaniel's ears.

"Do I look sexy?" Irene says.

"I want to show you something, Miss Tempesto Trewin."

I march Irene to the mirror. I put her hands behind her back. She leans against my chest.

"I'm already late, George. It was sweet of you to let me change in your rooms. Thanks awfully for the game."

"I'm not going to bite you. I'm going to play ventriloquist. I'm putting my arms where yours should be."

"No sudden movements, George."

"Mouth the words to my song as if you knew them."

"I look like Kali," she says. "Or an octopus."

"Watch the mirror and listen.

"Happy talk, keep talkin' happy talk,
Talk about things you'd like to do . . ."

Irene's head bobs in tempo with the song. She giggles at herself in the mirror.

"You got ta have a dream,
If you don't have a dream
How you gonna have a dream come true?"

"That tickles," Irene says, swatting my hands as they scratch her flat stomach instead of belting out another chorus.

"Always leave 'em laughing."

"You've a good sense of humor, George. I'll say that." Irene picks up her tennis bag and kisses me good-bye. At the door, she turns back. "You never said whether I was sexy."

"You're very cute, Miss Chubby Cheeks."

"I'm very sexy, actually."

"If you say so."

"Call me," Irene says. Then, arching her left eyebrow, she adds, " 'It's not the men in my life. It's the life in my men.' "

Irene sits in front of the mirror brushing her hair. She stares at the pictures of the Maharaj Ji in the Mark Cross frame where I used to be. One hundred and twenty strokes—count 'em—before breakfast and bed—she's eligible for the *Vogue* Olympics. After a shower, her hair smelled like mown hay. She never let me touch it with my hands or my hairbrush. But sometimes when we woke up her hair blanketed my face. I loved nuzzling into that Happy Hooker's mane.

She wore panties and bra in my era. She wouldn't take

off her nightdress until the lights were out. But now she's
Miss X-rated and Liberated. She sits there with her robe
open, with her breasts edged out so I can see the firm,
pug-nosed nipples. She's got a fishwife's tongue, but those
breasts are still friends. The first pleasure of our marriage
was making their acquaintance. No more grabbing BT.
No more Maidenform clasps to jimmy. Those breasts
were Irene's dowry. They lay flat and full on her chest
like pizza dough. They were tasty.

The points I racked up!

The waitress puts two glasses of water on our table. She
hurries away in search of menus.

Angie stares out The Peach Tree window. "I took a
bath on the College Boards. Five hundred in English.
Five-fifty in math. What'd you get, Meli?"

"Six hundred across the board."

"They posted the term grades. I held at nineteenth in
the class. You moved up to twelfth. Faggot!"

The waitress swoops down on us with the menus. She
takes out her pad. "May I help you?"

Angie gulps down his water. "Can I pinch your ass for
a quarter?"

"What?"

"Can I please have another glass of water?"

The waitress refills our glasses. We order the usual—
two egg creams and a large plate of French fries.

Angie waves at a girl passing by.

"I'd like to dip my wick into that."

"Fuckable."

"Who is she? C'mon, Angie. I gave you the answers to
the Spanish test."

Angie bites a French fry. "Helen Popkin. She's my
cousin. Bitchin', huh?"

"The one from Scarsdale?"

"Herself."

"Does she really do it?"

"They don't call her the Finger Bowl for nothing."

"Round heels, huh?"

"The roundest."

"Fix me up, Angie."

"You couldn't handle the action, Mr. Six-Hundred-Across-The-Board."

"I bet I could."

Angie smiles. "Is this a challenge?"

" 'You betcha, Red Ryder.' "

Angie takes out his pen and turns over The Peach Tree doily. He scribbles on it for five minutes. He slides the paper over to me. "Read the small print."

THE SEX SWEEPSTAKES

Rules of the Game

French Kiss	1 pt.	(First Base)
Hickie	2	
Breast	3	(Second Base)
Bare tit (BT)	4	
Tit to mouth	5	
Crotch shot	6	
Downstairs	7	(Third Base)
Hand job	8	
Blow job	9	
Around the world	15	
Home run (*with protection*)	20	
Home run bareback	30	(The Grand Slam)

"Sign on the bottom, lunchbag," Angie says. "The winner gets to name his present. And I know just what I want."

I write my name. "Don't be so cocky. The game's not over till the last out."

Angie takes back the pen and completes the contract. "You're the intellectual, Meli. You keep score."

"Only the laundress will know how excited I am."

"Remember The Kid's motto: 'When in doubt, whip it out.' "

We shake on it.

There he is: Elvis Presley II. He throws his clothes around the room as if he owned the place. He's got one of those small asses, the kind that fits snugly into the newest clothes. He wears no underwear under those hip huggers. Bum-boy. Fag-bait. He's green. He's got no intellectual qualifications (guitarists don't need degrees). He hasn't even fought for his country.

How can Irene let his hand stroke her back? He has calluses on his fingers from thumping that electric guitar. I was never callous.

Doesn't Irene understand that she's nothing but an instrument to him? He'll step on her like his wah-wah pedal. He'll smash her to smithereens the way he does his Fender 500 on stage. The kids love it. But adults? If I could see Irene, I'd explain. The English don't understand about psychiatry. Anybody with the rudiments of Erich Fromm can see that the guitar symbolizes a woman. FL's libido is fixated at a masturbatory level. He can't feel for others. A guitar won't talk back, Irene, it's a lover and a weapon. He needs electronic sensation to penetrate that crush of tight skin and tattoos. He's deaf from amplifiers, numb from dope, played out from all those one-night stands. What security will you have in twenty years when they're not playing his music? The man's a mental midget. What will you talk about then? You'll be fifty-three—almost dead. He'll be enjoying the prime of life.

The treehouse is great cover. I can even make out an occasional word. "Him," Les Paul is saying to Mary Ford. They're talking about me—laughing, comparing notes. They probably think of me during their kinky capers to give their coupling a little juice. I was a six-penny man; he can't even balance three on his ding-a-ling.

Irene laughs. Her teeth are alabaster white from years of careful brushing.

He sits on the corner of the bed and picks his toes.

Irene sprays herself with the perfume atomizer. Joy by Patou. My favorite scent ($85 an ounce). When I gave it to her two Christmases ago, drunk on eggnog from the Prescotts' Yule Fool, she said, "Perfume's a spiritual deodorant. Keeps the decay from smelling." Flighty twat.

"Good," I heard Lady Chatterley saying to Mellors Hendrix. I've thought of bringing my skeet gun here. It'd be as easy as the binoculars. I could pepper them with shot: scar them for life. I could kill them both at once, or one at a time. A *crime passionnel*. Why bother? When Bo Diddley leaves her and she's hysterical, calling his name up the hill as the red taillights of the Bentley slither around the bend, maybe I'll come out of hiding and comfort her. Maybe I won't.

Irene stands between his legs. He kisses her belly. He follows the rivulet of hair with his nose until it comes to rest on her belly button. Irene was always hairy. She should've shaved more. In the winter, she was elegant cashmere on the outside; but inside, Spanish peasant.

She's tossing the chiffon robe behind her. She's on her knees. The Woman's a thirty-three-year-old, married groupie! A society scrubber!

"Nobody will remember you got a fourth," Irene says, taking the Oxford English Honours List from *The Times* and throwing it in the wastebasket outside Waterloo Station.

"I will."

"You're a talented, wonderful person."

"I wanted to go back to America feeling in fat city. My credentials in order for the cruel world. Believe me, I've never failed at anything before."

Irene takes my arm. We stroll along the embankment. "Is this an omen, Irene?"

She kisses my cheek. "You studied too hard."

"I really need that vacation now. Are you coming with me to Greece?"

"That depends."

We lean against the embankment railing and stare across at the Houses of Parliament. "I thought we'd agreed."

"Don't be angry, George. I like you very, very much. I know you respect me. I know we trust each other, and that what we have is special."

"Then it's settled."

"I don't want to displease you, George. But couldn't we just sleep beside each other?"

"I've heard your abortion lecture. There are plenty of girls in this town who'd love to go on an all-expenses-paid holiday for two weeks. I've known many women, but who's counting? I don't need waves, especially not now."

"If you want it, George, then I'll do it."

"Girls tell me I'm very good."

"I've long ago given up trying to please myself. I just don't know if this is right for us."

"Nothing is unnatural."

"We'd be in the same room, the same bed, the same shower—everything. That guarantees twenty-four hours a day together. I could wake up and find you near me."

"My tutor guaranteed I'd be vivaed for a first.

"Next week, then?"

"OK."

Irene hugs me. "I'd almost forgotten that something nice could be guaranteed."

Irene's hair cascades over Buddy Holly's lap. She puts his old dog deep into her mouth—no hesitation, no talk. Last night, it was probably *Last Tango in Paris*—one brick of Blue Bonnet margarine up her wazoo. Tonight, they're running through *Deep Throat*. Irene's got none of that icy coldness—the killer's heart. She's famished but gentle. She likes performing this unnatural act. The first time Irene did me, she made me wear a Trojan. That must have been as big a treat as licking a Good Humor in its wrapper.

He leans back on the bed with the palms of his hands. His legs fold around her. His eyes are shut. Irene's body sways with him. She looks up. Her mouth is shiny and still eager. He puts his hands on her shoulders. She kisses them, then bends back to her dinner. Her tongue scrapes every ridge. Her hair falls in her way. She frees one hand to brush it back so she can see her delight more clearly. Her head rotates with the movement of his body. He pushes himself deeper into her mouth. This woman's a pelican!

They make me sick. They don't have the decency to turn out the light. Somebody could be taking the night air. Love is mystery. Love is quest. The old slap and tickle. These two tear at each other like dogs.

Where's the romance?

Where's the love-play?

"Read me the erogenous zones," I say to Angie, both hands on the steering wheel, the rubber sole of my white bucks too heavy on the gas pedal. We wind our way along the Merritt Parkway.

"This is neat," Angie says, turning up the radio.

"In the glove compartment."

"Shoo-dooten-shoo-be-dah. Shoo-dooten-shoo-be-dah. In the still of the nigh-ight, tell me you love me, hold me tigh-ight. For I love only you—ooh. Promise you'll always, always be true—ooh!"

Angie opens the compartment and pulls out the paperback of *Love Without Fear*. "Don't sweat my cousin, Meli. You'll go into second standing up."

"First date?"

"I got pelt with her friend. Met her outside Temple Emanu-El. I didn't know her name."

"Where'd you do it?"

"We took a cab ride through Central Park. Those panty girdles are murder." Angie slides down in the seat, keeping his balance by propping his saddle shoes on the dashboard.

"Try page fifty."

" 'The degree of stimulation which is attained by both partners from mouth to mouth kissing is usually heightened if the love-play proceeds downwards toward the genital regions. The neck provides a pathway, for it is highly sensitive, especially to the tongue kiss . . .' "

"These erogenous zones could mean big points."

" 'Most women like to have their breasts kissed. They say no word, but move their breasts invitingly toward the lover's mouth. The tongue kiss around the breasts and applied to the nipples is usually found to be the most stimulating to both partners.' "

"You think the girls know about this?"

"The clitoris is really the buzzer. Opens all the doors. Listen to this! 'The clitoris is a small organ just above (though inside) the lips of the vagina. Masturbation of the clitoris usually ends in clitoral orgasm. This is a very powerful mechanism of erotic pleasure. One thing is certain—sexual intercourse should only be indulged in when there is a natural desire to express mutual love.' "

"Does it feel like a wong?"

Angie holds up his pinkie. "The size of a fingernail. When you find it—wow!"

We turn off at Purchase Street. "That's Winston's house. His father owns the Hope Diamond."

"Who gives a shit when we've got the clit."

"I once went down to his office. He's a little man, smaller than us. He took me into his vault. He made me hold out my hands. Know what he put in them? Packets of thousand-dollar bills. I had a half-million dollars in my hands. I was thirteen."

"Stop the car. Stop the car!" Angie says. I pull over to the side of the road just before his cousin's driveway. "A nookie cram course. Look at this." We inspect a diagram marked: "Appendix B: Genitalia."

Angie looks at himself in the mirror. He flattens down the front of his hair. " 'Mirror, mirror on the wall, who's the fairest of them all,' " he says in falsetto. Then, deeper, he adds: "You are, big boy."

The girls are already on the porch waving hello.

"Whoever loses on points pays for the gas," Angie says. He pinches my nipple as we roll into the driveway.

In thirty-five years not one woman ever clamped the Wailing Monkey (position 45) on my sturdy rod. And I asked. From that first moment, I was ready. I read that manual backwards and forwards until I was twenty-five and married. I knew the highways and byways. I could hum the five rules to sexual harmony like Gilbert and Sullivan. 1) Learn how to love and make love. 2) Realize that love is as much for you as for others. 3) Don't neglect your body (three years on the grapefruit diet after she said I looked disgusting in my boxer shorts). 4) If possible get to know each other really well. (That's what it said.) 5) In love, everything is acceptable.

I forgot my dead father. I can't remember my mother's phone number or next season's video lineup or my new address. But those first unalterable, clear-cut rules in the art of love are branded on my skull. What did I earn for my diligence? (After all, how many other guys cared enough to read up on women?) Where did it get me? Answer: twenty feet up an oak tree, squatting in the shadows of a damp treehouse watching the marital congress over which I was president for two full terms of incredible productivity and prosperity being dissolved.

Eustace Chesser is Santa Claus.

This very minute, as Irene rubs down that Everly Brother, there are at least four million of New York's eight million sprawled on sheets and rugs. Couples of all creeds and colors are banging the bedsprings, whimpering in pleasure, panting "Did you come?" I got nothing on a silver platter. My father was right: You make your breaks. George Melish, you can take pride in that. You didn't loaf. You had to work your fingers to the bone for every piece of ass. You should've learned your lesson the first time. You followed that mythic clitoris like Ponce de Leon and the Fountain of Youth. He found Florida: you discovered child support. Schmuck!

Dancing is my best approach. I pull Helen Popkin and her 32-B's close to my Lacoste shirt. At five-foot-two, her head rests just below my shoulder. I angle my head toward hers. I do a few dips and a quick turn. I inch closer.

"Not so fast, mister," Helen says. Her hand slips off my shoulder and pushes me gently back.

As proof of my good intentions, I do the Deerfield

Pump. Helen leans back in my arm. We talk as we spin around. This is how Fred Astaire does it in *Shall We Dance?* and how Miss Harris teaches. Nothing touches.

"I don't mind the camphor balls, do you?"

"It's typical of Angie's grandmother," Helen says. "This beautiful house and she treats it like a closet when she's away."

"She's a nice old lady."

"She's a tightwad. She'll only pay for my college tuition if I go to Smith."

"I'm aiming for Yale."

Helen smiles at me. "Who's your favorite author?"

"F. Scott Fitzgerald. 'So we beat on, boats against the current, borne back carelessly into the past.' Fitzgerald wrote that when he was twenty-seven."

"You're cute," Helen says, pecking my cheek with her lips. An arid kiss, it leaves no memory.

"You're not bad yourself."

Girls are like fishing—don't rush and keep your tip up. My tip is up. I pull my Shetland sweater as far down as it will stretch. I put on Little Richard for a change of pace. We lindy. Each time Helen moves close, I spin her away in a new step. I make her look good. We do the Jersey Bounce. I break her into my body. Both hands around my neck, her tight ass brushes each knee. I pass her between my legs and yank her back up. She's shiny with sweat, and breathless. She's holding my hand at the end of the dance.

Angie and Jane come into the living room. He's got her sweater around his neck; her blouse is unbuttoned to the third button—a good sign. Angie's lips have a red haze around them. "Keep it down, you guys. I don't want breaking and entering on my report card."

Angie turns down the lights and puts on Frank Sinatra.

Helen and I dance cheek to cheek. Angie swings Jane around and looks at me. He flashes five fingers.

I bend down and lift up Helen's chin. We kiss gently.

"My kisses don't come cheap," she says. Angie turns out the light. Helen and I go behind the sofa. Angie and Jane stay by the fire.

Helen's tongue wedges in my mouth. I put my legs between hers. I feel her move beneath me. Her breasts grind into my chest.

"May I touch you?"

"Don't spoil it, George."

My left hand works its way up her rib cage. She puts her hand on mine. "No. I'm not that kind of girl."

"It would mean a lot to me."

"Only the outside?"

"Cross my heart."

I kiss her ear. I breathe heavily into it. This does nothing for me; but Angie says next to Spanish fly it's the best thing—and I need the points. Her chest is heaving. Her legs tighten around mine. Her skirt rustles.

"Don't, George. Please?"

"They're so beautiful."

"I'm a virgin."

"I respect that."

The left hand's as important for bras as it is for basketball. I fast-break up her chest, feeling my way along the patterned cups of her bra to the strap. A quick snap of the thumb and index finger and I'll have scored. "Goddammit."

"It's in the front, George." Helen pushes up and unclasps her bra. She leans back as my fingers slip under it.

"Helen?"

"Darling?"

"Would you touch me down there?"

"Don't ask me."

"I wouldn't ask you if I didn't respect you."

"You'll talk like all the rest."

"That's the difference between men and boys. Boys

talk. I'm a man." I push up on my elbow and look at her.
Helen's shirt is off, her bra dangles around her shoulders.

"Promise this isn't just physical."

"I really think you're special."

Helen takes my hand and starts to lower it into extra
bases. I should be thinking of her, but I'm thinking of
Appendix B—

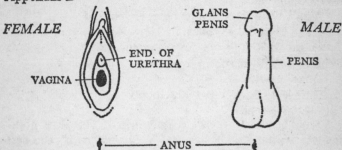

FEMALE

GLANS PENIS

MALE

END OF URETHRA

PENIS

VAGINA

ANUS

My body shivers. My pants are wet. (Thank God the
lights are out.) I pull my hand back. "I don't want to take
advantage, Helen. I want to save something for later."

"Touch me, George."

"Next time, I may really touch you. I may engage in
the full stimulation of love—everything from top to bottom. I'm a very passionate person. I may do things you've
never felt. But I will never lose control, Helen. I will
never take advantage."

Helen hugs me. "Will you take me to the Fourth of
July dance at Old Oaks? I'll have a tan. I'll look great."

"That'd be fun. I'd hold you very close. I'd touch your
knees under the table. We could talk."

I kiss her cheek. She giggles. "You like to talk, don't
you? And read."

" 'A little learning is a dangerous thing; Drink deep or
taste not the Pierian spring.' Know what I mean?"

"Are you saying that relationships should be a mixture
of the intellectual and the physical?"

"That's it."

"Most people don't realize that."

"I'll call you."

"Lester Lanin will be playing in person."

"Can we sit at a table by ourselves?"

Helen kisses my eyes. "When you call, if my father answers, hang up."

"You're with a gentleman now, Helen."

Later, on the way back to New York, I pull the car into a gas station. I honk for the attendant.

"How long does sperm live, Angie?"

"Long enough."

Angie leans back with both elbows over the seat.

"I'll pay, Angie."

He grins.

With me, Irene had to have sheets over her. Fucking was like fighting your way through a clothesline. With him, she rolls on my king-size bed like Isadora Duncan.

I wear my wedding ring. I don't know why. Irene doesn't. It was no two-dollar Motel Kit from Woolworth's I slipped on her finger, either. That was good enough to get Helen and Sue and Jeannie past the front desk. But Irene got the real thing and I got a lifetime's free pass to her all-star body.

That ring was safe harbor. I remember touching it as we went hand in hand through our first New York cocktail party. We'd been in the city four months. I'd been editing the *Life* house newspaper and was angling for the science desk. What do you do? people would ask. "I'm a writer." What do you *really* do? they'd say. I'd touch Irene's ring and think of the shower we'd take later and feel that nothing else mattered.

When I joined ABC, I bought a ring for myself. It gave me an air of maturity. It said to everybody, including

Irene, I was not to be tempted; I was at work. Now, when people ask me what I do, I just lay the name ABC on them. I can see them relax. They take note and imagine the rest. But I still catch myself touching my ring finger. My gold band was never blessed, but it made me feel lucky.

I consider us a double-ring ceremony, Irene.

As I tiptoe to my room, the light behind their door clicks on.

"George," Mom whispers. "You're late."

"I doubled with Angie. His cousin in Scarsdale."

"What about those nice girls from Miss Harris', George? There's nothing wrong with gentile girls. I went to a convent."

" 'Night, Mom."

"Sleep tight, George."

I stuff my underwear down below the dirty sheets at the bottom of the hamper. I look at myself in the full-length mirror. Stomach flat. Muscles tight and bulging. Underarm hair coming along.

I sit on the edge of the bed. I glance at the pinup of Rita Hayworth kneeling in her negligee on silk sheets. I say my prayers.

Helen would look like Rita in the raw.

In bed, with the lights out, I smell my right hand. Helen's perfume and perspiration are still on it.

I roll on my stomach. I put the pillow under my chest. I slide against the clean sheets.

"Don't say anything, darling. I'm going to give it to you. I'm going to burrow inside you. I'm going to ram you . . . so deep . . . so deep you'll choke. Relax, Helen. I'm good. Put your legs around me. That's right. Wider. Higher. Oh Rita, marry me . . ."

The shiver again, and the tingle. I lie on my back. The dampness feels nice against my skin.

The soiled sheets don't matter. Maddy'll change them in the morning.

I can't believe I was wrong about you, Irene. I've been educated to know quality. ABC pays me handsomely to make casting and script decisions. You were perfect for Mrs. George Melish. Innocent, eager, attractive, you were the right counterpoint to my urbane gregariousness. Pictures don't lie, Irene. What about us sitting suntanned and smiling at that seaport *taverna* in Greece. That used to be in your bedside table with our love letters. We were such a nice couple. Many people remarked on it. They needed us to be happy. We still could be.

Strike that. Listen to her moan! She'll wake the children. She's got the morals of Nineveh, my wife! Has she no shame?

Bless me, Father, for I have sinned. It has been one week since my last confession. These are my sins:

I have lied to my parents.

I have had unchaste thoughts.

I have taken the name of the Lord in vain.

I have forgotten my morning prayers.

I have eaten meat on Friday.

I have had sex with a woman.

"Was this coitus?" says the voice in the darkness behind the screen.

"I don't think so, Father."

If she'd just open my letters, she'd see I've changed. I'm slimmer than I was—the snapshots show that. My check-

book balances and I pay my own bills. I wash the dishes.
I spend more time off the job. I'm not like Joe Cocker in
there, I don't dress messy. If people look at me, they
know I've had an East Coast education. But, in the par-
lance of the underground papers, I'm "into pleasure." Dig
it, Irene. My office has Mies van der Rohe furniture; my
apartment has a waterbed and a Jacuzzi Whirlpool for
tandem baths. I've got a two-year subscription to *Swhopper,* the magazine "For People Who Dare To Be Different." This separation has done more for me than
Wonder Bread.

And she said I was stuck in my ways.

She told the marriage counselor that sex wasn't that
important. (I am good. And getting better.)

"I want something of my own to look forward to."

"This is what's sending me up the wall. *This!*"

"The phone rings and it's for George. The dinner parties, including our close friends the Prescotts, are his
business acquaintances. With two small children to look
after, what's for me? I never knew he'd be so successful."

She made me sound like an Ivy League Lon Chaney.
Now that I'd landed myself on Boardwalk was I supposed
to go back to Baltimore Avenue? As they say in Hollywood, her unhappiness was "bankable." It was her most
fundable asset. I could see Mrs. Bogner was moved. Sure,
Irene was a foreigner; I was only third-generation myself.
OK, it was sad that her father choked on a piece of steak
and died. And worse that she'd felt like an orphan in her
own home even when he was alive. But we were together.
We had a family. We saw interesting people and did interesting things. In television a show's success is measured
by its share of the audience. Anything less than thirty-
three-and-one-third percent and you kill the show. Our
marriage had higher happiness numbers than that. It de-
served to keep going.

"I feel I should be doing more with my life."

"The Could Have's, the Should Have's, the Would Have's—that's all dream time! What counts is what *is*. If you're unhappy, forget about your almost-free verse and do something."

"See," she said, turning to Mrs. Bogner, a pleasant white-haired lady whose book *Let's Love Right* is in its ninth large printing. Irene held her arms wide and her palms up as if she'd proved Einstein's theory of relativity.

I didn't stamp my foot or point an accusing finger during our session with Mrs. Bogner. I was very quiet. My calm maturity was a dramatic contrast to Irene's predictable hysteria. I told her so afterward at the coffee shop. Irene has an annoying way of cutting off an argument. She flies that beautiful hair in your face. She turns that aquiline nose to the side and recrosses those thin, sharp knees. I tossed a quarter on the table. "Well, I'm leaving. If you want to sit here doing your lame impersonation of the Sphinx, you've got my permission."

"That dig about my almost-free verse wasn't funny either, George."

"At least I didn't go into a This-Is-Your-Life-Irene-Melish routine."

"You always belittle."

"Those are jokes. They're not nasty. They're a way of having fun."

"At my expense."

"C'mon," I said, chucking her under the chin. "Let's go."

"See, George. I'm a plaything. A doll. I want to be a goddess."

"And I want to be Jeff Chandler."

"Forget it," she said and stood up. We walked back to the car in silence. She never mentioned the incident again.

George Melish is ready for pleasure! My senses are on

Red Alert. My orifices say All Systems Go. Chinese basket jobs—why not? Twenty-four-hour marathons, followed by Tantric orgies—how sweet it is. Casanova's my name, scoring the game. Since I walked out that door, baby, I've been in training for the Permissive Society Pentathlon. There's a cornucopia on every corner. And nothing disgusts me, sweetheart, not even my own dreams. If you weren't chickenshit, you'd study those snapshots. Eat your heart out! You gave up a stallion for a quarter horse.

Coach Davis asks for the basketball and blows the whistle. "You guys are slowing down on me. You've got to be sharp to beat Poly Prep. You've got to concentrate your energy. You can't let up. You can't lose your edge. Tomorrow, we'll scrimmage. Thursday, it's light practice and work on our set plays. Friday, I want you all to have a nap before the bus picks us up at five-thirty. You won't be home from Brooklyn before eleven, so tell your parents."

Angie leans over to me. "We'll have to change our date."

"Melish. Angell. This isn't study hall. Shut up. Or get out."

"Sorry, Coach."

"You want to be on this team?"

"Yes, Coach."

"We've been pointing for this game all season. I told you at the beginning that I could make you into winners if you gave me one hundred percent. Winning is a habit. We train hard. We hustle. We win big. This is the last game of the season. I don't want you guys easing up. I want this game. I want it bad. I want you to want it so bad you can taste it. Sometimes, when you people interrupt when I'm talking or horse around during drills or come out onto the

court looking sloppy in old whites stinking from yesterday's practice, I think you're a bunch of bushers. I'm not
in this business to coach bushers. If you don't care about
winning, you shouldn't be playing. I've never been on a
losing side. Once you get on that winning road, you want
to stay on it. It's something that sticks with you through
life."

Angie raises his hand. "Some of us have a history makeup exam on Friday afternoon, Coach. We won't be able
to have our nap."

"I'll talk to Mr. G. I don't want any of you thinking
about anything but the front of that hoop for the next
three days. Understand?"

"Yes, Coach."

"Yesterday, I was in the locker room late. I don't know
who it was. But one of you—I could tell by the shorts
pulled down around his ankles—was sitting on the john
pulling his pud."

Angie nudges me. I concentrate on Coach's mouth.

"I don't want to know who it was. Anyhow, I can tell
by how you played today. Let me tell you a trade secret.
This is no bull. Keep your hands off your meat, boys.
Don't waste yourself. 'He who beats it depletes it.' Bob
Cousy told me that. Remember it. When you play for me,
you give one hundred percent or you don't play. You eat
special food. You keep special hours. Discipline. Control.
That's the name of every game."

"I'll say," Angie whispers with a wink.

"Are you with me, fellas?"

"Yes, Coach."

"Then let's hear it!"

"WE'VE GOT THE TEAM. WE'VE GOT THE FIGHT . . ."

"Is this my Varsity? You sound like fairies. Let's get
up! 'Talk strong, you walk strong.' "

"WE'VE GOT THE WILL, WE'VE GOT THE

MIGHT. TEAM! FIGHT! WILL! MIGHT! C'MON INDIANS FIGHT TEAM FIGHT."

"That's more like it. Now hurry down and shower. And for God's sake, keep your hands to yourself."

Huff and puff—go ahead. Heave on that bed like sailors coming about in a stiff wind. It's no fun up here, honey, but I can take it. The plywood splinters are tearing my cavalry twills. But I'm here for the test.

No, it's not comfortable. It was never comfortable. But I'm a tough competitor.

"Could you slide up a little bit more, Helen?"

"Don't stop now, darling."

"The steering wheel's killing my shoulder."

"Kiss me."

"I can't hold you and kneel on the drive shaft. My leg's asleep."

"Is that better?"

"Yes."

"Good."

"All through the dance, I wanted to be on top of you like this."

"I can feel it, George."

"How does it feel, Helen?"

"Sharp."

"What else?"

"Oh, George."

"Darling."

"The door handle's jabbing my neck."

I push up, take off my tuxedo jacket and fold it under her head. I maneuver myself back on top of her. "Can you feel me now?"

"Not yet, dear."

With my feet against the glass, I get good leverage. I push with the momentum of three men. Her eyes are shut. Her breath hisses as she sucks it in through clenched teeth. My hand slips beneath her crinoline. Her fingers follow mine down the inside of her thigh. "Take off your underpants."

"No, George."

"Don't you trust me?"

"I don't trust myself. I haven't gone this far with Bobby Ziegler and I've been dating him six months."

"But I'm different. You said so."

"We have to save something, George."

"There's you and me and now."

My hand is already touching her. The wiry tuft—so much for such a small girl. The dampness.

"Not there," she says, shifting my finger to the spot.

"Isn't that good, Helen?"

"Yes."

"I think I'm falling in love with you."

Breathing heavily, Helen looks up at me. "When will you know?"

On the ride back to her house, Helen sits with her arm around my shoulder. We listen to the music.

"This is my favorite song," Helen says, kissing my ear. " 'I give to you and you give to me, true love, true love . . .' "

"Grace Kelly sang it in the movie. She's got class."

Helen tells me not to see her to the door. "I'm not a prude, George. A girl's got to think of the future. Nobody wants spoiled goods."

Once she's out of the car, I roll down the windows and blast the radio. I get the car up to a hundred miles an hour on the Merritt Parkway.

The doorman must think I've been riding horses when I walk bowlegged past him.

"You all right, Mr. Melish?"

"Sure, Frank."

Maybe this is what Jerry Lee Lewis means when he shouts, "Great balls of fire." The pain won't stop. I sit on my bed and hold them. I try lying on my back with my knees up. My balls have swollen to the size of oranges, so heavy I feel they'll drop off. The pain is worse than my football injury. At least then the doctor was on the field immediately. The crowd understood and applauded me as I was carried off.

Now I hobble to the basin and fill it to the brim with cold water. I lift my throbbing nads carefully over the edge. They soak against the smooth blue marble.

I say good night to Rita, and ask God not to let it happen again.

Dear Irene,

Even on my new waterbed—the waves rippling against my back, buoying me up like dolphins keeping a shipwrecked sailor afloat—I have the same vision. I swear it's real. My bed is full of windows. Dozens of them. Through each is a different woman I've known lying nude on the floor. Each is making love to me.

I saw this for the first time in our four-poster the night George, Jr., was conceived. I stayed up reading, remember? I never doubted we would succeed. Planned parenthood. A doctor, a calendar, a bankbook, a pill. We did everything right, and on time.

I never told you because you would have been jealous and asked questions. Who was Helen? And Sue? And Jeannie? I stayed up half the night watching me at it. I was incredible. So were they.

Each time we made love after that, I'd wait anxiously for you to go to sleep, so I could see myself multiplied dozens of times. I promised to love and to cherish you. I promised to covet no one else. And I kept my vows.

But even as I kissed your forehead and said, "I love you," they would be there. "The Late, Late Show" has nothing on me. You once complained that I was "rough" in bed. That was on purpose. I was sending myself through your womb and impaling the writhing bodies of all those nubile vixens. I was trying to kill them or fuck them or something . . . Do you understand?

I've never told anybody about this. I'm glad I didn't tell you when we were still on speaking terms. I wouldn't have known what to say. When you grow up, you put away childish things, right? I was—I still could be—a happily married man.

George, the father of your children.

P.S. These pictures are me on my new patio. I have a nice view of the East River and Carl Schurz Park. I liked the Hudson River from our bedroom better.

P.P.S. Please accept the enclosed check for the kids. You're not the only one with pride. What's a man work for but to give his family the best of everything?

"You're not going to show them that?" Sally says, pouring herself a brandy and looking at her husband reflected in the liquor cabinet mirror. "George is a professional writer."

"The Class of 'Thirty-six—with all due respect—was Yale's greatest class," Prescott says. "Stewart Alsop, John Hersey, Brendan Gill, me. Every five years we publish this book on ourselves. We write our own biographies."

"John C. Prescott—ABC's high roller," Sally says. "You'll have to report snake-eyes for the next installment."

"We didn't have a TV in Manhattan," Irene says. "But I watch it a lot out here. You get very involved with these soap operas. I suppose I'll be too busy when the baby arrives." Irene touches her stomach and looks at me.

"I know," Sally says. "Don't I, John?"

Prescott lights his pipe. He reaches up and takes a gold and blue book from the shelf behind him.

"Let's do something. Let's dance," Sally says, feeling behind her head for the barrette and releasing her streaked hair so that it falls gracefully over her shoulders. "George and Irene aren't interested in nostalgia. They live for now. I love your generation." Sally smiles and touches my shoulder. "I always wanted to dance like you people do. To twist and shout, and have nobody guiding me. At Sarah Lawrence, I studied movement with a disciple of Martha Graham. Sarah Lawrence taught me the difference between art and entertainment."

Prescott takes his bifocals out of his pocket. "The Book Committee sends out a questionnaire. Serious things. Matters of sociological interest." Prescott thumbs through the book. "Here's a funny one," he says. " 'How many times a week do you do what Kinsey writes about?' "

"What was the most?" Irene says.

"The average for a forty-eight-year-old man is one-point-four times a week."

"I just bought this record," Sally says, kicking off her shoes and feeling the carpet in her stocking feet. She's wearing an ankle bracelet. "These dishy boys with bangs and collarless Pierre Cardin suits."

"You mean the Beatles," Irene says. "I heard them at the Cavern, before they became famous. They've been around."

Sally puts on a record. "I love this song. 'It's been a hard day's night, and I've been workin' like a *dawg*.' "

Sally begins to spin around the room.

"You'll hurt yourself," Prescott says.

Sally leaps by him, knocking the book out of his hand. "I'm dancing," she says. "Louder."

Prescott gets up and goes over to the stereo. He snaps it off. "I think that's enough, dear. Please?"

Strands of hair stick to Sally's forehead. She grabs the record off the spindle and goes out to the patio. Prescott hurries after her.

"They're a little strange," Irene says. "Did you notice the ankle bracelet? Very non-U."

"We've got to get used to older people."

"You were a big hit," Irene says. "I don't think he likes me."

"Make more of an effort. You never know when they'll be useful."

"I've never heard of secret societies, Mory's, the Green Cup. I'm shy."

"You've got the guts of a burglar. Look how you caught me."

"Don't say that." Irene gets up. She takes my arm. We walk out on the verandah. Prescott is standing next to Sally. She draws her hands over her forehead and smooths her hair.

"I've written scripts before, you know," Sally says.

"I've read them."

"Darn good. Too good."

"Don't be so dramatic," Prescott says. "The Shermans are still up. They can hear."

"THE SHERMANS ARE BORING!" Sally screams, breaking the record and heaving it in the direction of their house. "THE HANCOCKS ARE BORING! THE FEENEYS ARE BORING! SNEDEN'S LANDING IS BORING!"

"We'd better go, George," Irene whispers.

Prescott looks over his shoulder at us. He forces a grin and rolls his eyes.

"We really should be going," Irene says to Prescott. "It's been nice to finally meet somebody in the neighborhood."

Sally turns around and leans against the verandah railing. "I'm a writer, aren't I, John?"

"Sally's been printed in magazines," Prescott says.

"I won the *Vogue* essay competition my senior year at college. 'Fashions for the Fifties' was the title. They gave me a job."

"I'd hardly call myself a writer, yet. I've only been at *Life* a year. But it's a good stepping-stone."

"Have I read anything of yours?"

"Last week, they ran a twelve-page color insect spread. 'Factory of Love: The Termites.' "

"Did you write that?"

"I did the captions."

"Tell me one of your captions," Sally says.

"Don't get him started, Mrs. Prescott," Irene says. "He's an *idiot savant* about what he writes."

"I'm on the science desk."

"Go ahead," Sally says. "Tell me one you're working on right now."

" 'The Oyster's Virgin Birth: Certain oysters off the coast of Spain and Normandy are male and female by turn. These unique hermaphrodites (captured in action above by *Life* photographer Horst Eberstedt and his time-lapse camera) are a one-man maternity kit. When one is female, it sucks in the sperm of the next-door oyster. A few days later it turns into a male and fertilizes the same or another's egg.' "

"I love 'one-man maternity kit,' " Sally says. "Punchy."

"We don't want to exhaust our new neighbors before they've settled in," Prescott says, slipping his arm around Sally's waist. She takes his hand away and comes over to me.

"I know about words, George. Believe me. I have the articles to prove it. Let me tell you one thing about writing. It isn't enough. The word comes from the body. Did you know that? Not just the throat. A word is shaped by the resonators down here behind your back and in your diaphragm. If you just write a word, it cuts it off from the body. It eats away a chunk of your soul because it's not connected to the body. That's why I've postponed my writing career for the drama. I was the only woman in Bergen County experienced enough to play Masha in *The Three Sisters* for the Farleigh Dickinson theater festival. I wanted to make full use of the body, you see. I wanted to say more."

"Darling," says Prescott. "You've ripped your skirt."

Sally looks down at her dress. "You'll excuse me, won't you?" she says. "We don't like splits of any kind in this family." She walks away.

I slip into the bathroom before we leave. I can hear Irene and Prescott talking by the front door. On the wall in front of the john is a mirror in the shape of a television screen. At the bottom, it reads: "Smile, You're on TV." Next to the mirror is a framed postcard to Sally from e.e. cummings thanking her for the poem she'd sent him. The postmark is June 3, 1955.

Nylon stockings and underwear are draped and drying on the towel rack behind the shower curtain. I pick up Sally's underpants. Blue silk. Size 3. Slowly I crumple them over my face.

"Forty-fifteen," Irene says, scooping up the Dunlop two-dot with her racquet and walking back to the baseline.

"Forty-thirty."

"Are you sure, George?"

"Yes, I'm sure."

Irene bounces the ball in front of her left foot three times. She pauses; then, taking aim, rifles her first serve to my backhand.

I swipe at it. The ball ricochets at a crazy angle off the end of my wood racquet. It flies over the fence and onto the Prescotts' lawn.

"Game. Set. Kiss from a handsome man," says Irene.

I turn my back to the net. I fling my racquet as hard as I can against the wire fence. "Fucking son of a bitch!"

I hear Irene's sneakers padding around the net. "C'mon, George, look at me. Say you had fun."

"I'm stronger than you. I'm faster. I should be able to whomp you. Six-two, six-one, six-zero is no fun. I don't want losing to become a habit."

"I've been playing all my life, sweetheart," she says, trying to hug me.

"I can't even beat a pregnant woman. I was terrible."

"Maybe I just played well."

"You didn't play well. I played lousy."

"Darling, if you insist on charging the net with every shot, you'll never win. I'll lob you to death."

"The Yale Club gives lessons. I'll stay in town twice a week. You'd like that, wouldn't you? I'll study tactics. I'll learn a drop shot. I'm going to wipe your ass off the court."

"Tennis isn't like school, George. That's why I love it. The body's instincts are as good as the mind's. When you're on form, you're not aware of one or the other. It's just you—swinging, planning, battling."

"I know. Wimbledon Junior Championship. Grass courts. Doubles with Tony Trabert. I've heard it all before. If you're so fucking good, why can't you get the score right?"

"I made a mistake, OK?"

"You make that mistake at least five times a set. It throws my concentration off. Would you like it if I called you Heavy Hips or Little Miss Teardrop?"

"I didn't do it on purpose."

"Apologies aren't enough. I look forward to our weekends. Tomorrow, I'll be back in my cubicle breaking my ass to meet a deadline."

"You have two degrees, George. You don't have to stick it."

"I'm sick and tired of your childish, competitive antics."

"You want me to cry?"

"That's it! The Wounded-Mother-To-Be routine."

"Please, George," Irene says. "Here comes Mr. Prescott. Be nice."

Prescott ambles down the lawn in his yellow slacks and sneakers. He picks up the ball and waves hello with it in his hand. "How do you like the court?" he says coming toward us. "The clay hard enough?"

"I'm not playing with you anymore, Irene. That's it. That's final. I'll play with the guys at *Life*. I'm tired of all your emotional zingers."

"All right, be that way. Frankly, it's no fun for me playing with a novice."

Prescott opens the gate to the court. I pick up my racquet and sweater and start to walk out. "Why don't you rally with Gorgeous Gussie, John?"

"I was just going to ask if you'd mind."

"Irene's Wimbledon caliber, you understand. We don't want that championship style lost by playing against your garden-variety dilettante."

I hand Prescott the racquet.

I walk up the road to my house. Behind me, I hear the steady rhythm of their rally. Suddenly, the sound stops. "Nice shot," Irene says.

Where does she get off? Answer me that. Melish—you pussy-whipped Protestant-lover—you put her on a pedestal. You lofted her pootie-tootie so high above you that you were blinded by the glare off her Guccis. You took a nice London girl with a shrub for a family tree, whose largest charge had been the Dublin Horseshow, and introduced her to the sophisticated glitter of the New York scene. She was as plain as British beer. But you always had taste, Melish. You were sensitive to color. She found her way to the good boutiques like a sleepwalker to the refrigerator. Pucci became her middle name. Remember the great voluptuary calm of walking with her in the springtime, running your hand over her brilliant black, pink and silver behind! You built her into a stunner! You taught her about eye shadow, and color combinations. Those earrings you bought. The large, circular Florentine gold ones for daytime; the green jade pendants for night. Gorgeous. People stopped and stared at us in the street. The Managing Editor from the forty-third floor sent memos asking us to dinner. You made her into an asset. *Women's Wear Daily* asked us to pose twice. I have to be fair. Over a candlelight supper, Irene was sensational.

But it's not talk she wanted, was it? She wanted to be thumped like Leadbelly's guitar. She grooves on a long tongue licking her face and the nape of her neck, leaving its slippery trail all over her body like a hyperthyroid snail. Frank Zappa handles her like a microphone—yanking her up to eye level, twisting her about. Spittle sparkles all over her. Her pouting lips never stop moving. She's just a kid—the mother of two. There's more to love than feeling. Ecstasy doesn't last. (Anyway, it's counterrevolutionary.) And in the clear light of day you need something stronger, deeper, more enduring. A relationship based on a firm moral foundation. That's what you have, Melish, *Lux et Veritas*. They don't elect a guy Class Secretary unless they're sure of his staying power.

"This is a very important question," Mom says, pulling her chair closer to the Crown Derby gravy boat and spooning out the gravy. "Sol? Are you listening? Your father never listens."

"I'm listening."

"More water, Mom?"

"Get it yourself, George. Tell Maddy to hurry up with the potatoes."

I bring back the water pitcher from the kitchen and sit down. Maddy follows behind me, holding the silver vegetable dish with both hands and hobbling in her black-laced shoes. She stops to the right of each of us. "Mind your hand, George. It's hot."

"I was trying to say something serious to your father," Mom says. "This is about the only time in this house we get together. At Henry Fonda's—before the divorce—they held a family meeting once a week. Everything was decided by democracy. That's what we should have."

"Hank's kids are pretty talented."

"What's that supposed to mean, Sol?"

"Nothing."

"Then why say something like that in front of George? Only children have enough c-o-m-p-l-e-x-e-s. He's just as good as anybody."

"I didn't mean that."

"That's what it sounded like."

"Well, Fonda's kids are earning, aren't they? Little jobs here and there."

"You want George to have no childhood like you did? You want him to pay his own way? Sometimes you sound like a grocer instead of a film producer."

"Vera, I'm eating."

"The doctor said it would be risky to have another child. I wanted to adopt, but you wouldn't. George could've had lots of brothers and sisters to play with—a real family."

"I played with him."

"Sol, I don't call gin rummy a child's game."

"What was the question you wanted to ask, Mom?"

"Sometimes, Sol, you make me sick. I have to do everything—raise George, order the food, balance the books."

Dad chews each piece of meat twelve times, like he tells me to do.

"How's the meat, Sol?"

Without looking up, he says, "Eh?"

"What do you mean, 'eh?' That's twelve dollars' worth of rib roast. It's the best Gristede's had. I talked to Ralph on the phone myself. He promised me the top cut."

"It's tough," Dad says.

"It is not."

"Mine's like horsemeat, Vera."

"Have mine, Sol," Mom says, handing her plate across the table toward him.

"I don't want yours. I've got mine—four dollars' worth of Arab stallion."

"You won't eat veal. You hate ham. You're bored with meat loaf. We had lamb twice last week. I don't know what to feed you. The man's impossible. He complains about everything. It's not easy keeping this house, cleaning up after you. And I don't get very much thanks. That goes for both of you as a matter of fact, thank you very much."

"C'mon, Mom . . ."

"Don't 'c'mon, Mom' me, George. A little flower once in a while. A box of chocolates. Something for all the trouble I go to. Neither of you care. You're too damn selfish."

Mom starts to cry.

"Vera," Dad says with his mouth full. "Don't be ridiculous."

"You won't eat garlic. You won't eat fried foods or foods with spice. I've had it up to here." She starts to move her hand up to her throat, and spills her glass of water.

Dad and I laugh.

"It's not funny McGee."

She rings the bell for Maddy. "That woman hears what she wants to hear." Finally, Mom wipes up the water with her napkin. She dries her eyes. "George and I have been talking about college. I went up to the Parent-Teachers meeting last weekend. They say college admission is very difficult. The New Deal babies . . . We should start planning now. Do you have anything to contribute to this most important decision of your son's life, Sol?"

"Where does he want to go?"

"He's undecided."

"I don't care where he goes. It's up to him. As long as he doesn't flunk out, that's fine."

"Is that all you have to say? Do you know that Mrs. Gottlieb has already taken her son, Michael, for special tutoring? In one year, Michael moved up from twenty-fourth in the class to fourth. Last year, he didn't have a hope. Yesterday Harriet Gottlieb was telling everybody that Mike's going to Harvard. George is number twelve. He's not low, but he's not high enough to be nonchalant. He's what they call a borderline, Sol. He needs every break he can get. He needs your help as well as mine. The boy works like a dog."

"I can get him into Notre Dame."

"Notre Dame?"

"I met Father Hesbergh at the Stork Club. He said to me, 'Sol, when your boy gets old enough, we'd love to have him among the Green and Gold.' "

"Sol, do you realize what you're saying? That's a safety college! Nobody's got that on their list. Our son's not going to a safety school. Is that what we paid thirty-five hundred dollars a year to send him to prep school for?"

"A lot of great people have come out of there."

"Name two."

"Johnny Lujack and Bronko Nagurski."

"Who are they?"

"Football players."

"This is serious, Sol. Only the Top Ten get into the grade-A colleges. George practically wrote Mike Gottlieb's last biology report. George is going to need a little push. At least show an interest in your son's education."

"Where do you want to go, George?"

"Yale."

"Where's that?"

"New Haven."

"That's good."

"You know, George, you should think about Williams," Mom says. "Foxy Sondheim's son—Stephen, the one who's writing the lyrics to *West Side Story*—it'll be the biggest hit in New York, I won't be able to get tickets for my charity—well, Steve went to Williams and really blossomed. They taught him how to rhyme. He took composition courses. He wasn't more than twenty-five when Lennie and Jerry picked him for the show. Williams really prepares you."

"Williams is a little small, Mom."

"Small! Listen to your mother for once in your life. President Garfield was a graduate. Herbert Lehman and Elia Kazan. Mrs. Sondheim says Williams has almost as many people in *Who's Who* as Harvard."

"I wouldn't mind Connecticut Wesleyan."

"Oh, George," Mom says throwing her napkin on the table. "Who's heard of that?"

"Academically, it's very good, Mom. You can live in dorms. You don't have to join a fraternity."

"Whatever you want," Dad says. "So long as when you're finished you can earn a buck."

"Is that your advice, Sol? You'd let him go to college without a fraternity?"

"I don't know from colleges. I was at the University of Hard Knocks. Believe me."

"We believe you, Sol. The paper route. The struggle. All that. Times have changed."

"When I was a kid, you had your paper route. Six in the morning, I got up. No money for a bicycle or a cab—I walked. Forty-three stops between Broome Street and Waverly Place. Three-and-a-half miles before eight in the morning. All on an empty stomach. I don't mind telling you, there were days when I got home for breakfast that I had frostbite. I earned three dollars a week. I gave two-fifty to Mom and Dad. The spare change was for candy and cigarettes. You could get three Turkish Delights for a nickel. The minute you were old enough to get your working papers—*voom*—into the street. Hustling. My father—your grandfather, may he rest in peace —took home fifteen dollars a week. In those days, it went a long way. Not like kids today. No allowance. No extras for dances or clothes. We had it tough. Money didn't grow on trees. I was seventeen before I bought my first hardback books: a secondhand edition of Gibbon's *Decline and Fall of the Roman Empire*. One buck for six volumes. Resold it the next week for three dollars."

"Sol, if I wasn't around, you'd be in the poorhouse right now."

"Your mother buys dresses the way most women buy candy."

"Go into my closet! Come on! Let's go and look. I haven't had a new outfit for two years. I'm embarrassed to walk in the Easter Parade."

"I don't begrudge you the money."

"You do, Sol. You have no idea of prices. You charge everything."

"All I know is this—it's dog eat dog out there. The fittest survive. Here we are in a Fifth Avenue apartment sitting on Chippendale chairs, eating prime rib. All the amenities. That didn't happen by luck. You've got to work for it. Now, George is a hard worker. I've noticed that."

"A lot of help he gets from you with his studies."

"The best thing I can give him, Vera, is the price of tuition."

"That's what we're talking about."

"George, what do you want to study?"

"I think I'll major in English, Pop."

"Now this—if you don't mind me saying so—is stupid. This I can help with. What can you do with English, George? You already have a beautiful vocabulary. You're well-read. Study something that will help you when you get out."

"With a university degree, Pop, they say I should be earning eight thousand dollars on my first job."

"No kidding?" Dad says. "They have it easy—these kids coming up."

"Sol, this is why a good university is important. At Yale or Williams, George, you get a nice quality of boy. Good families. These are the kinds of contacts you could use in later life."

"Your mother's right there. It's not what you know, but who you know. Get that degree and get the big bucks. If you want to come into the film business, I've got some friends. You don't even have to go to college for that."

"Sol, George has to go to college."

"I'm tired of this discussion."

"We don't ask much of you, Sol. Only once in a while we'd like a little attention to important details."

"Look, George. You go where you want. You should have an education. You should become—God willing—a rich man. You're not bad to look at. You've got a pleasing personality. You've gone to the right schools. We always wanted this for you. Your mother and I never had it. Just don't waste your time on English. All you could be is a teacher. What kind of life do they have?"

"He wants to be a writer, Sol."

"Oi vey. I deal with writers every day. What kind of security is that? It's hand-to-mouth. Do your writing on the side, George. Advertising. Public Relations. Television. If I were starting out today, that's where I'd be."

"Dad, I've got a date."

"Where?" says Mom.

"Angie and I are doubling."

"Isn't that the boy who was suspended last year for cheating?"

"It was only a French vocab test."

"You don't see Jerry Frank or Mickey Baum anymore. Don't lose your friends, George. Keep up with them. You'll never know when you'll need them."

"What's the girl's name?" Dad asks.

"Sue Kelley."

"Congratulations. Hear that, Vera? He's finally met a mackerel snapper."

"Sol!"

"I don't think that's funny, Pop."

"It's no joke. It's the truth. You love me, right? I never tell you wrong, do I? Our name was Mellischevitz for seven generations until I changed it. Your mother complains that I don't talk at dinner. But I'm watching. I like sitting back and hearing you speak. You talk with good language. We didn't talk the way you do when I was a kid. At night, I walk around the house and turn on the lights above the paintings. I give each *nature morte* two minutes' attention. I look at your jade collection, and the

fishing rods. We've come a long way in my lifetime,
George. We're going farther. 'Melish'—I like the name. It
still sounds new to me after twenty years. It's a good
sound. It rolls off the tongue—sweet and decisive."

"Dad, I really have to go."

"Get going, then. Go to college. Improve the strain.
You think you got that turned-up nose by luck?"

"Oh, Sol!"

"It's time the boy learned."

I fold my napkin and push in my chair.

"You forgot something," Mom says.

I kiss her, and Dad.

Jenny tucks her knees underneath her miniskirt and leans
back against a cushion on her bed. Above her head is
pasted a collage of film faces cut out from fashion magazines. Paul Newman, Sophia Loren, Elizabeth Taylor and
Steve McQueen smile behind her. In the corner is a picture of Dad and John Huston on the set of *Crazy*. "I
know why they sent you to talk to me," Jenny says.
"Some friend."

"I know about study methods, Jenny. Listen to your
Uncle George. First, you can't work with the Dave Clark
Five blaring in your ears. Second, you've got to clear all
that clutter off your desk so you won't be visually distracted."

Jenny laughs. "But I am distracted. I love movies.
Where do you think all your baby-sitting money goes?
Film books, double features—that's where. Movies are
what I want to study. Not this geometry junk."

"You've got one more year at school, Jenny. When you
go to college, you can major in film. I've got nothing
against film."

"They do."

"Let me handle them."

"How do I know they'll listen to you?"

"Leave it to me. I got you on the set of *Crazy* like I promised, didn't I? Do your work, and get good grades, and stop worrying your parents. I'll do the rest."

Jenny leans over and puts her hand on my knee. "Mr. Fix-It," she smiles. "You're a groove."

Jenny gets up and walks me to her desk under the gabled window that looks out on the lawn. She rummages through a drawer. Outside, Irene and John are talking over a chess game. Sally strolls out with the drinks. Her ankle bracelet glints in the sun.

"Bard, Antioch, NYU, UCLA—they all have film courses," Jenny says, holding up the catalogues.

"Jenny? Why does your mother wear an ankle bracelet?"

"Dad gave it to her when they first got married. He was very romantic in those days."

"What does it say?"

" 'To My Last Mistress,' " Jenny says. "That's between us, OK?"

A. Whitney Griswold, the President of Yale, stares down at us from the Woolsey Hall rostrum. He stands as muted and streamlined as a Brooks Brothers mannequin. In front of him are hundreds of freshmen like myself: clipped and scrubbed, name tags pinned to our tweed jackets, lucky pennies wedged into our Weejuns.

Angie squirms in his seat, doodling on the orientation schedule. I listen.

"During the next four years, Yale will be your home. We welcome you to the family knowing like any parent that your time with us will be filled with discoveries and disappointments, but confident in your ability to meet the challenge. As a group, you are more highly qualified than ninety-nine-point-seven percent of all Americans entering university this year. Not only your parents, but your country expects much of you."

We were the Ivory soap of a generation and proud of it.

I missed the pill, the revolution, drugs, coeducation. Have I missed passion? Is that something to miss?

The BBC is offering us their "Uncle Vanya" with Laurence Olivier. We need something to cut into the "Forsyte Saga," but the basic arithmetic has me worried. I lie down on my sofa, smoke a cigar and figure the numbers. This is my routine when making a big decision.

I decide to reject the proposal. The film's not in color.

The cleaning lady barges into my office. She apologizes. She says it's very late and that everybody on the nineteenth floor has gone home. She hands me a note wedged under the door and excuses herself.

I stare at my picture of Irene holding Tandy and little George. The note is from Prescott. It says: "Command is a lonely vigil."

> *"Here lies Irene,*
> *One score and three,*
> *Who gave to worms*
> *What she refused to me."*

"Don't think me silly, George. I can't do it on my mother's bed."

"We could put the mattress on the floor. I used to be a trip counselor. I'm great at camping out."

I sit by the window listening to the hee-haw of a London ambulance racing down the back streets of Belgravia. I think about the exam two weeks ahead.

"Your eyes are very far away," Irene says, putting her hand on my shoulder. "It's not good to dream."

"Why not?"

"It just isn't."

"You meet a better class of girl that way."

Always lumbered. My skull feels like a ninety-pound pack-basket. I pull my memories along with an imaginary tumpline around my forehead to distribute the weight. My neck is taut. My head tilts toward the horizon of my dreams.

The day the injunction arrived, I wired her:

> YOU CAN'T ESCAPE THAT EASY STOP
> YOU ARE IN MY DREAMS STOP AND THEY
> AREN'T WET

Now she wears dashiki dresses and peace shirts. A Van Cleef & Arpels silver fish dangles from a small chain around her neck. She's of the Let-It-All-Hang-Out-Within-Reason school of philosophy since she met Johnny Cash. That's all I was asking. I was ahead of my times.

"I'm embarrassed, George."

"Nothing's unnatural in marriage."

"Love is sacred. We weren't married to behave like animals."

"What about the Reverend Charles Bury and all that talk about the Great Chain of Being and the nesting instinct?"

"He didn't tell us about kinky nesting."

"At least animals don't feel guilt."

Almost eleven years. 3,857 days. That's all it took for her to come around. I could've stuck it. I could've been as good as him. (I am as good as him.) He's not as young as he looks. His cock's not headline news either. We're only seven years apart. And FL's talk about "doing your own thing." What is that? The history of American capitalism. Freedom is dollars and cents. I have the big bucks, too; but I have to work nine to five for it. That's *my* gig, baby. All right, ABC is the Establishment. But what's Atlantic Records? And Warner Brothers? And ASCAP? FL was a *Playboy*'s Musical All-Star, complete with a collegiate caricature. How middle-class can you get!

I should charge admission. I really should. Bo Diddley can't even diddle. He can't cut the mustard. He's standing up. He doesn't know how to strike while the iron is hot. He's been with her nearly a year now and he doesn't know to kiss her armpits. That's the buzzer.

Irene stands up and stretches. She's yawning. If Frankie Avalon could see that from the crapper, he'd hit the road. You can't just pound away at Irene. You have to jazz her with language. After all, she's English. She's a verbal person. Irene's got a greyhound's ribs. Sharp, lean, dramatic against that smooth skin. You can count them like a side of beef. She bends over and picks up his clothes. The woman is a nut for order. Why bother, Irene? A raunchy pair of tie-dyed blue jeans. A sweat shirt with a corny number on the front. U.S. Keds. I didn't throw my clothes around. I pulled my own weight in the house. I took care of my things. Clothes meant something, they were a sign of respect. The first time we made love on that Greek beach I folded your things and mine. When we were married, I bought a silent valet. I took care. Remember that, Irene?

"He won't listen to me, Sol."

"George, will you do me a favor? Will you go down to Brooks Brothers and buy yourself some new pants and a jacket? You want us to be the laughingstock of Manhattan?"

"Dad, I don't need them."

"Are you allergic to looking nice?"

"I didn't raise him to be a pig, Sol."

Dad goes to his walk-in closet. He opens the door. The smell of camphor fills the room. His suits—all twelve of them—are in a straight line. His shoes, which Maddy keeps polished, are standing at attention below the outfit they complement. There is a hat rack, a tie rack and a small dresser with an El Morocco ashtray holding studs and collar stays. A brown leather flagon of Of Thee I Sing cologne stands next to it.

"People know me in this town, George. Misbehave, or look sloppy, and it's a reflection on me."

"Us," says Mom.

"Dad, all I said to Mother was that I don't need any more clothes. I don't want khakis."

"No backtalk, young man. When I walk down the street—my Spanish chukka boots from Peales, the custom-made tweed jacket that Gregory Peck gave me after the last picture, my trilby from Harrods—people show me immediate respect. What am I looking for—a woman? I feel good. I know I'm neat and clean. I don't offend—like some people. I'm not a ball of wrinkles you'd think had been sleeping on the Bowery—like some people. Good clothes give you confidence. They make others confident in you. If I'm waiting on a corner for a taxi, the cabbie automatically pulls up to me. You can lay book on it. I give off a sense of responsibility. I'm telling you this for your own good, George. You'll be going to college soon. You should know."

"If I've told him once, Sol, I've told him a hundred times."

"For your father, George. Do it for me."

"OK, I'll go. But no khakis."

"Look at the shine on those shoes. You can see your

face in them. I never leave the house without a pressed handkerchief and clean shirt."

"Try giving him a handkerchief, Sol. You'd think it was cough medicine. He hides them in his bureau under the sweaters."

"Oh, Mom."

"It's true. You act like a beatnik sometimes."

"Mom!"

"It's Angie, and all those boys you hang out with. We wanted you to have a nice childhood."

"It's not Angie."

"All I know is *I'm* neat as a pin. You didn't get these habits from me."

"Or me," says Dad.

"If we're going, let's do it now."

"Has he got an overcoat, Vera?"

"Threadbare. It's a rag. Frayed at the cuffs. Hasn't been washed in three years. The smell under the arms! Phew! I can't get it away from him, Sol."

Dad looks at me in disgust. "You wanna be an outcast? Will you please buy yourself an overcoat? Go to my tailor. Get anything you want. You'll freeze in that rag. Clothes lose their warmth, you know."

"The Melish men have a history of stubbornness," says Mom.

"If you don't respect yourself," Dad says in his final word on the subject, "who's going to?"

As the cab pulls up to Brooks Brothers, Mom says: "If we don't find what we want here, we'll try Abercrombie." She pats my hand.

The fifth floor of Brooks Brothers is for young adults. Mr. Jay has been our man since Mom bought my first jacket and short pants. He comes out from behind a glass

counter and walks us toward the rear. The wood floor
creaks. We stop to look at the stacks of sports coats
lumped on the tables.

"Won't you buy just one pair of khakis? They'd be
darling with this herringbone."

"Mother!"

"I was only asking."

I come out of the dressing room and step in front of
the mirror. Mom stands up and walks over to look at me
as I turn around in the three-sided mirror. Mr. Jay marks
the cuffs with chalk. "He'll have to have a little more in
the seat, Mrs. Melish," he says, chewing on his Sen-Sen.

"How do you feel, George?"

"Fine."

"Is this the newest thing, Mr. Jay?"

"Our classic look, Mrs. Melish. I've sold more of these
than any others."

"Not too itchy, George?"

"They itch a little."

"A few washings and they'll feel like racing silks," says
Mr. Jay.

"Don't mention 'wash' around him. It's a dirty word.
We'll have to chip them off his legs." They laugh.

Mom touches my leg. "They feel awfully heavy."

"They're pretty heavy."

"You sure you want them?"

"Yes."

"How many should we get, George?"

"Three."

"You can wear anything with them, George. Hounds-
tooth, herringbone . . ." Mom looks to Mr. Jay for help.

"Camel's hair. Plaid. Pinstripe."

"You wouldn't want a tighter fit?"

"No, Mom. This is how the guys wear them."

"He's just like his father. Knows exactly what he
wants."

Basic black. Not just the color of Mom's Chanel originals, but my wardrobe as well. True, Brooks Brothers pants were baggy. But this was their great advantage. It wasn't a fad, but a necessity. The whole lower half of the body was shrouded in $42.50 worth of woolen, absorbent shadow. As for the dura-grip zippers—known as "tiger teeth"—they were murder on the old joystick when humping. But this was nothing compared to the Rorschach blot that seeped easily and unexpectedly to the surface of the finest khaki.

"Pink shirts would look nice with this."

"No pink, Mom."

"What's wrong with pink and black? I gave you that shirt and tie last Christmas."

"It's pansy."

"I can never do anything right," she mumbles to Mr. Jay. "And watch your language. You're with a lady, you know."

By the end of forty minutes, we had two ties, a belt, the pants, a chesterfield coat ("Your father will be so proud") and a three-piece suit.

I look very thin in my three-piece. "Gray herringbone suits you," Mom says. She's right. The vest holds me in, and up. The pants' creases are as stiff and straight as a spine. I feel streamlined. Only a fifth of my blue, buttoned-down Oxford cotton shirt shows; only the knot and two inches of flashy striped tie peek out.

Everything matches.

'61

George Melish
ABC
1330 Avenue of the Americas
New York City 10019

Your corresponding secretary is now corresponding from better quarters down the road. If you don't know the address, you've seen the logo. ABC. In the trade, it's called Hard Rock. There's 30 Rock (NBC), Black Rock (CBS) and Hard Rock. I'm off to a good start as assistant to the head of programming. My old man used his *avoirdupois* with the studios to get me a bargain price on some of the golden oldies. *Run Riot* got a 54% share of the audience. RUSTY THWAITE, who was managing editor of the *Yalie Daily* when I was sports editor, gave me a write-up on the *Times* feature page, where you've been seeing his by-line. By the by, the head of programming is John Prescott ('36). Prescott's a neighbor and nature enthusiast. We're business partners off-hours, too. We've started an apiary in Sneden's Landing. Presmel Honey sells for $1 a jar. Any buyers?

Ran into BILLY WADSWORTH at "21." Besides being my ex-roommate, Wads has other distinctions. He's been promoted to VP of BBD&O's Creative Department. Wads produced a study of the networks which showed that ABC is gaining a larger share of the youth market. That's where my muscle is. We've already started to challenge the others in the prime-time race. Up to now, ABC has delivered five million fewer viewers per minute than the two other Rocks. Wads was recently divorced from the former Cissy Calhoun. They have a son, Brett.

VICTOR ANGELL reports that he ushered at BOB MARSH's wedding in San Francisco. Flying out to the occasion were BUSTER HARE, HENRY HUDSON, JUNIOR CUSWORTH. Angie photographed the wedding. Bob, who was briefly engaged to Jean Shrimpton, married another English model that Angie had snapped for *Harper's Bazaar,* Lulu Davis-Poynter. Angie was recently listed in *Town and Country's* "Ten Most Eligible Bachelors."

Class of '61, where are you? Six years ago this June we were all massed on the Old Campus, smoking tobacco from clay pipes, listening to Dean Acheson's pep talk. With the reunion coming up, let's have a progress report. I looked you all up in the Yale Directory. No one else is in TV. Won't any of you guys take the plunge? The money's great, and the secretaries are discreet.

James Taylor struts back to bed. He rests with his hands behind his head. He stares at the ceiling.

Irene says nothing.

Their hips touch.

His cock is at attention. He's back to square one, but he doesn't seem to mind. He's taking longer than a Warhol movie. When you've got a girl on the brink, you keep her busy. You play those erogenous zones like a pinball machine. Sweet nothings. Fast fingers.

This is what I hate about the permissive society: overconfidence.

"This is the last night, George," Irene says, rubbing up beside me.

"It was only a few days ago you said the coast was clear."

"That's right. And tonight's the last night. You want to?"

"No, I don't *want to*. Asking's not very romantic."

Mother raps on the door. "George, why is this locked? You've got nothing to hide from your parents."

"On the phone, Mom."

"What about the English exam?"

"Talking to Angie."

"Open the door and get off the phone."

"Wait a minute, Angie."

I hurry to the door and unlock it. Mom sticks her head in the room and looks around.

"I'm helping Angie with his homework."

"You work hard for your grades. Don't give away all your information."

Mom bangs the door shut. I flop back on my bed and pick up the phone. "You hear that, Angie?"

"Yeah."

"Sorry."

"What are you doing about the essay, George?"

"Describe her again to me, Angie."

"Her name's Marge. She's nineteen. She's flat-chested, and she thinks that taking off your bra is losing your virginity. She doesn't mind anything else."

"Many points?"

"We have to talk it over. When we drew up the rules, the possibility of nymphomania never came up."

"You're putting me on."

"Soixante-eat-your-heart-out-*neuf.*"

"Jesus!"

"I'm working up a little cheat sheet."

"Don't risk it again, Angie."

"Mr. Strauss is blind as a bat. You know the Angell motto: 'Rules are for fools.' "

"Memorize the first verse of Donne's 'The Good-Morrow' and the last four lines of 'Woman's Constancy.' "

"I'm not getting much sleep. I can't concentrate. This one's got a body that never quits. She owns her own diaphragm."

" 'The Canonization' is important. You know. 'For Godsake hold your tongue, and let me love.' You should memorize one of Donne's songs."

" 'Catch a falling star and put it in your pocket . . .' "

"You *have* been studying."

"Perry Como, putz."

"What's it feel like?"

"Like driving your spike into a swimming pool of mashed potatoes. Soft and forever."

"I can't wait for college."

"University nookie," Angie sighs. "My folks are going away for a long weekend. We'll be here alone till Monday. Let the phone ring five times. Hang up and call again. I'm not answering to anyone but you."

"I'm fainting, Angie."

"See you tomorrow at English class, lover." Angie hangs up.

I stare up at the Camp Caribou baseball bat for most improved in boxing. After a while, I sit back at my desk. I thumb through the *Elegies* and drain my Coke. "Love's Progress" catches my eye.

> *Who ever loves, if he do not propose*
> *The right true end of love, he's one that goes*
> *To sea for nothing but to make him sick . . .*

I write the lines out ten times—extra credit for the test.

Mom opens the door and then knocks on it. She walks over to my desk. She looks down at the books and my practice pad. She smooths my hair.

"That's better," she says, and takes the empty soda bottle into the kitchen.

"Now, Fred," Irene says, holding her arms out toward him. "Now."

He rolls on top of her. His long left arm reaches out toward the dimmer switch. It's getting hard to see. C'mon twenty-twenties, do your stuff!

Fred. What kind of a name is that for a rock star?

"George, now." Jeannie says. "Don't stop, darling."

I roll on top of her. My left hand reaches out toward my wallet on the night table.

Damn Wads. He gives you the Trojan. He tells you to get laid. When the moment comes, it's too dark to read the instructions on the foil. Stall, Melish. "Let's go around the world."

"I'll have to think about it, George. I want my education diploma before anything."

"I'm not talking about any trip."

I roll off her. I move down her body, my tongue making new trails in her flesh.

"Oh," Jeannie says. "I get it."

Keep her happy, Melish. Let her play. Let her tire herself out. Let her run under your boat and hide in the weeds. Your pole is strong. It can hold her. Then, haul her in.

I lie on my back. I pull her legs over my ears. I hear her sighing. Her legs clamp tight around my head. Melish, you are cool. I hold the Trojan up against the whitewashed background of the ceiling.

Slowly, big fella. You've waited nineteen years and nine months for this moment. Make it magnificent. Take your time.

I've almost got the little mother. Jeannie's legs press close together over my face—darkness. Give me a few seconds, sweetheart. I rub my head hard in her crotch. She wiggles—daylight. There it is.

Roll it down. But which way? Inside or outside? "Kiss me, Jeannie."

"I am kissing you."

"On the lips."

As I slide up her body, the rubber slips out of my hand. My fingers patrol the sheets. I pretend to tickle her. Fast thinking, Melish. I find it under a fold in the blanket.

My left hand is on her breast. My tongue is in her mouth. My left leg is kneeing beaver. All points of contact are being made. The plastic ring is in position and ready to be unveiled. I roll it an inch and tug. Another inch. Another tug. Slow and steady wins the race.

"Hurry, darling."

"Yes."

"Forget protection."

"I can't."

"Let me help." Jeannie's fingers find my work.

"Careful, Jeannie."

"I want you."

"Not too hard."

"Pull it on, George."

I yank.

"Pull, George."

The rubber flaps against my cock, split up the middle like an unzipped galosh.

"We can still do it, George."

"It's not safe."

"My fault, George." Jeannie's body relaxes. "It was beautiful anyway."

"I forgive you."

Jeannie—Princess of the Palmer Method, my Numero Uno—I can't talk to you now. I've got business at hand.

Irene found our letters. She knows about you. But she doesn't really know. You met me when I preached the gospel of "grace under pressure" to my ten-year-old campers, when I had them chugging beer at bedtime and dropping their pants on the highest Adirondack peaks. I was their initiation; and you were mine. You sang me your sorority song:

> *Awfully glad I am a*
> *Kappa Kappa Gamma*
> *A rootin', tootin'*
> *KKG.*

I didn't have the words for your sweet mischief. I do now. I can see you standing behind your relish tray at Saranac Inn. The boys called you The Relish Girl and you could strut your stuff in that white dress and "tenny pumps," as you called sneakers in Missouri. Once you goosed me with the roll prong. And I thought you were a virgin!

Jeannie, if you were here now, we'd rewrite history. I'd forget about the Trojans and buy that prophylactic spray. I wish I could remember your face. The pictures were destroyed in Irene's Living Room Putsch of 1963. Once every two years or so I see you again in a dream. The lips are full. The hair is black and cut short. The smile is that same gummy grin. I can still feel your father's rough fingers as we held hands around the farmhouse table saying grace. You should've married me like I asked. I was blue-chip, Jeannie. The writing was on the wall if you'd have been patient enough to read it. I was a good camper, twice voted best at Camp Caribou. I was *DKE* and Dean's List. That's something to build on.

Fred's on top. I can tell by his long hair.

The bedsprings wheeze.

He's leaning back like a limbo artist. He's probably chanting voodoo code words he's picked up from his black sideman. They have their ear to the criminal background. He's murmuring "Nommo," and "Mojo," and "Kintu."

They're not very coordinated. Ecstasy is a team effort. Gimbels has to tell Macy's.

Maybe *she's* on top?

Irene is singing in her sleep. Her hand is draped over my chest.

"Are you OK?"

"What?" Irene pushes herself up on her elbows.

"Night noises again."

"I dreamt you had three penises. I took the big one."

"Go back to sleep."

"Sweet dreams, George."

"Sweet dreams."

What am I, some perverse Pantalone? All the girls I see during the day—the secretaries, the starlets, the agents in open-toed shoes nudging me under the table—and I'm here with Irene. She's so corrupt, it's breathtaking.

Does this make sense, Melish? You spend half your week in the ABC screening room looking at rough cuts and reruns and at night you're still ogling shadows.

It never pays to sneak. You always learn too much, don't you, Meli? Still, it's part of what makes you an A-1 executive and a cool customer in affairs of the heart.

Images keep bunny-hopping into my brain.

Dad decking Mom. It was a good punch, owing much of its inspiration to Dad's lifelong adulation of Joe Louis.

First the screams which brought me tiptoeing to the door, kneeling by the keyhole. And then the shock of seeing it. Dad holding her by the arms and pushing her out of a clinch to get enough elbow room for a right-cross to the ear. I heard the pop of bone on bone. Then, shuffling on the balls of his slippered feet, Dad went back to his corner as Mom crumpled to the floor. Fists still clenched, Dad taunted her—"Go shit in a hat, Vera!" Mom crawled out of sight to the bathroom.

Banquet Night at Camp Caribou. Excusing myself from Uncle Jim's table and running back to his cabin to see the list of awards. The creak of the screen door. The room smelling of pine and dust. The cat mewing and jumping off the desk as I came close. Melish—Captain of the Blues, victorious in the color war; Number Three in the batting lineup with a season average of .382; fifteen lanyards and four wicker baskets in Arts and Crafts; Order of the Arrow—two days in the woods without speaking and only bread and water to eat. All this and not even an honorable mention for Best Camper.

I piss in Uncle Jim's fireplace.

Back at dining hall, Uncle Jim asks me to lead the singing. I tap my glass. I smile at the counselors and parents who will be taking their boys home the next day. Everybody joins in.

> *"We welcome you to Caribou,*
> *We're mighty glad you're here,*
> *We'll send the air reverberating*
> *With a mighty cheer.*
> *We'll sing you in,*
> *We'll sing you out,*
> *For you, we'll raise a mighty shout,*
> *Hail, Hail, the gang's all here*
> *And you're welcome to Caribou."*

Jeannie's letter. Finding it in her drawer with snapshots of us from the first summer at Saranac Lake. Hurrying to the kitchen before she returned from her last class. Locking the front door, then the back. Holding the envelope up to the teakettle's black spout. Keeping it over the steam until my wrist ached. Pulling the flap slowly open without a mark. Seeing his name—Dennis—and the last line: "When is lover boy leaving?"

Skip it, Melish. Think happy thoughts.

The kids rush at me as I walk in the door. They're in their pajamas and ready for bed. Irene's kept them up so I can see them. She's standing tired but smiling by the stairway.

Tandy leaps into my arms, a bundle of sweet smells. My hat falls off. George, Jr., picks it up and puts it on his head.

"Who's your favorite person?"

"Mr. Wonderful," Tandy laughs, pulling my nose and looking at me.

"And who's Mr. Wonderful?"

"You know."

George, Jr., butts his head against my intestines. "Batman!"

"Stop that, George! That's Daddy's hat."

"Batman!" he says, punching my leg.

"What's got into him, Irene?"

"It's your channel, darling."

I hold George, Jr., at arm's length and let him swing away. Tandy whispers, "Mr. Wonderful's the same as yesterday."

"And who's he?"

"Dadda!" Tandy says, jiggling up and down in my arms.

"Daddy! Daddy! Daddy!" George, Jr., screams sliding in his slippers on the wood floor.

I put the kids to bed. George, Jr.'s asleep before I've tucked him in. But Tandy wants to talk. She enjoys hearing the stories being planned for TV. She tells me whether she likes them or not. She makes up ideas of her own.

"George?" Irene's voice outside the room stops conversation. "Dinner's getting cold."

Tandy kisses me good night. "Can we keep the light on?"

"Mummy wants it out."

Tandy rolls over on her side. I turn off the pump lamp by her bed.

Irene says I shouldn't let the kids stall at bedtime. She says I should be stricter—more like a father, less like a friend. She doesn't understand. There's so much to say.

Irene never liked sex with the lights on. She said it was lower-class. It never bothered me. She said it was as bad as making love with your clothes on. That's pleasant, too. "You have a lot of Russian peasant still in you." Maybe so, but I liked watching the way she bit her lip, the flutter of her eyelids as she craned her neck back over the pillow. But the minute she'd click us into darkness her face became a memory, a damp phantom who vanished from me every time I was beginning to crawl and swivel my way inside her like a Marine commando landing at Guadalcanal. Then, the screening room faces came up like credits across the dark pillow. I felt bad about this, but there was no stopping them: Barbara Stanwyck, Ida Lupino, Gene Tierney, Joan Collins, Rita—always Rita. They all got pieces of my action. They let Irene do all the moaning and panting—the voice-overs. But they received me with silent respect and full pleasure. After a while, a pattern began to emerge. Prone, it was leading ladies. Sitting, it was secretaries. Sideways, it was Esther Williams (who else, sideways?). And on my back, with more time and less responsibility, Sally Prescott spurred me to incredible performances. She'd whip me with her hair. It tingled and tore my flesh like rawhide. I'd rip her black slip in half. "Stop it, George," I heard her whimper. "No, baby," I'd say, burying my head in her muff.

When it was over, Irene would turn on the light.

I snap on my key-chain light. The treehouse is full of crayon graffiti and broken toys. A spider has her male tangled in her web. They freeze in my light.

I know the scene, Spider. It's hard to get your rocks off without getting swallowed alive.

"The Bible should be read as the story of the species," says The Reverend Charles Bury, putting down his glass of sherry and picking up his pet turtle.

We sit in canvas deck chairs on his lawn. Irene reaches over and holds my hand. She glances at her engagement ring. She bends down and kisses it, then looks up at me. I smile back.

Mr. Bury produces a piece of lettuce from his pocket, and holds it in front of the turtle. "It's all in Genesis. 'And the eyes of them both were opened, and they knew that they were naked; and they sewed fig leaves together and made themselves aprons . . .' "

I start to giggle.

"What's so amusing?" Mr. Bury says.

"In the Garden of Eden lay Adam
Complacently stroking his madam

And loud was his mirth
For he knew that on earth
There were only two balls—and he had 'em."

Mr. Bury chuckles. Irene scowls at me. "You agreed to a church ceremony, George."

"The Church often uses Adam and Eve as a parable to dramatize sex as a necessary evil," says Mr. Bury. "But only sexually reproductive things die. So sexuality is Man's glory and his destiny."

"I thought Adam and Eve were banished because they ate from the Tree of Knowledge?"

"But, my dear, what is the first thing Adam and Eve make after their fall from Divine Grace? Top hats for their minds? No. Aprons!"

"In America, I had to stand up in church and swear I wouldn't see movies that 'dwelled on suggestive situations'—*The Moon Is Blue, And God Created Woman.* I left the Church when it declared Brigitte Bardot a mortal sin."

"George was raised a Catholic," Irene says.

Mr. Bury watches the turtle creep into the flower bed. "Man is like a bee. He fertilizes the egg, then dies. He sustains the community. That's his role."

"We don't want children right away, do we, George?"

"I've got a berth on *Life* magazine when we go back to the States. You need mobility when you start out as a writer. Kids would be the wrong move."

"*Homo sapiens* always underestimates the nesting instinct. We don't think of ourselves in the scheme of things. The chain of being. Without sex, there is no death; without death there can be no development of the species. We old turtles must die to make room on the evolutionary ladder."

"Let's change the subject," I say, standing up.

"I've always found Nature very comforting."

"George is afraid of death," Irene says. "I'm not. There have been times in my life when it seemed beautiful and very close."

"You call twenty aspirins and half a pint of whiskey Death? You passed out."

"But I thought I was dying."

Mr. Bury eases out of the chair and gets to his feet. He helps Irene up. "The theological problems will sort themselves out. What's important is the right spirit." He smiles at us.

Irene takes Mr. Bury's arm. "Now, my dear," he says. "What day shall this celebration take place? Thursdays are best for me."

They walk ahead of me inspecting the flowers and talking about arrangements. The word "obey" will be included in the ceremony; there will be ten ushers and bridesmaids; there will be a Bentley waiting to take us to the reception; we will take a short honeymoon in Paris and sail back to America that same week because I'm scared of flying.

Irene looks radiant in the garden. Around her, robins jab at the grass and flutter in the afternoon sunlight. I finish my sherry and inhale the aroma of a summer day.

If the marriage doesn't work, I can always get a divorce.

My cubicle at Time-Life was about the size of this treehouse, and as messy. Even then, I'd read the contents of my wallet to calm myself down when I'd feel that panic —like a monosodium gultamate rush from too much Chinese food—seep into me. I'd take out the same jam-stained note that Irene once shoved inside my breakfast croissant and stare at it. After a while, the memory of

Time's "People" or the column-inches of the so-called "new journalists" in the *Village Voice* or the faces of the child prodigies photographed with captions in *Esquire* would pass. No wonder Irene's scrap paper is so crumpled. "You're scrumptious," it says.

If they found me sprawled dead in a Bowery gutter with only this wallet, the police would have a helluva puzzle to piece together. Kangaroo leather available only at Dunhill's. My secret society pin—gold with blue enamel —which only Irene has seen. In case of death she's the one who's supposed to handle it, not the police. They'd inspect the pin, but our fraternal code—YITB (Yours in the Bonds)—would stump even the cagiest gumshoe.

Yours in the Bonds. Where are they now, my thirteen best friends? It's not male bonding I'm interested in. Maybe it was in those days. Coming down from the tomb excited and tired, wearing our secret robes, giving our secret handshake, forming a circle with our arms around each other to sing one of our repertoire of secret songs— "Here We Are Together." Maybe that was my problem at college. Maybe I was a closet queen.

That panel discussion. "Whither Media?" Here's the clipping.

> NEW YORK—According to a top programming executive of a major network, sex, not violence, is the major TV villain. "Our children are growing up with sexual overload," said George L. Melish, 33-year-old son of movie producer Sol Melish, speaking for ABC at a conference at the Waldorf Astoria today.
>
> "We have a responsibility to reality. Everything our children see and hear on TV—from

ads to late-night movies—gives them the feeling th t sex is everywhere, that they should and
could be miniswingers. This, as we know, is not
the case. We must make distinctions between
love and lust, relationships and romance."

Drawing a parallel with the amount of killing
on TV westerns and the fact that only 115 hom-
icides were reported in the nine infamous
cattletowns, including Dodge City, between
1866 and 1887, Mr. Melish said: "Women do
not collapse at your feet if you wear this cologne or brush with that toothpaste. Seduction
is still as hard as ever. Children who grow up
thinking it isn't are placed in a potentially trau-
matic situation. They are forced to perform before they are ready. The adult world makes
them feel they should be enjoying themselves;
and if they are not, they are confused and sty-
mied. This is doubly dangerous because the
youth of today believe both science and the
modern sensibility condone casual promiscui-
ty."

Mr. Melish, smiling at the applause which
greeted his remarks, said that ABC was putting
many of their mature films into cassettes, which
make it more expensive, therefore harder, for
the youths to be titillated. ABC is investing
heavily in sports and documentaries, he said.

George, Jr., and Tandy. Their faces pressed close to
the Photomatic window, beaming like jack-o'-lanterns,
snuggling cheek to cheek with their Old Man in the
booth. The police might suss the connection with the
clipping when they pull out the silver matchbook from
our wedding: IRENE & GEORGE, September 1, 1963,
embossed in script on the cover.

But how would the police finally finger you, Melish? Not by the 1916-D dime you keep in the secret compartment of your wallet for good luck. The cops will pocket that. Eight million people in Fun City, Melish; two million of them with chesterfield coats. What'd be the telltale clue?

This is how they'll find you—a Trojan Gossamer Tip. Who else in the city, aged thirty-five, white, upper middle-class, educated in the best schools despite the dried blood caked over both eyes and mouth from that final punch-up, would still be carrying a *scum-bag!*

Girls go on the pill at twelve now, Melish. Abortions are easier to get than a doctor to visit your home. In the beginning, with Jeannie, she wanted the foam. She said it was less bother. But to you, foam was for egg creams.

At the Saranac drugstore, they kept the Trojans behind the counter. Today, they're displayed like Chiclets.

I walked briskly to the counter. A lady came out from behind "Prescriptions." "Mrs. Breers" was pinned onto her smock above the words "Thank You, Call Again."

"Can I help you?" she said.

"Just browsing."

I strolled to the rear of the store. I studied the paperback books. Then the pharmacist appeared.

Quickly, I picked out a paperback, a can of Old Spice shaving cream, a tube of Colgate toothpaste and hurried to the counter.

"Anything else?" the pharmacist asked, as I deposited my goods in front of him.

"Yes."

"Take your time," he said. "The lady will be with you in a moment."

Mrs. Breers appeared again from behind "Prescriptions." "Did you want all these?"

"Just a minute."

Standing in the back, I checked the mirror wedged in

the top right-hand corner of the store. This was how the pharmacist watched for kleptomaniacs, and how I watched for the pharmacist.

"Is that the section you're looking for?" Mrs. Breers called to me.

"Yes, ma'am."

"Women's eye shadow and nail remover?"

"Oh, sorry."

"What exactly are you looking for, sir?"

"False eyelashes."

"They're up here. On the counter."

On the way to the front, I stopped to choose a box of candy. I took my time. When I looked up, the pharmacist had taken over from Mrs. Breers. I walked quickly to him. I added the candy and eyelashes to the other items. He rang them up on the cash register. Each chinking of the machine made my head lighter; my heart was sprinting.

"Is that everything?"

"PackageofTrojansplease."

He reached into a side drawer. "Eight dollars and twenty cents," he said, taking my money and flipping the little red and white box into the paper bag with the other purchases.

"Thank you." Thank you. Thank you. Thank you. Thank you. Thank you.

"What do you call it?" Sue says, sitting cross-legged and nude on the bed. Her hair's as golden as Dad's Oscars. There's a well-scrubbed Briarcliff glow to her fine face. She unclips her Tiffany earrings and bends down to inspect.

"Prontor."

"Prontor? Sit."

"He won't lie down while you're here."

"Where'd you find a name like Prontor?"

"Science fiction."

"I love you, but I don't *love* you, if you know what I mean," Jeannie says.

"For once in your life, George, listen to your mother. I know your father won't talk to you about these things. He won't even let *me* read *From Here to Eternity*. You're a good boy. You've never been any trouble to either of us. Now that Yale's accepted you, you can take it easy these last two months. I'm all for having a good time. But be careful, darling."

"Of course, Mom."

"I'm not talking about the driving."

"Mother, I know."

"Your father has built up a reputation in this country. His public respects his product, and he respects his public. Any scandal . . . Well, look what happened to poor Fatty Arbuckle or Dalton Trumbo. Keep your nose clean, George."

"Have you been listening on the phone?"

"I have not."

"You have."

"Susan Kelley is a wonderful girl. She comes from a very fine family. The Judge and his wife are two of the nicest people it has been your father's and my pleasure to know."

"Mom, I'm no Jack the Ripper."

"Is there anything you'd like to ask?"

"Mother!"

"Keep your mouth shut, Vera. Tell him *not* to do

something and he'll do it. Tell him *to* do something, and he won't."

"I love you, Mom."

"I've heard that one before."

"I do."

"Your mother's been in show business, George. She knows the ropes. Listen to me for once in your life."

"Sue and I have been going to the movies. I'm teaching her about the films. She doesn't know anything."

"And what do you know?"

"A lot."

"I mean about s-e-x."

"Enough."

"Just because I don't have a college degree, don't get short with me, Buster."

"I didn't say anything."

"I heard that 'Enough.' Read your lines better around here Mr. Undress-In-The-Closet-And-Come-To-Bed-At-Three-In-The-Morning."

"I'm late already, Mom."

"Will you listen to me?"

"How can I listen if you won't be specific?"

"You've always been a polite boy, George. I've raised you to show respect. Of course, it would be nice if you held your mother's chair once in a blue moon at dinner."

"Sue hates it if I'm late."

"Take a cab. My treat."

"We're going to *Picnic* at the Loew's State."

"If you go to the men's room in those theaters put paper on the seat. You never know who's been there."

"All right, Mom."

"I was young once. I know what boys are after."

"What's that, Mom?"

"There are clinical words for it."

"Pudendum?"

"Don't get fresh. I looked that one up after our last talk. It's from the Latin."

"Tomorrow, Mom. OK?"

"It means 'Be Ashamed,'" Mom says, walking me to the door. "Have a good time, darling."

I tell Angie about Sue. I show him the letter signed, "You have my warmest, nicest, grossest thoughts." Angie's happy for me. He slaps me on the back. He serenades me!

> *"Tell me why*
> *There's lipstick on your fly*
> *Sloppy blow-job . . ."*

Trying to get away, Helen pushes her spiked heel through the cushion. I force her back down on the sofa. "I've been dreaming of eating you out."

"Get off me, George."

"Every day in the stacks, I'd see your face. I couldn't wait to rough you up."

"You didn't write once in five months."

"I was thinking of you."

"You promised to take me to the Yale-Princeton game."

"It'll be better than last summer."

"You've asked somebody else, haven't you?" Helen says, turning her head away as I try to kiss her.

"Sue Kelley."

"Is she as good as me?"

"Nobody tastes like you."

"That's not what I asked."

"I want to squeeze you. And tear you. And bite you."

"Look at the cushion, George. You're paying for this."
Helen knees me. "Get off."

I grab her chin. I kiss her hard. I feel her relax under
me.

Helen looks up. "I'd like to see a basketball game."

"No talk."

"And go to Mory's and the Old Campus."

"OK."

"Be careful, George."

"I love you, Helen."

"George, I'm not even wet down there."

Nude, except for the whip he holds between his teeth,
George Melish crawls the length of the Persian carpet to
where Rita sits, legs crossed, in her butterfly chair. The
silver studs on her belt blaze like headlights as he ap-
proaches.

"I love you," Melish whispers, squinting upward to see
her face.

Rita takes the whip out of his mouth. She stands above
him and stares down without a flicker of recognition. "I
know your type," she says. "Just a thong at twilight."

"I love you, Jeannie," George Melish says, as he pulls her
down into the midwestern field. The camera moves in for
a close-up.

"I love you, Sue," George Melish says, whispering as the
confessional window slides shut. She puts the palms of
her hands against the wood. Melish mounts her from behind.

"Marry me," Irene says. "You can't leave me now."

The bedroom light pops on. That was quick.

Bill Haley is about as fast in the saddle as an old seventy-eight—three minutes and lift up the needle. They roll off each other. Irene's eyes are shut out of frustration. He's left her high, and obviously dry. "Men experience the desire to sleep as soon as orgasm has been attained. A woman rarely feels the same way, and so she feels hurt when, culmination reached, she is ignored." Page 166. Third paragraph. Bottom right-hand corner: "How to Manage The Sex Act." "Chuck Berry should've done a little headwork on the art of love. He just doesn't know how to pull out all Irene's stops. In ten minutes, I could've given him a cram course and whipped him into shape. It's the pioneer who gets to know the territory.

"Read it, Irene."

"No, George. It's embarrassing. A man of your age with a sex manual."

"I find it acceptable. *Honi soit qui mal y pense.*"

"The answer is n-o. I don't want you there. It tickles."

"Page seventy-three. Where it says: 'Many women find this is the only way to achieve orgasm.' "

"I don't care about my pleasure, George."

"You should."

"A woman doesn't have to achieve orgasm to have a sexually fulfilled marriage."

"I want to give you an orgasm."

"Did you come?"

"Yes."

"That's all that matters. Sex isn't parcel post, George. You don't have to deliver the goods every time."

"You don't think I deliver the goods?"

"I didn't say that."

"Last week, you said I was fantastic in bed."

"You are."

"How do you know? I was your first lover."

"You're very good, dear."

"I could be better."

"Turn off the light if you don't want to read."

"I am reading."

"I don't call *Vixens' Eden* literature."

"Don't knock what you haven't tried."

"Good night, George."

I crave flesh in my hands. Conquest is all that concerns me. Hate is my aphrodisiac. I am the true Lover.

I fought for your hand, Irene. You were the treasure. I battled Lord Trewin until the early hours of the morning. I endured his insults. Nobody calls George Melish unworthy. Nobody tells George Melish he has no resources. His abuse only strengthened my resolve. I was banished from the house too late to find a hotel. I trudged from the Strand to Knightsbridge but no one would take in a student without a bag in hand. Finally, I settled on a bench in Hyde Park, but the screams from behind the bushes made it impossible to sleep. Rain began to fall. It was cold. I was forced to find shelter—the Hilton men's room, where I lay beside a toilet bowl. I returned the next day, smiling and scrubbed. And I won. At the wedding reception, Lord Trewin raised his champagne glass to me.

Feeling must have dignity. Love must be heroic. I have heart. I have words to stoke my anger and keep love alive. I kept my word. I didn't undergo hardship to have my prize squandered. I hate waste. While you sweat and steam in front of me, Irene, I am vigilant. So is Rita. She never turns her back on me. She keeps the faith. She appreciates a pure passion. Don't you, darling?

"If she hadn't treated you like shit, George, if she hadn't cheated on you and forced you to take revenge, if she hadn't put your career in jeopardy—I would have been honor bound to stay away."

"Thank God you didn't."

"Run your fingers over my peaches-and-cream complexion."

"I love the look of you. The lure of you. I'd love to make a tour of you."

"There's poetry in everything you say and do, George."

"I'll never lie to you, Rita. *Paid to Dance* and *Girls Can Play* were grade-B flicks."

"Treat me rough, George."

"Like Iceberg Slim in *Pimp?*"

"No coat hangers."

"B and D?"

"Bondage and Discipline. I need it."

"That's the difference between you and the others, Rita. They were playing at keeping house. You mean business."

"I owe you so much, George."

"We're even."

Did you lindy to one song about adultery? Was there one TV serial that bruised the way this separation does? Did the poets on the syllabus write about love's revenge? Thirty-five years of mental Muzak. Always playing house, Melish. Domesticated by age eight with dolls and a dollhouse; dressing up like "Mommy" and "Daddy" at ten; dancing school and all the steps by fourteen; going steady in a dry run of sharing at seventeen ("Can I wear your I.D.?" Sue said); pinned at twenty in a dry-hump of marital happiness ("I want five boys," Jeannie said. "Enough for a basketball team"). Even my office—its sink and refrigerator, televison and cocktail cabinet, Bar-

nett Newman and Nielsen ratings stuck on the white stuc-
co walls—everything is an adult playpen with all the
comforts of home.

You were prepared for business, Melish. Loyalty and
hard work were the mortar of university life. The big
names you'd met at the Yale *News,* the famous faces
who'd sipped sherry in the Merton Common Room, or
who sat at the country club pool with your parents, would
now be on your Rolodex. The world was only a telephone
call away. This is how you'd been taught it would be, and
when John Prescott sat behind his imitation Louis Qua-
torze desk explaining the ABC strategy, the game plan
was already second nature. "Be first. Look first-class.
Seek prestige." You'd been educated to give off the sig-
nals of success. This was just how the world was supposed to bend. Your eyes wandered. The fishing prints,
the tacky wooden animal sculptures and Toby mugs, the
framed pictures of Hanna and Barbera cartoons he'd
originated—Prescott didn't have the polish or the hard
edge. At ABC, you could be golden. Prescott was offering
a new life and you felt the affection of a son.

"Don't you like the proposal, George?"

"Like it? It's right up under my chin."

I know my product. I specialize in plots and happy
endings. My stories—the stories my writers make for
me—are tailored to very specific demands. They sit in my
office. They take notes. I know when a scenario is weak,
where it needs to be cut and strengthened. If I don't like
what I see, I change it.

I don't like Irene's scenario. And I have plans for a
rewrite.

Mick Jagger reaches down beside the bed. He pulls up his
guitar from the floor. He props himself against the pillows. His fingers slide up and down the strings. Blind

Lemon Lorber: white boy blues. Driving a Bentley and talking ghetto; letting it all hang out in custom-tailored suits—anybody can do that. Change is easy; consistency takes guts.

The pillow Mother gave us was embroidered with a rabbit on both sides. The pink rabbit had "No" written beneath it; the blue one, "Yes." It was on our bed when I lifted Irene over the threshold. She slept curled up like a child. Her face was alive with wonder at her dreams. I wrote to Wads, "I kiss her awake. She unfolds to me like a flower. I am her sun."

'61

George Melish
Merton College
Oxford

Two news flashes from Angleterre. GEORGE "Steamer" BELL, Oklahoma's most important gift to politics since the oil depletion allowance, is making hay while his Rhodes Scholarship shines. From his rooms at Balliol, George is publishing a six-page newspaper called *Okie at Oxford* and mailing it to his would-be constituency back home. He plans to return from the Big O next year to study law and run for Congress. Issue 5, the latest, is all about Steamer's trip to Jerusalem to see the cave where Jesus was born. There's a picture of him on the spot, and also an editorial on the Arab-Israeli problem, which Steamer says is a real can of worms. As luck would have it, Steamer met JERRY STEVENS and his beautiful archeologist wife Barbara at the Wailing Wall. They were on a dig nearby. Jerry and Steamer were the powers behind the Yale Political Union. If you can steal one election, Steams, you can steal two. (Just joking.)

GEORGE MELISH, the man himself, is proud to announce his engagement to Irene Trewin, daughter of Lord and Lady Trewin of London and Oxfordshire. You guys can start addressing your letters to "His Majesty." I never thought I'd be the first of my roommates to marry. But when love walks in, it takes you for a spin. We plan to be hitched at St. Margaret's Westminster with a spectacular reception at the Dorchester. Lord Trewin—or "The Colonel," as his friends call him—is a WWII hero as well as a

99

real estate wizard. He parachuted four times into enemy territory in the south of France and was seriously injured on his last jump. He's known at Boodles as "the man who broke his back at Monte Carlo."

SANDY VAN MEGS writes: "MIKE WEYLAND, BILLY DeBRETTEVILLE, THUMPER TAFT and myself were graduated from the U.S. Marine Officers Candidate School. We've been trained as Advisers for a Southeast Asia assignment. They say the girls and the French food there are exquisite."

There are millions of people who'd pay good money for this bird's-eye view of Big Fred. Just to hear him sing his golden hits costs thirty-five dollars a head in Las Vegas; fifteen-fifty at Carnegie Hall; five at Shea Stadium. Think of the money I'm saving. Irene would be proud.

> *"Got a buzz on you baby*
> *Overamping on your charge,*
> *Got a buzz on you baby,*
> *Electric kisses make me large."*

Listen to that. In my day, he couldn't share a stool with the Kingston Trio. Two literary critics writing for journals that sell for over two dollars have called our Fred "the poet of his generation." Books are made from his lyrics. They're not written in Byron's *ottava rima,* or Pope's heroic couplets. Fred wouldn't be on Leavis' "line of wit." But next to the German mark, he's the best currency of exchange. Everybody has an opinion on the putz. You can't hop into bed with any of these young ones unless you do fifteen minutes on his style. They love it when I reveal I know him. I tell them about the meaning of rock lyrics. (I'm rather impressive on the imagery of light in *Sgt. Pepper*.) It took me a long time to learn the new lyrics. It took me a long time to learn the new dances— the fish, the boogaloo, the funky chicken. But I did it. I'm no sore thumb on the dance floor. I look as sexy as the next guy. Why do I keep remembering the mambo?

> *"Buzz like the current,*
> *Buzz like the bee,*
> *Buzz like everything you do to me."*

Every time he sings the word "buzz," Fred's chin juts out over his guitar like a clucking rooster.

Irene laughs. She joins in. A southern accent comes easily to the impoverished English upper classes.

> *"Buzz like freedom,*
> *Buzz like joy,*
> *Buzz like love*
> *'Tween girl and boy."*

Irene puts her arm around Fred's pimply shoulder and hugs him close.

> *"Oooo—eee!*
> *Got a buzz—*
> *An all-time buzz*
> *On my baby."*

"One more time!" Irene giggles.

Mother was right. I should've learned an instrument.

Melish, you were a musical Arthur Murray. Before you, Irene couldn't hold a tune. Her idea of a lyric writer was William Wordsworth.

That first year—when we were still struggling—I'd pull down the window to muffle the conga drums on Twenty-second and Eighth Avenue. I'd turn the lights low. I'd spin the great sounds. No candy-ass guitar and scratchy voice; but Nelson Riddle orchestrations—violins, percussion, brass—the works. We'd fox-trot cheek to cheek.

Irene was embarrassed by crooning. I don't know why.

"It's so soppy, George."

"Sit down and listen. I grew up to these sounds."

"You take it so seriously."

"Sing it the way Lena does, honey. Hiss the 's'. Stretch the vowels. Bite down hard on the consonants."

Lena was the kind of woman you had to tame. She had a hunger—sharp, fierce, eager, tough. Her rhythm was mine after three Scotch and sodas at the DKE "Happy Hour." "Listen to this, Irene:

> *"When I'm takin' sips*
> *From your tasty lips*
> *Seems the sugar almost drips,*
> *You're* confec—tion, *goodness knows,*
> *'Cause you're my honey—suck—le ro—ose."*

"Why can't she just sing the song?"

"Don't you get it? Don't you feel it? Lena's hot to trot."

"She's making a fool out of herself if you ask me."

"What about Ella?"

"I like to sing, George, but I'm no jazz baby."

"Listen closely, sweetheart. These are the only women who talked about love the way I dreamed it'd be."

"Sol? We're not finished eating."

"Ball game," Dad says.

"I haven't finished my coffee, Sol. Do you mind?"

"It's Padres against Antonelli," Dad calls back, disappearing into the television room.

"That man," Mom says. "You see what I have to put up with, George?"

"More coffee, Mom?"

"Thank you, dear."

"If it wasn't for me, this house would be in ruins. Bills wouldn't be paid. Laundry wouldn't get done. He expects everything on a silver platter. No wonder his first wife divorced him. The man doesn't know where to fine one single thing in this house. I have to do everything. It's not good for my heart."

"Sue wants me to escort her to her coming-out party."

"I like that girl, George. Be good to her. It means so much to a woman."

"I don't want to go."

"Why not?"

"It's white tie and tails."

"Are any of your other friends going?"

"Jane Parker's asked Angie. Tommy Newman is going."

"I'll buy you a set."

"But Dad said . . ."

"Never mind what Dad said. You should go. You're only young once. I've gone without before for you, George, I can do it again. I don't expect any thanks, just a little respect now and then."

"I don't know if I should go. It's better to play hard-to-get. Girls don't like if it you're too . . . obvious."

"She'd be very lucky to get a nice young man like you."

"You're not objective. You're my mother."

"My only advice to you, Mister, is don't be a pig."

Dad comes back into the dining room. He bends over the Grundig console. He clicks off the radio. "Can't hear the play-by-play."

"We were enjoying a little culture, Sol. Some people want to improve themselves."

"Any nuts, Vera? I'm hungry."

"You can't possibly be hungry. You just ate."

"Nuts have no cholesterol."

"I'm not feeding you again, Sol. If you don't eat what's put in front of you, then it's just too bad. Think of your kidneys."

"Giants got two in the first," Dad says to me, going toward the room. "Mays homered with one on."

"George, would you shut the dining room door? That's a good boy. You were saying about Sue Kelley before we were so rudely interrupted?"

"I've found a little illusion goes a long way."

"You don't lie to girls, do you?"

"Mom!"

"True love is honest love. Generally speaking, no matter what his faults, your father has been honest with me all these years."

"You never lied?"

"Did he say I did?"

"No."

"Often, when your father and I have been on the town, men have made certain proposals to me, if you know what I mean."

"In front of Dad?"

"Your father hates to dance. He might as well stay at home. But your old mother wasn't voted Miss Terpsichore of Pittsburgh, P.A., for nothing. It usually happens on the dance floor, during the rumba. I just say: 'I'm very flattered. But my family comes first.' "

"Want me to put on a record? He can't hear with the door shut."

"Even if he can, let's give ourselves a treat."

"George Feyer? Frank Sinatra?"

"Something classical. *Carmen Jones.*"

> *"Toreador-a,*
> *Don't spit on the floor-a,*
> *Use the cuspidor-a,*
> *That is what it's for-a."*

"A woman likes a man who's sensitive; who can appreciate the finer things. Sometimes you talk like a mental retard."

"Sue thinks I'm brainy."

"You can fool some of the people some of the time, Mr. Too-Big-For-Your-Boots. But I'm telling you this for your own good. Nobody wants a slob."

"She wants to go steady."

"You're not fast, are you?"

"You've got a dirty mind, Mom."

"Oh, this part is beautiful. Carmen is this seductive southern beauty. She meets Joe, who's supposed to imprison her. But she sings her way out of it."

"It sounds awful."

"Like father, like son. No sense of romance." She starts to sing.

"Mom. Your voice."

"Don't laugh, young man. When I was your age, I had a range of three octaves. If I'd had your opportunities, I could've gone into the opera instead of musical comedy."

The door opens. "Vera! The ball game!"

"Goddammit, Sol. I live here, too."

"All I ask is for a little peace and quiet when the Dodgers play the Giants."

"There are finer things in this world."

"Christ," Dad says and slams the door.

"Opera's so . . . melodramatic."

"You're a funny one, George."

"Why?"

"All this going steady and dates. What do you think passion is? Welling melodramatic emotion—that's what it is. If your father and I didn't fight, I'd be worried that the flame of love had died."

"Sue says she loves me."

"Do you love her?"

"I suppose so."

"There's no 'suppose' about love, George. There's only one love in a person's life. And when it happens, you'll know it."

"What do you call it?" Jeannie says.

"Godzilla."

"I love you, Godzilla."

"Does it have a name, Daddy?" Tandy says, pointing as we wallow in the bath together.

"The Thing."

The taxicab rumbles up Park Avenue.

"Do you understand what I'm saying, Sue? Does it sink into that pretty blond Irish-Catholic head of yours? 'An unexamined life is not worth living.' I don't want you as a decoration. You can't get away with being just a beautiful face with George Melish. Good looks are water off a duck's back to me. I've been with dozens of good-lookers —model-types. Some of them have very big breasts, and apartments of their own. You'd be surprised at how advanced these girls are. They don't have curfews. They don't push my hand away. They don't wear underwear.

But I ask myself, 'What do they have upstairs? What do
they want out of life?' They're only interested in enjoying
me in the fullness of the moment, if you get my meaning.
I think you want more than that, Sue. I could have my
way with you if I wanted. There are ways. You have to
work hard at going steady. We've got to help each other
grow. That's why we've got to read, to reach out. We've
got so little time, Sue; we can't reject any experience."

"Sometimes, George, I think you're too good for me."

"You'll grow. I'll help you. We'll share each other."

"Can I wear your I.D. bracelet, George?"

"What are you going to give me?"

Sue kisses me. We lean close together in the corner of
the seat. She takes my hand and guides it under the
rickrack border of her Lanz dress.

"I'll say yes to life, George. I promise."

"She said yes? Just like that?"

"Would you believe ten minutes after the run-through?
It's being in church that makes you want to fuck."

"It's a wedding, not a mixer, Angie."

"What's her name?"

"Griselda Duff-Jones. Irene's best friend. The maid of
honor."

"I'm a three-figure man now, Meli. But I've never had
an English girl. Do they really close their eyes and think
of the Queen?"

"Griselda's engaged to be married. He's a captain in
the Guards."

"My only responsibility's to bring the ring," Angie
says, pinching my nipple. "And I've got it, sweetie."

"Many people sitting on my side?"

Angie opens the vestry door and peeks out. "You think
it would be easier to shack up at the Hilton?"

"Cleaner."

"She won't have to sign the register or anything?"

"Who's on my side, Angie?"

"Vera just walked in. Big V's twisting her handkerchief. You know what that means."

"Who else?"

"Some Rhodes Scholar types. Cordovans and club ties. The other side's shoulder to shoulder."

"She's a great girl, Angie."

"I remember in 'fifty-eight, you'd put Jeannie on the train. You were bawling."

"Jeannie's married now. Two kids already. She was older than me, you know."

"Mom gave you a Scotch. You choked and blew lunch. God, you looked funny with your head lopped over the toilet seat. You kept saying, 'Jeannie's the greatest girl in the world.'"

"She was—until Irene. I was just a kid, then."

"We raised some hell, Meli. Had some fun."

"You don't like her, do you, Angie?"

Angie tweaks my cheek. He reaches inside his morning coat and pulls out an envelope. "I, Victor Angell, being the best friend of George Melish and of sound mind and body, do hereby declare the Sex Sweepstakes of the World a draw. The point system is hereby abolished. And, in so doing, the tell-tale evidence, the proof of the pud is returned, as promised, on the day of marriage."

"What is this?"

"Open it."

"She really is a good girl, Angie. Strong. Sensitive. Principled. She needs me."

"Open the envelope, schmuck."

"You kept these pictures?"

"And your letters. There wasn't enough room on the 707 for all of them."

"You threatened to show this one to Helen."

"My photographic talent was in evidence even at seventeen."

"Christ, I was embarrassed by that hard-on. You came into the bathroom, I remember. I was brushing my teeth after the party."

"It didn't take much to get a rise in your Levi's, Meli. One Nat King Cole record and Bambi Abrams backed up against the fish tank."

"With the lights out and the tank lit up, you could see through her crinoline."

"The next picture's a masterpiece."

"Look at us. Muff-diving on the Riviera. Thin as rails. Those goggles and snorkels cost us two days' food."

"All that underwater pelt we caught, Meli. It was worth it."

"Incredible."

The vestry door creaks open. "Can a mother say her final good-byes to her one and only son?"

"Hello, Mrs. Melish."

"Angie, have you got the boat-train tickets?"

"A-OK."

"And the ring?"

"In my pocket."

"Show it to me."

Angie produces the maroon box and snaps it open. "My hands are clean, too, Mrs. Melish."

Mother's mouth turns up at the corners. "Always the joker. Don't get too personal in your toast at the reception, Victor. And for goodness sake, remember to call George's mother-in-law *Lady* Trewin."

"I've gotten very suave. It's part of my profession."

"Your mother told me you were working for a fashion photographer."

"Bert Stern. I was just showing George a couple of my studies. Portraits."

"One other thing, Angie. Don't toast to absent friends.

The less the guests are reminded that Sol—Mr. Melish—isn't here, the better. I'm so ashamed I could die. But business is business."

"I'll be outside if you need me, Mrs. Melish."

"Thank you, Victor. It's nice the way you boys have remained friends all these years."

Angie takes his pictures from me. "We have so much in common, Mrs. Melish," he says, backing out the door.

For a long time, Mother stands still and gazes at me.

"I like your dress, Mom."

"Blue's your favorite color."

"I've never seen this quilted material in a dress."

"Make her happy, George," Mom says. "Make her happy."

"You're supposed to cry after the ceremony, not before."

"You've been such a good son."

"And you've been a great mother."

"You mean that, George? Really?"

"Yes."

"All these years, George, I've thought about leaving your father. He means well, but you can take just so much. We stayed together for you. It was worth it—for you."

"Every family has its ups and downs."

"Are you wearing the new shoes I bought you?"

"Too slippery for the marble floor, Mom."

"You're not wearing the pair with the hole?"

"What does it matter?"

"It matters to *me*. We're not off the boat, you know."

"Any more words of advice, Mom?"

"Your father and I spent our honeymoon night on a train, too. The Super Chief. Irene's not . . . I mean I was . . . Well, show business people know the ways of the world, George. Don't begin your marriage with a rape."

Angie sticks his head inside. "The music's started. I think my maid of honor's in the vestibule."

"Can you see Irene?"

"White veil. White sleeves. White stockings. White dress. I think she's trying to tell us something."

"Remember, when the Reverend Charles Bury announces the hymn, we walk out and take our places by the altar."

"Right now, she's standing like she's about to receive a tennis serve," Angie says.

"Anxious?"

"Determined."

The neon from NEW HAVEN MOTOR INN flickers across the bedspread.

"I can't marry you, George," Sue says. "You're too . . . irresponsible."

"Name one thing."

"Writing."

"It's a perfectly honorable profession."

"Do you happen to know how many writers actually earn a living by their work? Daddy was telling me. I think the military would make more of a man out of you than Oxford."

"We could starve for a while. All young marrieds do."

"Not me."

"May I touch you?"

"Goat," Sue laughs, flopping her head back onto the pillow.

"You're beautiful."

"Not bad."

"Just a rub."

"See, George, this is what I mean. Any adult would respect a lady's request."

I roll on top of her. "Take your pants off, darling."

"I've got 'my friend.' "

"It feels so good with your pants off. May I take them off?"

Sue arches her pelvis. I slip the nylon underwear to the bottom of the bed. I kick them down into the corner so she can't find them. We heave together.

"Not so hard, George."

Sue's eyelashes flutter closed. Her body trembles as I slide my cock faster and faster along her groin to the flat of her stomach.

"May I put it in, darling? We're safe."

"No," she says, her eyes clamped shut. "Oh, George."

"You're so good."

Her legs fold around me. I shove hard into her.

"Christ!" Sue says.

"Good, isn't it?"

She leans up on her elbows. "Oh, this is really great. Turn on the light."

"What's the matter?"

"My Tampax. The string. You've jammed it up me!"

"The Wedge, Conerly! Up the middle!" Dad leans toward the television set chomping his cigar.

"Sol," Mom says. "That cigar makes me nauseous."

Dad slaps my knee. "Third and three. It's all power, this game. Three yards and a cloud of dust."

"Conerly's a passing quarterback, Pop."

"Wrong, George. When you're in trouble, you keep driving. Find a hole. Bull your way in. Get your victories any way you can."

"Bet a dollar it's a buttonhook."

"Always expect the unexpected, George."

"Sol, do I have to vomit on the new carpet before you stub that thing out?"

"Look at that! Conerly's handing off to Webster! Straight over center. A hole so big you could drive a truck through it!"

"First down. Goal to go."

Dad turns to me and takes the cigar out of his mouth. "Football's a good teacher, George. Possession's nine-tenths of the law."

"Keep still, Sue."

"You're not going to use those tweezers?"

"It's a very small piece of string."

"I've got a two-hour ride back to New York tomorrow. For heaven's sake, shut the curtains."

"Stay calm."

"I can't go to my doctor. He's known me since I was a baby."

"Let me feel again." I put my finger deep into her. My fingernail touches the string. I try to inch it forward so I can draw it out with two fingers.

"Do you have it, George?"

"Almost."

"Goddammit, George."

"We need a better angle. The pillow's not good enough."

I take the Gideon Bible out of the writing desk. I shut the curtains. "This should give us some leverage."

"I should've stayed at the Taft."

"I think I've got it, Sue."

"Women die from accidents like this."

"Steady as she goes. There!"

When Sue comes back from the bathroom she gets into bed and turns away from me on her side.

"May I touch you?"

"Let me see your hands."

She looks at them. "Your fingernails are dirty, George."

". . . Wilt thou love her, comfort, honor and keep her, in sickness and in health? and, forsaking all others, keep thee only unto her, so long as ye both shall live?" says The Reverend Charles Bury.

"I will."

The weather-beaten pink rowboat is pulled up onto the hot sand fifty yards away. Our footprints pockmark the beach and lead to this spot.

"I can't go back to England without you. I can't start dating again. I won't. I'd rather kill myself."

"Why don't you take a dip, Irene?"

"Those spiny things are in the water."

"Wear your sneakers."

"Do you love me, George? Say you love me."

"I love you."

"How much?"

I hold my arms wide.

"Only that much?"

I stretch them wider.

"Love has responsibilities."

"I'm young. I've just finished exams."

"I wouldn't make a mess of it this time. I'd slit my wrists."

"The water's warm and soothing."

Irene laces up her sneakers. I watch her walk to the sea and bend over the waves. Salt water glistens on her tanned body as she splashes herself. Except for the shoes, she's nude.

I take out my pad. I write the name Irene Melish first in capitals, then in script. Finally, I make a chart.

+   Irene   —

Kind	Nervous
Attractive	Demanding
Good mind	Says what she thinks
(must read more)	No ambition
Loyal	Not crazy about kids
Sociable	Willful
Sense of humor	Cooking—fair
Trust fund	
Needs me	

Irene is treading water twenty yards from the beach and waving at me to join her.

I walk down to the damp sand. "Hold your horses!"

"The water's great, George. What are you doing?"

"Digging a hole."

"What for?"

"To see how deep I can get."

"Love me?"

I crumple the list and put it in the hole. I kick the sand back on top of it. "Love you," I yell and take a running dive into the sea.

Later, on the same spot, we lie together in the sun.

The surf spills over our ankles, sliding up to our thighs. "Did you come?"

"You're great, George."

I lived to see Irene happy like this—confident and calm. She never sang for me.

Sometimes I'd come home early. I'd stand at the window and watch Irene sitting in the wicker chair at the bottom of the garden. Her guitar rested on her knee. She sang to herself while little George played in his pen and

Tandy made earth pies. Even though I wasn't in the picture, I didn't feel like a guest passing through.

"Happy"—Mom's last request at our wedding. "Happy"—Irene's first word when I said I'd marry her. "Happy?"—the question I asked Irene when she'd sit silent and alone by the window twirling her hair. I know about happiness. It's my occupation. I give people their dreams.

Before she undermined my sense of timing, I could get a laugh faster than Groucho. She'd flash that accordion grin and squeeze my hand three times, which meant "I love you, very, very, very much." I did everything to please. She didn't like *Life*. I switched to ABC. She got nervous with some of my fraternity brothers, we dropped them. New York was a shock after London. "No waves" became our motto. That takes sweat, believe me. A man has to earn his daily bread. Irene and George Harrison can lounge around the house all morning. They can sing and go for walks. But I had a corporate ladder to climb. And don't think there weren't temptations along the way. Jackie, my secretary, is a knockout. She wears her suede skirt so high I can see the border of her underwear. After I left Irene, Jackie gave me her telephone number, saying, "What you see is what you get." But I'm no cradle robber. I don't want mercy fucking. When Prescott handed over the programming reins to me to move up to the twentieth floor, he said, "It's your turn to burn the midnight oil." It was a privilege. I made the front page of *Variety*. They called me a "whizz-kid." Prescott gave me credit for engineering the National Football League deal, the least he could do for me carrying him over the last eighteen months. At my desk, I felt like a broken-field runner—shifty, treacherously fast, instinctive. Everything from Dick Cavett to Howard Cosell's toupee was my territory. I inherited 290 projects a year and each required a different pace. I knew the pockets of power and how to follow them. I could feel the mood of the opposition and sweep around them. Each day, sometimes juggling twenty different productions, was a series of presentations, conferences, screenings. My decisions meant hundreds of thousands of dollars. I felt graceful and unfaltering. Irene accepted the long hours. She was happy for me.

Rita's silence annoys me. I'm no Hamlet. Action is my middle name. She crouches in the shadows at the other corner of the treehouse. The creaking must be her shivering. "I know how to hate, baby. The Jew of Malta has nothing on me. LeRoi Jones is a cream puff compared to what I've got inside."

"Use that anger," Rita says finally. "That's what Orson told me. Focus it. Make it pay."

"You've heard of Jack the Ripper?"

"He cut away his victims' snatches."

"And Cochise?"

"What about Cochise? Jeff Chandler played him for Warner's. You look like Jeff Chandler, you know that?"

"Cochise left his victims manacled and buried up to their necks in sand. The buzzards pecked them to death."

"George! You wouldn't?"

"I might."

"Kiss me, darling."

"First things first."

"Maybe when we're both married, George, we'll meet on the street. I'll be wheeling the baby down Fifth Avenue. You'll be hurrying to have lunch with your agent. Our lives will have gone their separate ways, but you'll always have a place in my heart. You'll stop and say hello. We'll talk about the good old days—about now. We'll rent a hotel room and make love."

"Nobody knows your body like I do, Sue. We'll do everything we used to do. We'll dive-bomb into each other. We'll explore. I'll cut out my pants pockets like the old days so your smooth fingers can find their way even in broad daylight."

"That's a promise, George. It'd be fun to have an *affaire* with you."

"I love you, Susan Teresa Kelley."

"I adore you, George."

A man wants to come home to a smiling wife, a nice dinner, and chitchat about the kids. He wants to enjoy his precious leisure time. He doesn't want soul-searching discussion—he can get that at the office. He wants the missus jaunty and playful and fun: in fact, he wants exactly what's lying on my four poster at 212 Palisades Road, Sneden's Landing.

Wait until Little Stevie Wonder gets Irene's tears. Nancy Neurosis'll spook him. The scowl. The rivulets of water following her crow's-feet and winding down her neck; or clinging to her nose like icicles. It's embarrassing. Who wants to stuff a psycho? It was my responsibility to calm her down. Melish, you were conjugal Compazine. A lover can just take his bongos and beat it; a husband has to face the music. Big Fred's always singing about the open road and the call of the wild. If Irene goes on one of her jags, she's had it. In the Age of Aquarius, there's no time for lamentation. It's good times or good-bye. I'm the only one who knows how to deal with her tears.

"In business, you learn to control yourself, Irene. Swallow hard."

"You don't know what it's like to wake up feeling permanently bruised inside."

"That's lovely to hear, really lovely. I'm out there working for us—you, me, the kids. I'm providing for our future. Be happy. You can't break into tears every time you have a momentary setback. Take a Librium or mix an extra martini. Work harder to take your mind off things. Maybe you should see a psychiatrist."

"It's not enough. None of this is enough."

"What more do you want? I gave you two healthy kids. You have a nice home. I worship you."

"I'm tired of being worshipped."

"That's what love is all about."

"I want some danger in my life."

"So? We'll move back to the city."

"This is no joke, George."

"You get married to be with somebody, to raise a family, to be happy. Show me where it says danger is happiness."

"Remember when you snuck into the garden after Father said you weren't to see me again?"

"I couldn't live without you."

"Exactly."

"I still can't.

"But it's different, isn't it? I remember those minutes. Taking bread out of the larder and walking toward the pond. She liked it when I fed the ducks. I did it every day when I was a child. Then, cutting behind the elm trees. My skin like needles. My palms clammy. My mind racing with worry if you'd be there, if she'd seen me detour."

"It was terrible, Irene."

"And beautiful."

"You can't romanticize fucking in a greenhouse. My trouser knees black from dirt. Rotten fruit staining your dress."

"Every word, every moment counted. I'd made up my mind to kill myself if they stopped me marrying you."

"We were just kids."

"But we were never careless."

"*I* was never careless."

"Don't start that again, George."

"*You* started it."

"Look at me," Irene says, She draws her fingers across her face. "When I married you, I had chubby cheeks, grease panels, thin hair."

"You're beautiful."

"I owe you a lot, George."

"But you're not satisfied!"

"No."

"When I grew up, the road map was clear. There was a good route and a bad one, Roddy McDowall or James Dean. I always traveled the main road. Blue-chip college. Good job. Nice neighborhood. Fun vacations. A well-organized portfolio. Everybody wanted that. When I went into television, it was the Cadillac of careers. People respected me for it. I was the only man in my graduating class of a thousand. 'Establishment' wasn't a swearword then. I didn't have to fight my way through protest picket lines to get to work."

"George, you're the nicest man I know. Don't cry."

"Bullshit, Irene. That's what they all say—what they all said. Mr. Nice, Mr. Right, Mr. Good Guy. Christ, you married me! I should be OK. Believe me, there were a lot of other ones—I mean quite a few—who would have been proud to be Mrs. George Melish. What's got into your head, Irene? You're not smoking marijuana with Sally Prescott, are you?"

"Don't raise your voice, George. The children."

"I'm not raising my voice. I'm excited, that's all. Don't you see how this tear bit can affect the kids? They'll think I'm an ogre. I'll be distrusted, feared. What am I, anyway, a wife beater? Before you know it, we'll have two yo-yo's for youngsters."

"Don't yell."

"Do you realize that I'm a hundred and eighty pounds and six feet tall. You are a hundred and ten and five-four. I could break your jaw. One punch. One jab. Cram your fucking white teeth down your throat for all this pain."

"Two months after I had George, we went to the Prescotts' party for Elton Rule. You're supposed to be at your best for the company president, but I felt lumpy and ugly. I wore that long red and blue Indian print dress you bought me. It hid my stomach pretty well. Until that night, I'd been in the house thirty-seven days in a row with the kids. I remember sitting next to John Prescott, feeling dazed and nervous about what to say. He began telling me about his fishing trip to Canada. He'd taken Jenny. He described the lake in the early morning and the eerie sounds of loons hidden by the mist. He talked about the art of casting and the smell of bass being fried over an open fire. He said he'd never known such tranquillity. I was flattered that he wanted to talk to me and not to Mrs. Rule on his right. The way he spoke—so quietly, so directly—made me feel very attractive. I'd almost forgotten I was young. Then I looked down at the food. I was cutting his meat for him."

"Why don't you just say you're horny?"

"But that's not it."

"You get enough sex. I know sometimes you're eager in the morning. But I've got responsibilities at the office."

"You don't listen, George."

"If you're bored, go to Hunter. Work toward a degree."

"Last week, I drove your mother home. As we approached the George Washington Bridge, I pointed to it and said, 'Bridge.' "

"You're going to a psychiatrist."

"Will you talk sensibly, George? It's not easy for me to tell you this."

"To put all these years of work, all these hours of dreams and tears into jeopardy. This is a fine way to show your thanks. You want to be somebody else? Who? Jean

Shrimpton? Jane Fonda? Mrs. John Prescott? At least for
the last five years you've been Mrs. George Melish.
Sometimes I think we've got nothing in common."

"We both love you."

"Jesus, you get me mad!"

I punch the plywood cabinet with a right jab. It dents
the wood.

I punch it again with a left cross.

Irene takes my hand. Standing, she turns her head slowly
toward me. "I, Irene, take thee, George, to be my husband, to have and to hold from this day forward; for better, for worse; in sickness and in health; to love and to
cherish, till death us do part, according to God's holy law;
and thereto I plight thee my troth."

Don't talk to me about troth. I've studied Anglo-Saxon. I
know its roots. I know the original: "trouþ." Price, my
tutor at Merton, used the word as an example of the Old
English thorn. He took a map of England from his book-
shelf and threw it in front of me. He dropped to his
knees. *"That,* Mr. Melish," he said, drawing his finger
carefully across the Midlands from Wolverhampton to
Leicester to Cambridge, "is where the 'þ' changes to
'th.' "

Troth. Truth. Betroth. Be-truthful. *B*etrothed. Maybe
that's why I liked Old English, it was a legacy of loyalty
that fits with our American heritage. It was dangerous out
there on the sea. Iron will was necessary. Loyalty was
cherished—the supreme virtue. We can still hold true to
pioneer values—the plighted word, good faith. What
could be more noble? More important? I've been trained
to swear oaths and believe in them.

At the Cub Scouts—the two pudgy fingers of my right hand raised, my mind dreaming of the merit badges I'd win—I swore:

> *On my honor, I will do my best to do my duty to God and my country and to obey the Scout law to help others. At all times to keep myself physically strong, mentally awake and morally straight.*

And I stayed straight. While other boys my age were sneaking into the bathroom with stolen copies of *Cavalier*, I was earning the Order of the Arrow—straight arrow. My initiation pledge—administered in the original Iroquois—is too long and too complicated to recite at this hour (but I remember it, believe me).

At the Little League, my first starting assignment— standing on second base, Bazooka bubble gum wedged like a marble under my tongue, holding the maroon and white cap over my heart—I believed in the flag I was swearing allegiance to.

> *I pledge allegiance to the flag of the United States of America. And to the Republic for which it stands, one nation under God, indivisible, with liberty and justice for all. Play ball.*

I went three for three in my debut, so it worked.

At the secret society initiation at Yale, I filed between two lines of Brothers to the Great Hall. They stood in their purple robes, hoods drawn up and pointed on their heads, their secret pins glowing on their chests in the candlelight.

> *"As the sacred portal opens*
> *Remember what this Tomb betokens.*

The Book, the Snake our emblems be—
Learning and immortality."

I stood alone at the altar. I drank from the gold chalice which, like the gold ceiling, had been donated by the Vanderbilts. I repeated my memorized oath from the Celtic Well of Wisdom.

> *"I am the wind that blows the sea;*
> *I am the wave of the deep;*
> *I am the bull of seven battles;*
> *I am the eagle of the rock;*
> *I am a tear of the sun;*
> *I am the fairest of plants;*
> *I am a boar for courage;*
> *I am a salmon in the water;*
> *I am the word of knowledge;*
> *I am the head of the battle-dealing spear.*
> *I am the god who fashions thought in the mind."*

When I had finished, the Number One approached me. He took my hand in his. He gave me a secret handshake. "Four-two-two," he said, whispering the holy numbers in my ear, each time pressing my fingers tighter. He handed me the key to the front gate. The brotherhood chanted in unison:

> *"The key is blessed as the cross*
> *Its bearer shall not suffer loss*
> *It will guide you through this life*
> *It will keep you free from strife."*

They circled around me. One by one, they stepped forward to embrace me. I hugged them back. I forgot my sadness at not being tapped by "Bones." I felt proud. I knew then that, if anybody said "Book and Snake" in public, I'd leave the room.

But these were just warm-ups, reprises for the ultimate troth. The Big T. "WHAT ABOUT THE VOWS, IRENE? WHAT ABOUT THE FUCKING VOWS!"

Irene walks to the window, slipping her nightdress over her head. "Did you hear anything, Pooper?" she says, looking back at Fred, who's now rolling a joint. "I thought I heard somebody screaming for help."

Funny about those little endearments, isn't it, Melish? You think they belong to you. I never let other girls call me Pooper. They can call me Sweetie or Beast or Stud; they can whisper the name of last night's lay in my ear, but not Pooper. That was Irene's word when we were very calm, and very content.

I stare at her. Her eyes are black as buttons. The moonlight gives her skin a soft sheen. To see her face unraveled from worry or anger has the riveting nostalgia of an old snapshot. I feel grateful to the darkness.

Irene goes back to the bed and steps out of her slippers. She dims the light.

The orange ember of the cigarette bobs up and down as they pass it between them.

I bet the sheets are clean and cold. I bet Irene's legs are smooth and slippery as she rubs against him. The pillow smells of starch and her hair. In the morning, she'll wake up tasting of sleep and feeling even softer.

You've made me avant-garde, Irene. Fidelity—that's really unconventional.

My hands are in my pants. My cock is hard. I wave it at them. I want them to see, and be ashamed.

A kiss is not just a kiss; any naturalist knows that. A kiss is a ritualized feeding movement. The mouth receives, the tongue provides. I'm the provider. I should feed Irene. A kiss is life-giving. Irene's grown strong on my mouth.

I'm the birthday boy, Fred. I can do what I want. Can you see me in your marijuana haze squatting here flashing my six-penny wantz like a vervet monkey? What makes me different from any other primate? I'm ugly as hell. Get a load of what's in store for you, fella. I'll stick it up your ass. I'll shove it in your ear.

I want you off my territory. I want you out of my dreams.

In the trade, Melish, you're known as the champion of the "step deal." Now, it's time for the first step.

I lower the rope ladder down through the treehouse door.

The "Avenger" is tucked snugly under a weeping willow. I slip into the front seat. The branches dip down over the windshield. Hidden from view, I can still see the moon and hear the waves from the Hudson as they wash up on the rock beach where the kids and I used to skip stones.

I rev the engine. I feel its power shiver up my wrist. The vibrations calm me down and take the lightness out of my stomach. I open the glove compartment and get out the magazine. Then I pick up the phone. In TV most business is done on these wires. I've mastered the five-second call. "Great. Beautiful. Let's talk. Get back to you." Speed doesn't help with the California boys, they still insist on calling at three p.m. their time. The telephone was my best friend at work, but Irene made it my worst enemy at home. I can see her scowling as she got up to answer during dinner. "It never rings during the day," she'd say, picking up the receiver. "It's for you." Afterward, when I'd come out of the den, she'd say, "Americans are so rude." Sometimes I'd get three calls a night. "They never want to speak to me," Irene said once when it looked as though the Smothers Brothers were going to walk off their summer series. I started to laugh. "But it's business." When the call was finished and I'd talked them back on the set, I came out to find Irene crying. She hadn't even finished her dessert. Her lips tightened into a vindictive sneer. "You wouldn't think of calling those lazy sods during your working day, would you? You'd wake them up at six a.m. or interrupt their lunch. This house should only be called in an emergency!" Well, this is an emergency, Chubby Cheeks. I dial the number.

"Is Fred there?"

"Who is this?"

"Sorry to ring so late. But it did say to call anytime, Freddie."

"I think you've got the wrong number, Mister."

"From the sound of it, this is my Fred. The Fred in the picture. I'm calling for a point of information. I read about you and your partner. When you say 'water games,' what specifically did you have in mind?"

"I don't know what you're talking about."

"You said, 'All reasonable requests promptly answered.' "

"Where'd you get this number?"

"Don't be coy. The advertisement."

"Variety?"

"Show business, are you?"

"I didn't say that."

"The advertisement says—and I'm looking at it as I'm sitting here—'Athletic couple with high marks in water games seek more good sports.' "

"Who is this? Bill Carpozzi? Noonan?"

"That's what I'm calling about, Freddie. I'd like to get acquainted. I'm in the area. I like the luff of your sail. I thought I'd drop by and you could adjust my rudder."

"I'm high, man. This is a bummer."

"It's very brazen of a show-biz type, Fred. I'm surprised you haven't been swamped with callers. Don't worry, genuine talent can always weather sexual scandal."

"What advertisement? Where?"

"Most people who advertise in *Swhopper* have box numbers. You write directly to the publication—418 East 88th Street, New York 10028—and they forward the letters. I've found this very unsatisfactory over the years. What with holiday delays and the criminal increase in postage—a lot of heartfelt inquiries go unanswered, know what I mean? And even when they do get through, it sometimes takes three to five weeks to make a connection and get grooving. So I was pleased that somebody had the guts to expedite matters and give their address and phone number. Your pictures make you both look so handsome and fresh. Good enough to eat."

"Nice talking to you, Mister . . ."

"You won't be disappointed, son. I'm the first caller, aren't I? Really, *Swhopper* reaches one and a half million people all over the country each month. The figure is certified accurate. Now if you multiply the sales by four—assuming that the average readership for printed material is four readers per purchased copy—you're both getting your faces in front of a lot of people."

"This is bullshit!"

"Honest injun, Fred. Page two. Volume three. The June issue. Very good position, too. Top right-hand corner. Let me describe it to Irene."

"Irene?"

"That's the wife, isn't it? You're in the 'Married Swingers' section."

"Man, I'm not from New York. I'm from New England. I'm not used to people calling me up, see?"

"What's your pleasure, Fred? Would you like to rim me? Are you into coprophilia? Do you dig eating shit, Fred? How about getting the missus in on this. We'll get a few of the boys over for a little *roulette intima.* You know, the Neapolitan caper."

"I could slam the phone down, Mister. But I want you to hear something. You're sick. You're a sick, sick sickie. An asshole. A creep."

"I'm your public, Fred. Don't disappoint me."

"There's no photograph. And no advertisement. This is a prank call."

"I'll put it in the mail to you and Irene tomorrow."

"Cocksucker . . . !"

"I'd say we had a case of false advertising here. Misrepresentation. Trading on the public's good will, Fred. Louis Lefkowitz and the Department of Consumer Affairs both should get memos. I mean raising the public's hopes, making them spend money to make your acquaintance. And then this blue language, Frederick. It's the limit."

"Get off the phone!"

"I hope your prick's stronger than your brain, Fred. I hear death in your voice. Your words have no pulse, know what I mean? No heartbeat. You're almost a ghost."

"Fuck you! Fuck you! Fuck you!"

"I won't let this color my judgment. I'll put in a word for you with interested parties. I have lots of friends. Be well."

I lean back and light up.

I'm so vicious, it's thrilling.

Fraternity Row echoes with music and the voices of laughing women. Little Anthony and the Imperials are singing "Tears on My Pillow" next door at Beta. Occasionally, a beer can clatters outside on the pavement.

The Heeler's Room of the *Daily News* is no place to spend Saturday night on a college weekend. The old Yalie Dailies cover the room from floor to ceiling. The stories, if you read closely, are mostly the same—Yale elects, Yale wins, Yale confers, Yale honored.

The door squeaks open.

"Melish, you son of a bitch. I've been lookin' all over for you." Angie props himself up by the Heeler's Bulletin Board. His black knit tie is undone. Both his loafers are held together by adhesive tape wrapped around the toes; even the bridge of his tortoise-shell glasses is stuck together by tape. Angie reaches into the pocket of his blue blazer and pulls out a half-empty gin and tonic. His right hand is stamped purple to show he's paid for the Freshman Mixer. Angie swills the drink, goes outside and heaves it at the Trailways bus parked beside Wolf's Head on Chapel Street. "Fuckin' Holyoke freshmen. A college of canoeists!"

"Strike-out at the mixer?"

"The Blue really wiped their asses, huh? Twenty-seven to seven. Fuckin' Harvard lunchbags."

"Let's get a hamburger."

"I'm staying stinko." Angie yanks the heeling ad off the bulletin board: a picture of President Eisenhower surrounded by reporters in the *News* boardroom. Underneath, it reads: "Make new friends." Angie throws it away. "What about the 'bright college years,' Meli? You spend eight weeks bustin' your chops for a newspaper. What about sowing those wild oats? That's what we've been waiting for, isn't it?"

"It's important to make a good start, Angie."

"I won't flunk out. I'll stay the same way I got in. 'Donation.'" Angie pinches my cheek. I tweak his nipple. He makes me laugh. "Come with me, Sweetie," he says, taking me by the arm and dragging me into the chilly November night. "I want to share the wealth."

Collars up, hands in pockets, we head for the freshman dormitories on the Old Campus. Trees line the way—they're covered with streamers of toilet paper heaved from pseudo-Gothic windows. We walk past the Harkness Tower, past the iron gates that I climb over at 2:00 a.m. after finishing my heeling duties, down the flagstone path to Vanderbilt Hall. At night, the Old Campus feels like the Kremlin—all towers and shadows. "Something I lucked into this afternoon. The Vanderbilts'd be proud. Her name's Shari. I'd say she's a townie. She's been here since five."

"A townie?"

"If they're old enough to bleed, Meli, they're old enough to butcher."

"Cool."

"This evening's strictly promotion. I told her my name was Griffith."

Angie walks me up the stairs to the second floor. He points to room 205 and checks his watch. 'You've got fifteen minutes. That's five more than the others."

I knock on the door. Nobody answers. I open it slowly. "Shari?" The lights are out. I fumble for the switch. I bang my knee on the phone stand. "Shit."

"I'm over here," says a voice. "On the sofa by the window."

"My name's George . . . Bill George. Griff told me to drop by. He's a great guy, isn't he?"

"Tell Griff I'd like another BLT and a cherry Coke."

I can see her silhouette—tits like wedges of cheese, a long pageboy.

"Let's turn on a light, Shari."

"No lights."

"Why not?"

"That was the deal."

"You sound pretty. A table lamp?"

"All Griff's pals kept to the rules."

I put my hand on Shari's shoulder. "Sit on my lap and we'll talk about the first thing that comes up."

"The verbal type," she says, sliding next to me.

"Actions speak louder than words."

Shari puts her hand in my crotch. I reach down and kiss her neck. She shoves her forearms against my chest. "No kissing. I hate kissing," she says. "I'm not getting mono again." Shari unzips my fly and feels in my Jockey shorts with her thick fingers. "Where is it?"

"Wait a minute. This underwear's tricky."

"I've got it," she says. "Now tell me how much you love me."

"You're a sweet person."

"Tell the truth," Shari says, tightening her grip on the neck of my cock. "Explain again how you've asked my father if you can marry me, how he's said no, how we're eloping to Europe."

"Are we going to France or England?"

"That's up to you, Billy."

"What should I say now?"

"Are we having a church wedding?"

"Certainly."

She kneels on the floor and puts her head between my thighs. "I want a Yale garter for 'something blue.' Will you buy me a Yale garter and put it on my leg?"

"My pleasure."

Shari looks up. "Eight Yale men have proposed to me tonight. Why should I marry you?"

"I'm eligible."

"Do you belong to a fraternity? Do you drive a car?"

"Yes."

"You're lying."

"I am not."

"You must be rich. Griff asked me to visit him next

week. My fiancés are giving me twenty-five dollars apiece."

"Kiss me there, Shari."

"You'll help me save, Bill?"

"Yes."

"I'll look beautiful with my braces off. No silver caps. No loose wires. A white smile."

"Let me do it to you, Shari?"

"Keep your peewee out of me, Mr. Speedy Gonzalez."

"I'm your fiancé remember?"

"But then I wouldn't be a blushing bride. Nobody touches me until I'm married."

The door bangs open. "Scram, George."

Angie pulls me into the room across the hall and slams the door. "Campus cops," he whispers, winded and sweating. He reaches into his pocket and swigs from a pint of vodka.

"The fire escape," he says, pointing to the window. "Meet me by the Arch."

I wait in the shadows watching the fire escape. Angie doesn't appear.

Suddenly, he's standing on the ledge of another window, feeling for the drainpipe along the wall.

"No, Angie!"

He rattles the pipe. It won't hold him. He stands back on the ledge and looks down at the courtyard. He takes another pull on the bottle and throws it back inside. He leaps. His legs hit the ground. He falls forward on his hands. He scrambles into the shadows of the Arch. "Close call," he says. We spring across the campus until we're safely outside the Freshman Gate and heading toward the *News*.

"Well, that was really a dumb move, Angie."

> *"My bonnie lies over the ocean,*
> *My bonnie lies over the sea . . ."*

"This is serious, for chrissake!"

> *Bring back,*
>   *Oh bring back,*
>   *Bring back*
>   *My bonnie*
>   *To me . . ."*

"We could be in big trouble."

"Somebody's roommate squealed. I hid her in the laundry room. Then snuck her out. Anyway, I've got an alibi."

"What's that?"

"I was with you at the *News*."

The destination sign on top of the windshield reads: "HOLYOKE EXPRESS." The driver beeps his horn to hurry the girls up. One leans against a Chevy convertible and vomits in the gutter. Two freshmen try to lift her into the bus. "I had a fab time," she says. "Bunny Brockway. Mary Seaton Hall. 289-3533. Switchboard closes at ten . . ."

"Fuckin' Holyoke canoeists," says Angie. " 'I had a fab time.' "

"C'mon, Angie. We've had enough excitement for one night."

The other girls straggle into the bus, opening windows to talk to their escorts. Some freshmen are writing down addresses of as many girls as they can. They prop their pieces of paper against the bus. From Beta, a chorus of voices shouts: "Stay! Stay! Stay another day!"

"Where do they get off?" Angie says. "They rush 'em in for one night. Then they rush 'em out. One hundred and sixty-eight hours in the week. And they call you an 'ass-man' if you spend eight hours with a girl."

"Yale is what you make it."

"I can't get my rocks off on Hegel or the ten reasons for the Depression."

"Twelve."

"It doesn't touch me, George."

"Sit down, Angie. Keep quiet."

"Go here. Go there. Eat this. Buy that. You meet them at the train or the bus. And then it's like running through one of the rat mazes in Psychology 101. Who has time for anything?"

"There's plenty of time for girls. That'll come later."

"These beautiful girls. These smart girls—all hiding behind their Peck and Peck armor."

The bus driver turns the ignition and revs the bus's engine. The bus doors shut. Angie bolts away from me and runs toward the bus. He leaps on the front of it. Shoes on the fender, hands clutching the windshield wipers, he's spread-eagled.

"I love you. And you. And you," he yells, kissing the tinted glass.

The bus starts to move. Angie holds tight. He humps the front of the bus.

The bus driver blasts his horn. Then his wipers start to move. Angie keeps his balance.

"Bulldog, bulldog, bow-wow-wow, Eli Yale!" Angie screams back at him. "Let them out!"

The bus driver speeds up, then slams on the brakes. Angie falls backward on the cement.

"Who is that guy?" someone standing next to me asks.

"Victor Angell."

"He's got a brass set of balls. Got to remember that name for Rush."

Angie's on his feet. The bus driver's flashing his lights, signaling him to get out of the road.

Angie drops his pants. His trousers are at his ankles. He's standing in the headlights' glare with his bare ass to the driver. He's bending over and peeking back at him between his balls and thighs.

"Gotcha!" Angie yells.

The driver swerves right and drives around The Red Eye. The drunken girl at the back of the bus has opened the window. The pink cheeks of her ass are wedged outside it.

"Bunny Brockway," she yells. "Remember me." Another girl throws her underwear at Angie's feet.

The girls are still waving to him out of the left side of the bus, as it turns the corner. Angie picks up the silk panties and waves back.

Sally sits in the white wrought-iron chair by the country club pool. The air smells of chlorine and clean linen. The kids are playing underwater tag at the shallow end.

"Sweet of you to entertain a tennis widow, George," Sally says. "John can't be bothered to go swimming, that's why we never joined the club. He'll play doubles with Irene all Saturday in the blazing heat. But he won't relax. He hates taking off his shirt. He's flabby."

"John's very well-preserved for fifty-five."

"There's no excuse for fat. I love being thin. Feeling my ribs in the shower. The lightness of my legs after I've shaved them. I feel close to myself."

"Let's face it, Sally. You're a great piece of ass."

Sally smiles with her eyes. "Not bad for forty-five, am I?"

"Medium rare, I'd say."

"Feel that calf," she says, putting her leg on my lap. "I rub my legs with baby oil, that's why they're so soft and shiny."

The waiter brings our food. Sally takes her leg away and pulls her chair close to the table. "I love avocado," she says, digging in. She savors it with her eyes shut.

"Have a bite, George," she says, spooning out some more and holding it up to my mouth.

"Can't stand it."

"This is really a treat."

"I've never liked it since I was a kid."

"You're an adult, now, George It's time to try again."

"Avocado's too rich."

Sally takes another bite. "It's almost as good as sex," she says.

"Sex doesn't have as many calories."

"You're really missing something."

"I'll have to add another item to that long list of George Melish regrets."

Sally runs her fingers along the inside of the green skin. She licks the vinaigrette off her fingertips. "You only regret what you don't try."

Mom is propped up in bed knitting a blue afghan she says is for me. "You're lucky to have a mother who takes an interest."

From his desk, Dad waves me into the room. "Howdy, stranger? Just thought you might like to schmooz for awhile. Like one of those college bull sessions." He turns off "The Late Show."

"Let it wait, Sol. Can't you see the boy's tired to death?"

Dad looks over his glasses. "You're the one who wanted this, Vera."

Mom works away at her blanket.

"How's Yale?"

"Great."

"They sure had a helluva football team. You getting enough sleep? And exercise?"

"Enough."

"They feeding you well? If you need any food—a late night snack sort of thing—we could always send . . ."

"The food's very good, Pop. You have to wear a tie at meals. That's a drag."

"It's good for you," says Mother. "Sorry, Sol. Go ahead."

"Go ahead what?"

"With what you were saying."

"I wasn't saying anything."

"You were about to say something."

"I wasn't."

"Yes, you were," Mom says, looking back at her afghan.

"Let me ask you this, George. Have I ever once as your father said anything to offend you or to criticize—except, occasionally, to tell you to take a bath?"

"No."

"You know, when I was a kid, I never passed a test. I've always said—haven't I?—that I didn't care how you did at your studies as long as you passed. That was more than I did. I was a horrible student, a schlepper."

"But you had talent, Sol. You were latent."

"Don't interrupt, Vera. I'm telling you I was a schlepper."

"Have it your way," Mom says.

"We got your report from Yale today."

"I did OK. Seventy-seven isn't bad for the first term."

"Of course it's not bad, George. Your father wasn't implying that it was bad. Whatever you do is OK with us. What's important is that you grow up to be a good boy, not your marks."

"We were shocked . . ."

"Surprised, Sol. At prep school, you got A's."

"I've been working hard."

"I said to your mother. He's a hard worker. He's not sloughing off. It's got to be something else."

"I was heeling the *News*. That takes a lot of time."

"If I don't take a vacation three weeks before I go on location, I lose the juices, you know. I'm tired on the set. I don't think quick. You got to learn to relax, George. You got to live it up once in a while."

"I'll do better next term."

"It's not work, you understand, George. It's the . . . I don't know how to put it. In Hollywood, when I first began producing before the war, we had this great young actor called Tyrone Power. I signed him for a picture. Got Hecht and MacArthur to script it. Tyrone came to me the day before we began shooting. He was a nervous wreck. He could hardly talk. He'd always been a quick study, but he couldn't remember a line. He wanted me to postpone the whole thing for a week. That delay would've cost me fifty-eight thousand dollars, which was a good chunk of our budget in those days. So I said to him, 'Tyrone, I'm sending you home and you've got to obey doctor's orders.' 'Whatever you say, Sol,' he said. 'Tyrone, I want you back in your hotel and in bed within an hour.' He left my office. I made a quick call. And when he got back to the Beverly Wilshire there was a beautiful brunette in his bed. He was on the set the next morning ready to shoot at seven. He was sharp as a tack. That's how I got the nickname Doc."

"Tyrone wasn't married at the time," Mother says. "We thought that maybe . . . We wondered if perhaps . . ."

"What she means, son, is how's your sex life?"

"There are lots of girls in New Haven, and they're all hot to marry Yalies."

"Your father wasn't talking about marriage, dear."

"I think it's important to get some experience."

"Tell him, Sol."

"If you want, I'll give you two hundred bucks."

"Are you telling me to go to a whore?"

"There's a place in the East Fifites."

"Your father didn't say anything of the kind, George. He just wants to make sure you're happy in all departments."

"I'd never go to a whore. Slam-bam-thank-you-ma'am."

"It's not like that, George. For two hundred dollars, they take their time."

"Sol!"

"Listen, don't worry about George Melish. He knows his way around the female anatomy."

"Sex is beautiful," Dad says. "I mean what happens between a man and a woman has no other ... I mean ... Beautiful, really beautiful."

"You don't have to spell it out, Sol. The boy understands. I knew it was first-term jitters." Mom holds up her cheek for me to kiss good night. "Who're you seeing tomorrow night?"

"Sue."

"Wonderful girl," Dad says, lighting a cigar. "Fine family."

I shut the door and listen at the keyhole. For a while they say nothing.

"Sol?" I hear Mom say. "The cigar. You want me to vomit in my sleep?"

"The kids nowadays," Dad says after a while. "They're all idealists."

"What do you call what we just did?" says Sue, standing nude by the window and staring across the Merton meadow and the smoky Oxford skyline. This is one event not typed up in the itinerary of the four-week tour the Judge gave her as a graduation present. On my desk behind her, the calendar shows only ten more study hours till finals.

"Soixante-neuf."

"You mean sixty-nine?" she says, turning back to me.

"You better believe it. There'll be more of the same if you come to Greece."

"That was it?"

Rita waits until I've finished my cigarette and stretched my arm over the back of the bucket seat. She slides next to me. "There's an art to getting even, George."

"I'm getting the knack."

"You can't be squeamish. Blood has a beauty all its own."

Rita's changed her dress to black satin, the same outfit she wore when she sang "Put the Blame on Mame."

"My father was a Latin-American dancer," she says. "I got the fire in my veins from him. He could kill a man by doing a flamenco on his chest."

"I was vicious, Rita. Admit it."

"A woman like me wants no pussyfooting. She wants to feel safe in a man's strength."

"The ad in *Swhopper*? The tongue-lashing I gave our Fred?" I say, slapping the steering wheel. "That was below the belt."

"Three minutes on the phone, one six-inch ad doesn't even the score."

"I devastated the bastards. They're a laughingstock."

"After what she did to you?" Rita says, smirking her *Pal Joey* smirk.

She pulls away from me. She pouts in silence by the window.

I step carefully back from the bushes and walk down the path to our house.

I can't concentrate. I feel bruised inside. My chest aches. Friends talk to me. "Good night," they say. Or,

"Thank Irene for us." Or, "Congratulations on the promotion." Their lips move. My face adjusts to the tone of their voices. But they float out of sight like figures in a dream.

All I can see is John resting his head on Irene's lap under a fir tree. She bends down. She kisses him. He brushes the hair out of her eyes. "My darling John," she says, and rocks him in her arms. They kiss again.

Later, in the bedroom, Irene is taking off her makeup. I lie on the bed with my clothes on. I kick off my tassled loafers. I feel tears inching down my face. I turn my head to the pillow so Irene won't hear me crying.

"The kids didn't make a peep," she says. "The party was a hit."

"I wouldn't know."

"Everybody said so."

"I wasn't feeling particularly festive."

"Stomach again?"

"My heart."

"Don't be silly, George. You're thirty-one years old. You get more like your father every day."

"He never saw his wife kiss another man."

"What's that supposed to mean?"

I hear Irene swivel her chair around toward me. I feel her eyes on the back of my head. I refuse to speak.

"Are you all right, George?"

"No, I'm not all right. I'm shattered. I'm fucking disgusted. I'm trying to be mature, but I can't hold it in. Not married seven years, and I'm cuckolded. George Melish, executive and cuckold. Where are my donkey ears?"

"You saw?"

"I should've gone back and got a kitchen knife and slashed that flabby fucker to bits. Stuck his limp cock down his gullet."

"Where do I stand?"

"You're off the chart."

Irene comes over to the bed and sits by the pillow. She puts her hand on my neck.

"He loves me, George," Irene says. "How can love for another person be bad?"

"I understand how somebody can love you. I love you. Don't make anything pure out of Prescott. He wants to get into your pants, like any man."

"He doesn't."

"Don't tell me about my own sex."

"He says I've given him reason to live."

"What about me? You're my reason to live."

"You've got your job."

"I've cared about only three things in my life. The office. The children. And you."

"In that order."

I grab Irene by the shoulders. She winces as if I'm going to hit her. I'd never hit a woman.

I shove her onto the bed.

"I'll tell you one thing, Irene. It's stopping. I'm not standing for it."

"In my whole life, George, all I've wanted is to be loved."

"You *are* loved. You've got a devoted husband. Two loving kids."

"John's interested in *me*."

"So am I."

"But you're not here all the time."

"Oh, that's great. I suppose you want me to be put out to pasture like Prescott!"

"John says he hasn't done any work since he knew he loved me."

"You think that's good?"

"At least he's got his priorities right."

"Do you want me to stop work?"

"Then we couldn't afford this place. You wouldn't be successful."

"Exactly. You can't work half a day and get the privileges I've given you. Why are you punishing me for it?"

Irene starts to cry. "The only bad thing is that you had to find out in such a cheap way," she says. "I wanted to tell you. I thought you'd be happy that I was happy."

"I'm the offended party, Irene. The tears should be for me. Did he tongue you? Did he touch your tits?"

"Of course not."

"Thank God for small favors."

"John's love is more *agape* than *eros*."

"He'll fuck you. Then he'll forget you. That's all he's after. That's your soul mate."

"He's your friend, too."

"When I give an order, it has to pack some clout. I'm pushing the concept of Eyewitness News—a team of wise-cracking reporters on camera who put some happy-talk between the headlines. I need John's support. He's friends with the News Department."

"John thought he'd lost the capacity to feel. I broke through."

"I'm the fair-haired boy at ABC. I can't have egg on my face."

Irene grimaces like a baby. Her eyes shut, her mouth opens and, slowly, she starts to wail.

"Don't expect sympathy from me."

She holds her arms out to me.

"It kills me, Irene. His daughter's almost grown. Our kids are just tadpoles. We've hardly had a family. You'd risk all that?"

"Hold me," Irene says.

"You started this, you finish it. It's cleaner that way."

"Don't take him away from me, George. You've got your job. I want John. We're equal."

Irene's eyelids are swollen and purple from crying.

"All these tears are for him! That really pisses me off. What about me? Me! What the fuck about me? Don't I get any sympathy in all this chest-beating? Aren't there a few tears for dear old Mr. Nice Guy?"

"I love you, George."

"You can't love two people."

"I don't love him like I love you. It's different."

"You have to make a choice, Irene."

"Why? I don't ask you to choose between your work and me?"

"What do you think you're doing now? Work and love are two different things. I have to work to eat. Love is love; it's something spiritual that takes years to deepen, to nurture. It's tough enough to love one person, let alone two. When somebody else comes into the picture, love is watered down. The focus of the family shifts."

"Love is infinite, George. What you give to one person isn't subtracted from another."

"Is he more romantic than me, is that it?"

"Love isn't a contest, George."

"Then what have I been training for all my life? Why did I learn how to dance? And to dress? And to support myself? I'll tell you why. So I could earn the respect of a good woman and have the resources to keep her."

"I have a chance for happiness."

"I've worked to make you happy. But what if your happiness is my sadness?"

"It doesn't have to be."

"Don't be a child."

I punch the pillow. I can taste my tears. "You were the only girl who ever loved me back the way I loved her."

"I still love you."

"How much?"

"Ten out of ten."

"Well, you're still off the chart with me."

"I want to be treated like an equal."

"You are."

"I'm just a straight man."

"Well, you're the one who's played the biggest joke."

Irene laughs. "Come to bed, darling."

"You have to earn love, Irene. It's not just sweet talk. And kissing."

"I can't listen anymore. I'm too tired."

"That's what I hate. He hasn't earned the right to love you. He hasn't suffered anything with you."

Irene turns out the light. I undress in the dark. The sheets are still wet where I've cried. Irene waits a few minutes, then snuggles up to me, pressing my arm close to her body.

"Let's make love," she says.

I straddle her. I pretend I'm staking her to the ground. My cock is rigid and unfeeling. After a while, her body shivers and she relaxes with a sigh beneath me.

"George?" she says, finally. "Tomorrow, be sure and brush your teeth."

"Go on, Rita. Get out! Take a walk!" I lean across and open the car door.

"That's right, George. Don't face the truth. Don't make a scene. Walk away."

"Irene's still my wife."

"She's a bitch."

"Basically, she's a good woman."

"She cast the first stone."

"I'll handle this my own way, Rita."

"You'll give up. You'll be a good camper about it."

"Are you calling me soft?"

"You're not exactly Orson Welles."

"Hit the road, Rita."

"Make me."

"I don't like roughing up women."

"Try it for a change. Use your heart instead of your head."

"Irene's the mother of my children."

"You hardly see them thanks to her."

"She's my inspiration."

"You haven't spoken to her in eight months. Did she answer one letter?"

"My happiest times were with her."

"She spoiled your fun."

"That bitch!"

Rita takes a cigarette from her bag.

I light it.

She blows smoke rings in my hair. "Can I shut the door now, George?"

The intercom buzzes. "You busy?" Jackie says. "I've got something I think you'll want to see."

"You wearing a bra?"

"Have you seen the numbers on the Rita Hayward anthology?"

"My mind's been on other things."

"I called Mr. Prescott. His secretary said she expected him about one."

"Did you get Irene?"

"I'll be right in."

Jackie pushes open the door with her bony shoulder. Her hands are filled with papers. She twitches her tight little twenty-four-year-old ass to the edge of the white Formica coffee table where I do my reading.

"Exhibit A. The *New York Times*. Headline: 'Foolproof Film Series.' 'ABC's, eight o'clock series—"Evenings with the One and Only Rita Hayworth"—is easily the best format conceived by the station this year. *Pal Joey,* its first offering, was tonic and welcome. The film clips of the great Rita Hayworth talking about the film and how it was made had the vitality and details of a TV special. The biweekly series looks foolproof. It's going to be a long season for ABC's competitors in this crucial weekend slot . . .' "

"Call Jack Gould at the *Times* and leak him the news about Ava Gardner being next season's heartthrob. Get Les Brown on *Variety*. I want him to do an interview with me."

"The show got a forty-seven percent of the audience."

"Tell Brown that, too. Tell him I want to explain my strategy. He's doing a book on TV. He'll want to know."

"Exhibit B. New York *Post*. Leonard Lyons. 'Rita Hayworth at Jack and Charlie's "21" talking about the TV screening of *Pal Joey*. "It gave me a real boost to be interviewed. The telephone hasn't stopped ringing," said the voluptuous redhead, who's just been offered the lead in *Applause*. "From now on, my heart belongs to ABC." ' "

"Let me see that."

"Lyons printed a picture of her," Jackie says.

"We'll take a full-scale ad in both papers. Use her quote."

"One of the girls went over to Broadway and got this made up for you. Everybody's excited."

Jackie hands me a pink and black bumper sticker. It reads, "My Heart Belongs to ABC."

"Get Irene on the phone."

"I've tried four times this morning. She's not in."

"Somebody should be there. It's twelve-thirty. The kids should be having lunch."

"You never call her before three."

"She said she'd be in. Why isn't she in?"

"Calm down, George. She's probably taking a walk."

"I'd like to know where she is, goddammit. That's natural, isn't it? She could've been in a car accident. Something might have happened to the kids. She could be violently sick, even dead."

Jackie picks up the phone and dials our number. "If you want a victory lunch, I'll be at the Sixth Avenue Delicatessen," she says, handing me the receiver. She closes the door behind her as she leaves.

"Hello?"

"Irene?"

"Yes."

"This is your husband."

"Is something wrong, George?"

"Nothing's wrong. Did you read the *Times* this morning?"

"I was out."

"I know. I called four times."

"Can it wait? I've got to feed the kids."

"You have time for Mr. You-Know-Who. You can damn well give your legal husband a few minutes of the day."

"Why drag him into it?"

"I can't help it. When you're not at home, I imagine things. That bastard never leaves me alone. When he was my friend, I never thought about him. Now that he's your lover, I can't get him out of my mind."

"He's not my lover."

"You'd like him to be."

"Did I say that?"

"It's like a banner headline across your face."

"Read me the *Times*."

"Where were you all morning?"

"I took the kids roller skating."

"Where was Mrs. G.? A housekeeper's supposed to be in the house."

"She didn't feel good."

"Put her on the phone. I want to speak to her."

"Why?"

"Do as I say."

"I sent her to the doctor's."

"Very convenient."

"George!"

"Call her up and tell her I want a letter from her doctor saying at what time and when she came to his office."

"Don't you trust me?"

"Why should I?"

Irene starts to cry. "Come home, George."

"Don't be childish."

"We could walk up to the waterfall and talk about us. I never see you in the daytime."

"Don't cry."

"Then don't make me sad."

"You started this, I didn't. I have the right to protect what's mine."

"Do you love me, George?"

"Uh-huh."

"Say it."

"I love you, OK? I wouldn't be so upset if I didn't. I want to share this with you. It's not every day that ABC has a winner and I'm responsible."

"That's nice."

"Nice? It's fantastic."

"I didn't do anything wrong, George."

"If *I* hid things from you, if *I* went off with somebody else, you'd go crazy."

"I'm here, George."

"You'll force me to be promiscuous."

"Let's drop the subject."

"I want my little squirrel to be happy. Playing. Nestling close. Squeaking her pleasure."

"I'm not an animal."

"You're my Little Squeaker."

"I'm a woman."

"Tempesto Trewin, I remember. Why don't you get a sitter and come in for dinner? We'll celebrate."

"Let's have a quiet night together, George."

"Why is it always what you want to do?"

"That's a laugh."

"Why am I always Mr. Bad Guy, Mr. Kill-Joy? You've got a fantasy about me that doesn't exist."

"That's what you think."

I hang up.

"Anything else?" Jackie says on the intercom.

"Call Irene and tell her I'll be home at seven. Order some flowers from Goldfarb's."

"What kind?"

"The usual."

I put on a cassette of the Ray Conniff Singers. The first number is "Moonlight Becomes You." I cut out Rita's picture from the *Post* and slip it under the plastic covering of Irene's photograph on my desk.

I stare at it.

"We've got all afternoon, Rita." I take off my wedding ring and turn up the music.

Rita stubs her cigarette into the "Avenger's" ashtray. "She really put you through it."

"I'm a nice person. Most women would jump at a chance to marry me. Of course it took time to adjust to Irene's idiosyncracies. But I did. I helped her to help herself."

Rita laughs and does her lips in the rearview mirror.

"What's so funny?"

"I just remembered an old nursery rhyme—

"Punch and Judy
 Fought for a pie
 Punch gave Judy
 A knock in the eye."

"I don't think that's funny."

"You will," says Rita.

"Irene's a darling," Mom says, taking my arm as we walk up Fifth Avenue. "You've made a fine choice."

"I think so."

"You know, George, if you don't have a son, the name Melish won't be passed on."

Irene unbuttons her shirt. Her right breast sprawls out through her feeding bra. She pushes Tandy's little hands away from the lumpy ridges of her nipple and plugs it in her mouth.

"Do you have to feed her during 'The Beverly Hillbillies'?"

Irene sits cross-legged on the sofa watching the TV. "If I don't start early, George, it'll be another late night."

"Would you mind putting your breast out of my line of vision? I find it very disconcerting."

Irene glances over at me, flicking the hair out of her eyes. "I'm feeding."

"Well, would you go to the bedroom? It embarrasses me."

"Why should it embarrass you?"

"That's an erogenous zone."

"A mother doesn't think of it that way."

"Well, a man does. He doesn't want his tit puked on or hanging out like a Hungarian salami. A breast is something a man dreams about. You just don't flash it around."

"George, you've seen it before."

"Mom never breast-fed me, and I turned out all right.

It ruins their shape, she told me. God gave you such a nice pair, Irene. Why spoil it? It's looking a gift horse in the mouth."

"Oh, so you think it's funny?"

"Go to sleep, George. Let's try and stop this."

I kick back the sheets and feel my way along the bookcase. I turn on the light.

"It's three a.m., George. It's freezing out, and you're standing there with nothing on." Irene starts to laugh again. "Sometimes, I think you enjoy this."

"I'm a mockery. I can't look anybody on the street in the eye. My whole life's turned upside down because of you. I trusted you implicitly. And then Kissy-Face is my reward. Do you love him?"

"I love him."

"How can you have the bad taste to love that lard-ass creep, that Protestant peewee? I thought I married someone a little more discriminating than that! They have a clinical word for his kind of thing—obsession. You should see a psychiatrist."

"George, you wanted straight answers."

"Does he show any remorse? Is he sorry for what he's done?"

"We don't talk about you."

" 'We'? That pisses me off. You and I are 'we.' John's not a 'we.' "

"Don't go on at me."

"I'm trying to make you see. I'm trying to put some sense into that thick little head of yours."

"You make sense, George. But does love have anything to do with sense?"

"Here it is. I've found it. 'Vow, substantive . . . A solemn promise made to God, or to any deity or saint . . .'"

"Are you finished?"

"That is the *Oxford English Dictionary* definition. And in 1963—almost seven years ago—we took vows at St. Margaret's Westminster. We knelt down. We prayed. We signed the register. We exited to Handel's *Water Music*. We were joined in *holy* wedlock."

"We should have said, 'I'll try' instead of 'I do.' "

"I'm not even a Protestant! I did it for you. This is taking Love Thy Neighbor too far. I'm putting my foot down."

"All right, George."

"I believed . . . I believe in our marriage. What you and he did was sacrilegious. It was going on for months before I knew about it. Remember, Charles Bury asked, 'Do you take this man to have and to hold from this day forward, for better, for worse?' And you answered, 'I do.' Not 'I could.' Not 'I might.' But 'I fucking *do*.' Understand?"

"I do," says Irene, turning back on her side.

I knock on the bathroom door. "What's going on in there, Irene?"

"Nothing."

"I smell fire. There's smoke coming under the door. Are you OK?"

"I'm doing the spring cleaning."

"In the middle of October? You could suffocate."

"I'm fine."

"We agreed—no locked doors. Open this door!"

Irene's still in her cotton nightdress. Inside the bidet a pile of papers flames up.

"Dad just gave us this fixture for a wedding present. That's Italian marble you're staining."

"You asked Sue Kelley to Greece."

"Are those my letters?"

"Who is this Jeannie? You sent her *The Art of Loving,* too."

"That's my property. Who gave you the right to open my desk?"

"I was writing thank-you letters. I have to write one to Sue Kelley for the cheeseboard."

"I have a right to my memories. They were happy times."

"I came over with one case of new clothes and five books."

"I married *you.* That's what counts."

"I'm getting rid of all these memories."

"What is this? The Living Room Putsch?"

"She's got her nerve, saying you were too young to get married."

"You found that one?"

"That's not all."

"It serves you right for snooping."

"You said you were studying for exams that Friday. You said you couldn't see me, Mr. Diligence. You were seeing her on her four-week round-trip excursion fare."

"I wasn't getting much sex from you at that time. I needed a little physical release."

"Release? I stayed home that weekend. I cried the whole time. My mother nearly drove me crazy with questions. 'Where's George?' 'I thought George was taking you to the boat races?' "

"That's water under the bridge."

"Imagine coming across the Atlantic to find this."

"I was keeping them for old times' sake."

"I hate that little mousy debutante."

"Sue was pretty."

"You call that pretty?"

"She was on the cover of *Seventeen.*"

"Stupid, insipid, boring, backbiting, cheap little bitch," says Irene, marching to the living room.

"You wouldn't say that if you knew her."

"And I'm not having her for dinner. Don't start that again."

"She's nice."

"I'd like to rip those false eyelashes off her blue eyes."

"How do you know Sue had blue eyes?"

"The pictures."

"What pictures?"

"The ones you kept in the manila envelope," she says. "Here they are." Irene tips over the wastepaper basket. The Kodak color prints float to the floor. "More food for the fire."

"They were the only ones I had."

" 'To George, Yours Till Niagara Falls.' 'To George, I'll Keep Weaving Till You Return—Penelope.' You fell for that? All those cloying American signatures, that semiliterate neatness with the cute circles over the 'i.' 'Puddles of Purple Passion.' 'Love 'n Hugs, SWAK.' And what about the girl who put her lip print over the picture?"

"That was Jeannie. She threw me over for a pharmacist from Des Moines. She didn't know what she was losing."

"Well, she's gone for good."

I flop down on the sofa. "How many times do I have to say I love you, Irene?"

"Show you love me. Call up Sue and say you never meant those things. Tell her she was just a good lay. Don't even say she was good. Tell her she was stupid and that writing her about me was unforgiveable. Tell her to go fuck herself."

"Don't be ridiculous. It's in the past."

"Not yet. Not for me."

Irene rummages through the presents on the dining

room table. "Here's that bloody cheeseboard. Blooming-dale's, eight-seventy-five. I'll show Miss Glamourpuss how much her present was appreciated."

"Come back here, Irene."

Irene runs out the door before I can reach her. She gets to the incinerator ahead of me. She jams the cheeseboard down the chute. It clatters seven flights to the bottom.

"Feel better?"

"Two-timer."

"I married *you.*"

"I loved you so much. I wanted to be with you so much at Oxford. But I was afraid to put all my eggs in one basket again."

I put my arm around Irene and walk her back into the apartment."

"She gave me the Chagall print."

Irene takes it off the dining room wall and tears away the backing. She crumples the print and throws it out the window.

"She gave me the frame, too."

"We may need it," Irene says, putting it in the closet.

Irene sits next to me and rests her head on my shoulder. "Let's move, George."

"We just got here."

"I want to go someplace where we can start fresh and equal."

"Don't be silly. We were lucky to get this apartment."

"I hate walking down New York streets and thinking you were once here with one of them."

"You weren't like this in Greece, Irene. You said you didn't care if I had other women when we were married."

"I didn't know I'd love you so much."

"Another campaign promise?"

"I meant it then, George."

"I'm the same guy you married. I haven't changed."

"How could I show you who I was? I couldn't risk losing you."

I lift the top off the hive and pull up one of the slats of honeycomb.

"I told Sally to send her outline for the soap opera to you, George," Prescott says. "I said it was no longer my department."

"I've read it."

"I told her to remember that a doctor or lawyer was the best kind of soap hero—a professional man has mobility, money, and meets women at dramatic moments in his life. But Sally's stubborn, she still thinks a city journalist is a good idea. She wants to put ideas into soap opera. 'Action is character,' I told her, 'ideas won't sell one commercial.' "

"It's not bad."

The bees cluster near the honeycomb. Prescott puts the smokepot on the ground and stuffs it with a dry rag. He bends down to light it. "I don't know what's good or bad anymore, to tell you the truth. In the fifties, when Oliver Treyez brought me to ABC from advertising, I was sure I knew what the public wanted. I got lucky with my share of programs—'Batman,' 'Shindig.' ABC's still sprinting."

"I like the pressure."

"After fifteen years, no matter how much you want to run, the legs won't respond. You lose your nerve."

Prescott takes the smokepot and levels it at the bees who cling to the honeycomb. They start to scatter. They swarm around the netting of our pith helmets. "Why does smoke get them so excited, George?"

"They think the hive's on fire."

"Can you see the queen?"

"She'll be somewhere in the middle."

"She'd better be. We paid ten bucks for her. Plus transportation from Florida."

"A honeybee can't live alone, John. She needs a family."

"Sally could live alone."

"Irene couldn't."

John points to a robber bee who dances cautiously in front of the hive. Smoke has distracted the guard bees. The robber bee moves easily into the hive. Finally, the bees detect him.

"Bet they maul the robber. They'll rip it apart and shove it out of the hive. They won't let it near the queen or the honey."

"You're on," John says.

The hive bees close in on the intruder. It doesn't move. They poke it, and the robber suddenly goes passive. It offers them food on its mandibles. It tucks in its tail. It lets the hive bees feel it with their antennae and even pick it up.

"If the bees don't get him now, they've missed their chance. Soon, he'll have the scent of the hive. He won't seem different."

I pry open each of the remaining beehive frames. John dowses the bees with smoke and then holds the pan for me to deposit the oozing honeycomb.

"You know what's great about beekeeping, George? You not only have the fun of watching the little fellas. You have them working for you, too. I bet we could sell this honey for a dollar a jar."

I put the top on the hive. "How's the robber doing?"

Prescott kneels down and inspects the entrance. "I'm not sure, but I think he's guarding the hive."

We take our time walking down the path to the house. John goes ahead with the honey. He's surefooted and

slow. We must look like astronauts holding samples of
moonrocks.

"I was thumbing through the yearbook a few nights
ago," Prescott says. "So many in the Class of 'Thirty-six
pooped out—drunkards, playboys, suicides. Suddenly, I
started to laugh. I had this incredible feeling of luck."

"You make your breaks."

"Elton Rule took me aside yesterday and said they
might need me on the twentieth floor. Director of Market
Development."

"Do you want it?"

"I believe in shooting as high as you can. But I'm not
sure."

"Think positive, John."

"Rule's very pleased with you. You're a feather in my
cap, George."

Irene is waiting on the lawn. "Hi, honey," she says,
waving and then disappearing inside the house. She comes
out with a camera. "The third annual harvest of Presmel
Industries should be preserved for posterity." Irene laughs
and arranges us in front of the pine trees. She paces off
eight feet and adjusts the lens.

"Why don't you get a Polaroid?" Prescott says.
"They're so simple and fast."

"I like old-fashioned cameras," Irene says.

"You get a beautiful picture in sixty seconds."

"That's just it," she says, taking aim. "I like waiting to
see how things turn out."

Irene takes our picture. "Lunch is ready, if you gentlemen would like to partake."

"Can I do anything for you, dear?"

"Everything's set up on the porch, George. You know
where to sit. I'm in the middle."

I put my arm around Irene and stroll her to the patio.

"Where's John?" she says, as we're about to sit down.

"He's taking off his netting."

Irene laughs. She walks to the front door. "Come inside, John, and bring your honey with you."

The phone will ring. At first I won't answer it because Jackie is taking off her blouse and I'm swilling back the last drop of ouzo she's brought for the dinner. Then, since it might be business, I'll pick it up. Jackie is undoing the buttons of my Arrow 366 blue pinstripe. Her nipples strafe my bare chest. I put my hand on hers. I ask her to stop.

It's the police.

Irene's been found dead.

As her next of kin, they want me to identify her. It's the least I can do.

I'm stunned.

I fight back tears.

Irene was a two-timing jezebel but she didn't deserve this. She was a naive, vindictive chippie, but she was my best friend. She turned against me after I'd brought her across the sea and given her a new life, but the evil that she did will not live after her. I will be loyal to her memory.

The revolving red light on top of the police car makes the whitewashed front of our house look like it's ablaze. The police have cordoned off the weeping onlookers, but they let me pass. The photographer from Homicide walks around to the corpse sprawled on the welcome mat, snapping pictures from every angle. Tears are in his eyes. He hands me his Polaroid Instamatic. "Here," he says. "I can't stand to look at this anymore."

They lift the white sheet off the limp corpse. It's Irene. Her body has been severely gashed. Knife wounds, almost invisible to the naked eye, riddle her torso. Her breasts are gone. The police reason that they must have been ripped away by the hood of a speeding XKE, the only

sports car low enough at her height to account also for
her mashed pelvis. The police break this to me gently.
What will I do without her?

The police drive me home. The children are beside me
wrapped in blankets, bewildered and crying. One police-
man offers me smelling salts. I refuse. I've got the funeral
to organize.

"Was it her?" says Jackie, as I come in the door. By
the look on my face she knows the answer.

The policemen lift Tandy and George, Jr., into the
bedroom. Before they leave, they shake my hand.

"I don't believe in marriage," Jackie says, when they've
gone. "But I want to raise your children."

"Let's talk about it later."

The funeral was simple. That's the way Irene would
have wanted it. I carry her coffin down the nave by myself. The organist plays Handel's *Water Music*.

Halfway to the altar, I stop. Prescott and Big Fred are
standing together in the same pew. Their heads are
bowed. They can't look me in the eye.

Tandy and George, Jr., stand on either side of the mahogany coffin. I speak the eulogy in front of it. The reporter from *The New York Times* scribbles while I talk.
" 'The way she wore her hat. The way she sipped her tea.
The mem'ry of all that. No, no, they can't take that away
from me. We may never, never meet again on the bumpy
road to love. Still, I'll always, always keep the mem'ry
of—the way her smile just beamed, the way she sang off-
key. The way she haunts my dreams. No, they can't take
that away from me.' "

Outside, Sally lifts up her veil of black Spanish lace.
"Can I do anything for you, George?"

"Will you marry me?"

Tears trickle down her high cheekbones. She kisses me
on the forehead. "I'll come to you tomorrow," she says.

Riding up the elevator to my apartment, I say to the

kids, "You have to be brave little Indians. Your Mommy's gone away for good. We have to help each other."

"Are we going to live in the city from now on?"

"Yes, Tandy. I'll pick you up at dancing class and after parties."

"Can we have bunk beds, Daddy?" asks George, Jr.

"If you want."

"I want to sleep with Daddy," says Tandy.

"OK, darling."

I open the door to 15-G. "This is your new home, kids."

The dining room table is set for four. The candles are lit. The napkins are pressed. The magazines are neatly stacked on the coffee table.

Soft hands, smelling of perfume and cold cream, cover my eyes.

"Jackie?"

"No."

"Sally?"

"No."

The children giggle. I open my eyes and turn around.

"How did you find me, Sue?"

"I read the papers."

"I saw your engagement in the *Times*. I would've written. But she was the jealous type."

"I married the kind of man you said I'd choose."

"Remember the old days, Sue? The New Haven Motor Inn? Trader Vic's. Saying good night at your doorstep— me listening for the Judge's footsteps, you hitching up your skirt so I could touch you there? You never wore underwear."

After the steak dinner, George, Jr., goes to sleep on the sofa. Tandy's nestled up at the foot of the waterbed, covered in Mom's afghan. Sue lies next to me.

"Am I still the most beautiful girl you've ever seen?"

"Yes."

"I've missed you, George."

"Welcome home."

The "Avenger's" clock reads 10:06—time for the scorched earth policy. Staying to the left side of Palisades Road, away from the street lamp, I sneak back up the hill to my house.

"Why can't you just enjoy the walk, George?" Irene says, stopping halfway up the hill. "Hold hands. Look at our house. And the river."

"Why couldn't *you* be strong, Irene? Why did you give into temptation?"

"All I did was kiss him, George. That was two months ago. I kissed men before I met you."

"But you didn't tell them you loved them. Prescott's like dope to you, some kind of emotional fix."

"All John wants is love."

"Don't you think I get urges? I'm a good-looking, successful man. Don't you think there are thousands of women I could love? Of course there are. But I don't. I won't. What makes marriage sacred is boundaries."

Irene says, "Nothing's changed between us. I'm still the same person. I'm still your devoted wife."

The moon's gauzy whiteness makes the sky seem too close. I pick up some pebbles from the side of the road and pitch them at the street lamp. "Did you contact the psychiatrist, like I said?"

"Yesterday was my first appointment. I'm going again Friday."

"I think it's the right thing. Get a third opinion. We're too close to this, Irene. Without absolutes, there's madness."

"Things are absolute only if you make them absolute."

"What did your psychiatrist say?"

"He didn't say anything."

"Did you tell him about your crying, and the early childhood bit—making your mother sign a contract she'd play with you one hour a day? About how I've helped you? About how lenient I've been about this?"

"I told him."

"Was he shocked?"

"He didn't show any emotion."

"He must believe that loving two men is wrong. He must have had something to say about adult responsibilities, didn't he?"

"I'm not going to talk about it."

"Before Prescott, there were no secrets. I've never lied to you. You knew everything about me. I even showed you my secret society pin."

"You're not supposed to talk about it."

"I pay the bills, don't I? Who is this doctor?"

"Dr. Jerome Freiman. Park Avenue and Seventy-seventh Street."

"It's a cut-and-dried situation. Anybody can see that. You're jealous of my success, although why I'll never know. It's all for you. I've been reading R. D. Laing, to make some sense out of this. You've got yourself into a double bind, sweetheart. You're a fucking schizo."

"Don't be silly, George. Dr. Freiman worked with Laing. He's a nonadjustive psychiatrist."

"I don't care what he is, as long as he puts some sense in your head."

"He doesn't believe in cure."

"Don't get technical. I bet you didn't tell him everything. Did you speak about how close we've been? Our whole idea of marriage?"

"No."

"Jesus Christ!"

One of my sidearm curves ricochets off the lamp post.

"He probably thinks I beat you. I bet you make me out to be some Madison Avenue schlepper."

"You want me to be another Vera Melish?"

"At least she's got Dad's best interests at heart."

"A glamorous puppet."

"Tell me one thing you said to the shrink. Anything. Don't freeze me out."

"We talked about sex, if you really want to know."

"Oh, that's lovely, isn't it? It's not a matter of sex, it's a matter of perspective. You know the man five minutes and you're counting our orgasms. You won't even kiss me you-know-where."

"I don't happen to like crawling down a sewer."

"Did you tell him that?"

"Yes."

"Have you no shame?"

"Vera. VERA!"

The silk pillowcase is stained from Dad's perspiration. He's propped himself up in bed. He sits like a boxer's second with a towel draped around his shoulders. The shooting script of *Crazy Sunday* rests on his lap.

"Go into the closet, George. Get those pictures of me with General MacArthur and President Kennedy. They're behind the cardboard box of film stills."

"What do you want them for?"

"Do as I say," he says. "When the *Times* reporter comes, I want him at my desk. I want those pictures on it, next to the Oscars."

Inside the closet are two shelves. One for Dad's hats, the other for his clippings. Each film is a leatherbound volume with gold lettering on the binding. The box is beneath them on the floor.

"Vera! Vera!"

I dust off the pictures with my handkerchief.

"Can't that woman hear? I'm weak from sweating like a pig all night. I've got a major motion picture that starts casting in three days. I need a little cooperation around here."

I place the framed photos on his desk next to the statuettes.

"All these interviewers want the same star angle," he says. "The real drama's the finance. You know how hard it is to get studio backing these days? *Crazy* has a ten-point-three million dollar budget, the second biggest at Universal since *Mutiny on the Bounty*. Let me tell you, it's an honor. They're in trouble. They're scared. They want a producer with a track record, who can hold the reins tight, who can drive to a fast finish. Sol Melish still has muscle in this industry."

"What if it bombs?"

"In Hollywood, George, it doesn't matter if you lose, as long as you lose big."

"Vera!" Dad shouts, closing his eyes. He reaches over and picks up the phone by his bed. "Vera? Didn't you hear me? . . . I don't care if it's the butcher . . . I've been calling for ten minutes . . . I've got this guy from the newspaper coming . . . I've got to have some nourishment . . . I think the temperature's up again."

Dad hangs up. He takes a thermometer out of his bathrobe. He shakes it and puts it in his mouth.

"Irene and I are thinking of moving to Sneden's Landing. She's not very happy in the city."

Dad points to the thermometer. He grunts his disapproval.

"Yes, Sol?" Mom says, standing at the door.

Dad puts on his glasses to read the thermometer. "A hundred and four!"

Mom takes the thermometer and holds it to the light. "A hundred point one, Sol," she says. "Now what do you want to eat?"

Dad thinks for a second. "Soup."

"What kind?"

"What've you got?"

"What do you want?"

"Lobster bisque."

"I don't think we've got that. I'll see."

Mom comes back from the kitchen. "Pepper pot. Cream of mushroom. Asparagus. Vichyssoise," she says, ticking off the names on her fingers.

"What else?"

"Bean. Vegetable. Minestrone. Chicken noodle."

"I can't stand noodles. Cholesterol."

"I'll strain the noodles, Sol," Mom says. "Now put on your dressing gown and sit in the chaise longue."

Dad stands up, a little wobbly on his feet. He eases himself into the purple and blue Sulka bathrobe with his monogram on the pocket. He takes an ascot off his tie rack and adjusts it around his neck. He stares in the mirror over his desk and smooths his hair back behind his ears. "I just wanted a tint," he says. "So, your mother gets the girl to come in. 'Brown,' I said. 'I want brown.' It's red, my hair. I look like a goddamn cockatoo."

He walks hesitantly to the chaise longue and flops down on it. "It's terrible when you get old, George. Your body's brittle as an egg, but you still want those touchdowns," he says, putting the script on the table beside him. "*Crazy*'s a great property. After it's in the can, I'm going to take the plunge. I'm going to make the greatest film of all time. Gibbon's *Decline and Fall of the Roman Empire*. Ever read it?"

"No."

"Sixty-thousand dollars for your education, and you haven't read the greatest book ever written? It's got everything. No copyright restrictions. Violence that defies the imagination. The foundation of law as we know it. The rise of Christianity and the Jews. Lots of location shots—Britain, Switzerland, Turkey, Egypt. The Romans were everywhere. Look at the newspapers. What do you see? Degradation. Chaos. Incredible wealth versus tyranny. Great discoveries. That was Rome! And what a cast of characters—Cleopatra, Mohammed, Jesus, Caesar, Hadrian—everybody's a giant."

Mom walks in with a tray.

"I think my temperature's way up there, Vera."

"You'll be all right, Sol. Eat your soup."

"Did you call Dr. Kammer?"

"He's not making house calls. He says you'll be fine."

"What's he know? I tell you, I'm sick. Give me the telephone book, I'll find somebody myself."

"Sol, you wanted soup. Now eat."

"Take a whiff of this room, Vera. It stinks."

"If you'd open a window, Sol . . ."

"Is Maddy cooking with onions?"

"No."

"It's onions. I know an onion when I smell it."

"I'll get the Lavender Haze."

I wrap the napkin around Dad's neck, while Mom straightens his bed and sprays the air freshener around it.

"Did George tell you Irene's complaining about his apartment?"

"Eat, Sol."

Dad lifts the soup spoon to his mouth.

"Good?" Mom asks.

Dad spits out the soup. "There's salt in this soup, Vera!" he says, coughing and wiping his tongue with the napkins. "You know I can't have salt."

"Sometimes, Sol, you're impossible," Mom says, taking the napkin from his neck and brushing the spittle off his robe. "Next time, get it yourself."

"It still stinks in here," Dad says.

Mom sprays an aerosol mist above him. "Can you smell anything? Anything at all?"

"No."

"I'm so glad," Mom says and walks with the tray into the kitchen.

Dad watches her leave. "Don't let Irene push you around, George. You're the boss."

Maddy knocks on the door. "There's a gentleman to see you, Mr. Melish."

Dad picks up the script and puts it on his lap. "Send him in."

"You can come up now, Daddy."

Tandy's voice startles me. I put down *Variety* and look over at Irene sitting by the fire. She's in her bathrobe. A towel is turbaned around her wet hair. She's clipping her toenails on my *National Geographic*. From here, I can see the stubble on her legs.

Upstairs, the door to Irene's dressing room is open. Tandy has her face close to the mirror. She's putting Elizabeth Arden's "Frankly Fuchsia" on her lips. Her mouth is a long, shiny pink gash.

"How do I look?" Tandy says, seeing my reflection in the mirror and swivelling around on the stool to show me.

"Where's the beauty mark?"

"Oh."

Tandy takes the eyebrow pencil and puts a large black dot on her chin. She turns around. "OK?"

Seeing Tandy stacked up on her mother's three-inch silver heels, with the pearl choker and the silk slip is as heady as an injection of B-12. "If Grandpa Sol was alive, he'd put you in movies. Shirley Temple didn't have your stuff."

"What stuff?" Tandy says, tying the Saint Laurent scarf to her wrist.

"Never mind, young lady." I kneel down beside Tandy and dab rouge carefully on her cheeks. I blend it in.

"Honey, you should use more of this. Your face looks thinner. The cheekbones stand out."

Tandy looks at herself in the mirror. She likes what she sees.

"You look like Rita Hayworth."

"I look like Tandy," she giggles, running to the door. "The show begins in two seconds."

"Did you memorize what we practiced?"

Tandy's head juts around the side of the door. "One second."

I sit on Irene's dressing chair and applaud.

Tandy struts out from behind the door and circles around me. She draws her scarf slowly across my face. Her little behind bumps from side to side punctuating each line of her song.

> *"Take back your mink,*
> *Take back your poils,*
> *What made you think*
> *That I was one of them goils."*

I'm laughing so hard I have to lie on the floor to catch my breath. "Where'd you get that business with the hips?"

"TV. You like it?"

I hold out my arms. Tandy falls into them. My face is blotched with her perfumed, sticky kisses. "You slay me, kiddo."

Irene grabs a bough of the weeping willow as we glide around the bend in the river. Across the meadow, we can see the front of Merton in the sun and Oxford's old city wall. Our punt hugs the bank. I plant the pole upright in the shallow, muddy water. I slide close to her. "Love is an impossibility."

"How do you know, George?"

"All women are alike."

"There's nothing greater than love between man and woman. That's what we live for."

"Someday—I hate to be frank about this, Irene, but there's no use gilding the lily—you and I are going to have intercourse. And that means orgasm. If this shocks you, I'll stop."

"I'm listening, George."

"Then, you'll see what I mean."

"When?"

"At orgasm. The consummation. The peak. The 'climax' of love, as they say in the textbooks. At the moment when, according to you there should be spiritual communion, each partner is concentrating on his own pleasure—this incredible sensation."

"I wouldn't know."

"It's true. Believe me. Read Sartre's *Being and Nothingness*. We're trapped on this reef of solipsism."

"I don't understand."

"There's nothing we can do about it. Our lives are one long subject-object struggle. You see me as an object of desire. I'm drawn to you. When you seduce me, I'm an object in your eyes. Your subjective will triumphs. You're free, a being-in-itself. I'm captive."

"But that's not true. I love you. You love me. Admit it."

"I respect you too much for love. I can't love you and allow you to be free. It's phenomenologically impossible."

"You mean there's no way that two people can have a mutuality, an enduring bond?"

"Put it this way: I think you're the most beautiful woman I've ever seen. Since I've met you, I've wanted to sleep with you. I admit it. I'd like to ask you to come to Greece with me after exams. But when I lure you—and I could lure you—I'm making myself into an object for you and for me. We're trapped, Irene. Life's absurd."

"Love isn't absurd."

"What have I been saying? Our bodies are all we have. We're locked inside them. Marriage doesn't change the name of the game."

"There's no way of breaking the circle?"

"We're stuck in this pocket of despair."

"An enormous nothingness?"

"That's it, Irene. Vast, eternal, meaninglessness."

"Why talk about such depressing things on such a beautiful day?"

"We have to face facts sometime."

"What does that leave us, George?"

"The moment."

"What else?"

"Lust."

The doormat says WELCOME. But the door to our house is locked. Another of Irene's come-ons.

There's a knock at the door.

I push back my chair from the desk, toppling the neat stacks of books that are piled around me arranged according to exam topic. The room stinks of dirty socks and cigarettes. "Just a minute."

I put on my robe. On the back of the door is taped a sheet of foolscap with "50" written on it. I cross out fifty.

Only twenty-five study hours left.

When I open the door, Mom is standing in front of me. She's holding her alligator bag. Her mink coat is draped off her shoulders.

"I'm leaving your father," she says. "I couldn't stand it anymore, George. I threw some things in a bag and took the first plane to London. He'll miss me. Aren't you going to ask me in?"

"Come in."

She puts her bag down beside the easy chair, and then walks the full length of the room looking things over. She opens the window. "Last week Kitty died," Mom says, finally. "He was only married to her three years. The way he acted you'd think he was married to that gold digger for a lifetime. She didn't do anything for him. I was the one who made him meet people. I was the one who introduced him to the money men in New York. For two nights he wouldn't come to bed. He sat up in the living room. I had to have the chair cleaned." Mom runs her calfskin glove over my coffee table, and stares at her fingertips. "George, this place is a slum. Do you have a mop? Ajax?"

"I've been studying ten hours a day."

"Poor baby."

"And then these girls . . . Would you believe Sue Kelley arrives Friday on her tour?"

"What happened to the aristocrat you wrote us about? You know who I mean? The one you said was like Bea Lillie."

"It's too much. I wake up every morning with this weight on my chest. Like a cat's been sleeping there. I've even thought of throwing myself out the window. But I'm only on the second floor."

"You'll do fine. Don't let a negative thought into your head. Don't I get a kiss?"

I kiss her.

"There's a person right here in Oxford who prays for people. Very reasonable."

She wipes her lipstick off my cheek. Tears trickle underneath her prescription glasses. "Sol paid for her funeral," Mom says, holding my chin firm as she scans it for a sign of red. "She's got family. For twenty-three years, she collected alimony. Do you know what a blanket of sweetheart roses costs today? It's almost a year's tuition at Oxford."

"I guess Dad felt guilty."

"Guilty?" Mom says, dabbing the handkerchief on the tip of her tongue and rubbing harder. "That man should be mortified! I haven't bought a new dress in a year. Until this *Crazy Sunday* is firm, we're poor as church mice. 'Sol,' I said, 'let her be cremated. Four hundred dollars, plus the cost of the urn.' 'You won't let *me* be cremated,' he says. I've given that man the best years of my life. None of this ashes to ashes crap. He's going to be buried next to me!"

The garage smells of gas and grease.

I turn on the light.

My workbench is still in its place. The number-four nails. The electric drill. The hammer. Presmel Industries boomed here before The Big Crash.

The stack of *National Geographics* hasn't been touched. The amount of bare tit in that six-foot pile of educational material could stretch around the island of Manhattan. Why couldn't Irene and I live serenely in Nature? If we could've swum naked, if we'd foraged for our food, she'd have had too much to do.

Irene's taken my baseball bat off the den wall. It's leaning beside the canoe paddle I got for the Waterfront Award. The print's smudged and dusty. The blue and gold Camp Caribou insignia is almost gone. The least she could've done was wrap them in paper so the wood wouldn't warp and the inscriptions wear off.

I look in the rag box for something to clean them. All I can find is a tattered piece of Pucci silk signed "Emilio."

"I like buying you things. It makes me happy."

"What do you want for your birthday, George?"

"Nothing."

"You must want *something*."

"To make you happy."

"You never want anything. Whenever I ask you what you'd like, you won't say. I want to get you something special, something you really want."

"Go ahead, Irene. Put on the dress."

"It's gorgeous. I can't choose presents like you."

"I got the idea from Lee Radziwill. I saw her walking down Fifth Avenue. She was wearing a dress something like this. Hair drawn back. Freckles like you. Gold earrings. I'm a sucker for the Bendel look. It never dates."

"This isn't too gaudy?"

"You look great."

"I do?"

"Now, that's the way I like to see you."

The Reverend Charles and Mrs. Bury stroll us through their garden. The children root in the bushes for the pet turtle.

"It's nice of you dears to think of us. How many years? Five, is it?" Mrs. Charles Bury says. "We always consider you one of our successful marriages."

"What a beautiful bird," Irene says, pointing to a branch high on the copper oak.

"An oriole, my dear," said Mrs. Bury. "She seems to have settled with us."

"Nature's typecasting," says The Reverend Charles Bury.

"How do you mean?"

"The brightly colored birds, sad to say, are also the most fickle."

"George?"

"Huh?"

"Are you asleep?"

"No, I'm not asleep. I don't sleep much these days."

"Hug me."

"What's wrong, Irene?"

"I had a terrible dream."

"You want to talk about it? You want me to get a pad so you can write it down for the psychiatrist?"

"Do you love me?"

"Let's hear it."

"I've had this dream a few times," Irene says.

"I suppose I'm the bad guy, as usual."

"I am walking along a road. Nearby, I am conscious of a precipice."

"That's me. George Melish—Mr. Precipice. Louis Abyss."

"I'm afraid of heights, so I don't go near it. I hear a moaning . . ."

"Probably Prescott beating his meat."

"Behind me is a boy. I go to him and see that he's got a pebble in his mouth. I kneel down and pick it out. Another appears. Each time I pick away one of the pebbles, the boy's mouth gets wider. Soon, the mouth is a cavern, and I am inside. His molars are stalactites. His front teeth stalagmites. The more pebbles I clear away, the deeper I go into the cave. At the far end of the cave, I think I see light."

"I suppose light symbolizes truth, and you think you're moving toward the truth?"

"My heart's really thumping. Feel it, George."

"Well, what you've done to our marriage has nothing to do with truth. With self-indulgence, yes. With violence, yes. With pride, yes. But truth, no."

"What's that got to do with it?"

"Do you love me, Irene?"

"Yes, George."

"If you love me, you wouldn't hurt me."

"I'm not hurting you. Your life hasn't changed."

"That's not for you to say. I can't concentrate at work. I'm making mistakes."

"Go to sleep, George."

"You're the one who woke me up. You're the one who started it. You couldn't be faithful seven years. People looked up to us. Our marriage was unique. You don't scratch every time you have an itch."

"It's different, now, with us."

"It's better than it was. Love isn't the bloom, it's the fruit."

"I agree."

"How can you agree, Irene? If it's not the same, it's because you've made it impossible for it to be the same. You've introduced an element of cynicism."

"I don't think I've done anything wrong."

"That's were you're mistaken."

"Don't make it ugly, George. It wasn't. It was tender and urgent and romantic. I want it to continue."

"Why should you have what I don't, Irene?"

"You don't want it."

"Haven't I been a good husband?"

"Yes."

"Haven't I been generous?"

"Yes."

"And this is my payment?"

"George, doesn't it seem strange you're praising yourself like this?"

"You forced me into it. Everything we've stood for, everything I've given you is being put down."

"It doesn't have to be that way."

"I can adapt. I can take it. I'm an adult."

"Stop pounding the headboard," Irene says, kicking back the covers and getting up.

"Where are you going?"

"To get a tranquilizer. I'm depressed."

"You're not the one to be depressed."

When Irene comes back, my reading lamp is on. I'm finishing *Pimp* by Iceberg Slim.

"It's nice to see you smile," Irene says, kissing my cheek. "A penny for your thoughts."

"Pimps have to keep their women in line. No chiseling. No emotion. Pimps don't brook shit from anyone."

Our antique desk—the first thing we bought for the house —is part of the woodpile, shoved against the back wall of the garage and weighed down with logs. Irene's not going to discard me as easily as that.

Did I make up our marriage or did it happen? We invented it together like we invented ourselves. The notes under the egg cups were real. The children, giggling and nestling close to us in bed, were real. The tenderness, the care, the plans, the pain. Didn't that count for anything? Why do I have to abandon my dream of marriage because she wasn't good enough to live up to it?

Irene takes her glass of orange juice into the living room and puts it on the desk. She lifts an airmail form from her bathrobe pocket and opens it carefully with the letter opener.

"What's that?"

"Letter from John," she says, reading it and then sliding the blue paper into the top drawer.

"Can I see it?"

"No."

"Don't be silly, sweetie."

"He's sent it to me, George. It's mine."

"What's mine is yours. What's yours is mine."

"Most of the letters are for you."

"You read my mail, Irene. We don't keep anything from each other. Please, may I see it?"

"No. And that's final."

"I work for John Prescott. We're business partners and neighbors. What's he got to tell you that he can't tell me?"

I grab Irene's hand as she tries to lock the drawer. I pull out the letter. "You're a stubborn little monkey!"

She bites my arm.

"Oow! That hurt!"

"Give it to me, George."

"Catch me."

She chases me out the door, down into the basement. I go through the inside garage door and lock it.

"Are you man or mouse?" Irene yells as I scan the letter.

"He's having a good time fishing in Canada."

"Open this door!"

I unlock it. Still out of breath, Irene brandishes her glass of orange juice at me. "If you don't give it to me by the time I count three, George Melish, you've had it!"

"You wouldn't dare."

"One!"

" 'The sun beats down on the boat. Time melts away. And it is good.' "

"Two!"

"John thinks he's a fucking Hemingway. You know: 'I went to the bathroom, and it was good.' "

"Two and a half!"

"Can't I have some fun with you? Throw that, Irene, and I'll paddle you."

"Three."

The juice stings my eyes. It drips down my neck and stains my pajamas. "Where's a rag, Irene?"

"Serves you right."

"Take the goddamn thing."

"There's orange juice all over it," she says, wiping the letter and walking back upstairs.

The stillness is frightening.

I take the flashlight out of my back pocket. Carefully, I inch the top drawer open and lift off the covering layer of newspaper.

Irene's packed away our wedding picture.

We're standing together by the sundial. My arm is around her. She's snuggled close, and looking up at me. "Say something," the photographer said as he knelt down on the grass to get this picture. Why couldn't our words be preserved along with our faces?

"I have a friend for life," Irene said.

"I'll be good to you, darling."

Waiting in the dark by the open door, I can hear Maddy snoring in the bed next to mine. The clock in the hall chimes four times. The night-light throws a spooky yellow glow on the ceiling.

I get up and walk over to Maddy's bed. I touch her forehead. I rub her lucky sweat on my eyes and face. We'll be safe until they get home.

I tiptoe into the hall and look down toward the front door.

I walk up and down my room. I talk to Jimmy, my clown-doll, who keeps me company.

I hear the elevator door slam shut. There's a jingling of keys and a click at the door. Suddenly, I'm wide awake.

"Sssh! Sol!" I hear Mom saying.

Dad mumbles something, and then giggles.

There's a rustle of clothes. Then, a thud.

"Vera," Dad is saying.

"Coming," Mom whispers.

I sneak another look down the hall. Dad is in his tuxedo, lying on his back. Mom is laughing.

I get into bed. I pull the covers over my head and cuddle Jimmy close. When Mom comes in the room, I snore. She bends over me and gives me a kiss.

Her breath has that sweet smell it always has after a late night. The smell I hate.

Here they are. Tucked under our wedding album. My letters to Irene from Oxford—fresh, adoring, before hurt. And his:

> July 12, 1969
> 3 P.M.

Irene dearest,

I should be at a meeting, but I begged off.

I'm glad to be stepping down from this job. George is a natural at it. He really knows much more than me. And his show-biz connections are better. Today, he showed me his new letterhead. I remember when I first took over, everything seemed so important.

Whether I'm one of those TV execs who fails his way to the top, this promotion to Market Development pleases me. More travel, more time away from the office, more hours with you. Now, I won't feel out of touch. You once said, "G. can't live without me." It still makes me jealous, but neither can I.

I know you're a "housewife" and that "George mustn't be hurt," but any moments spared to hold hands on long walks and bird-watch (remember the oriole?) will be cherished by your most devoted,

J.P.

We had a model marriage. Everybody said so.

Irene's the one who proposed, not me. Irene's the one who was afraid to travel alone, not me. Irene's the one who wanted to be cuddled after nightmares, not me.

I gave her children to give her a purpose. What does she mean I couldn't live without *her?*

The woman's laboring under delusions of grandeur.

Mom stands up and straightens her skirt. "Take care of your father," she says to me.

"Don't worry, Vera. I'll eat down at the Club."

"Maddy has the instructions," she says. "Everything is taken care of. Don't forget, Tuesday you see Dr. Novick and next Thursday the tax people are coming to the house."

The announcer says: "Last call for Flight Six-twenty-five to Paris, boarding at Gate Seven."

"Let's not have any emotion," Mother says. "I'll only be gone for two weeks."

"Have a good time," Sol smiles.

"It won't be much fun without you."

"I only fly when I have to—on business."

"Don't do anything I wouldn't do, Mom."

"Don't be fresh, George," she says. Then—holding out her arms—"Anybody want a good-bye kiss?"

One by one, we line up to kiss her. First Dad, then Irene, then me. "I'll miss you," she says.

"You're only going for two weeks," Dad says.

Mom bites her lip. Her chest heaves in a small spasm of anguish. She opens her purse and pulls out three letters, each individually addressed. "If anything should happen," Mom says, "think of me once in a while." She turns and walks quickly onto the plane.

I open the envelope. It's a million-dollar flight insurance policy. On the back is written: "It's the least I could do. Devotedly, Mom."

There's no time to read all Prescott's letters. The weight of them in my hand makes me ache inside.

I never knew he wrote so many. All the time she was getting up early to make me breakfast, Irene was pocketing his postcards before I saw the paper and the morning mail. I gave her permission to see him twice a week during the daytime. I said nothing about correspondence.

Irene walks off the court.

"Aren't you going to congratulate me? That's the first time I've taken two straight sets. The lessons sure paid off."

She wipes her face on the towel she's draped around her shoulders. "Why do you always start getting at me before we play?"

"All I said was, 'I suppose our marriage contract was *caveat emptor?'* "

"Can't you just accept us?"

"Us is you and I, Irene. Not Prescott."

"He's a very good friend. Why shouldn't I see a very good friend?"

"Things will proceed as normal. We will go there for dinner on Saturdays. They will come to us on Wednesdays. Jenny can baby-sit. But under no condition are you to see Prescott while I'm at work."

"That's unfair!" Irene says, crying. "What have I got? I can't even beat you in tennis now."

"I work my balls off to get this promotion. I'm finally

on my way. You helped give me a push. I'm not on the job one hour and you spring this on me. Do you know what it's like walking through a business day acting like a choirboy and feeling like a killer? *That's* unfair!"

I smash my Dunlop two-dot as hard as I can. It arches over the fence and into the woods. Leaves fall slowly down from the clump of trees where the ball has caromed. "You mentioned Prescott's name in your sleep last night!"

"I'm not responsible for my dreams."

"You were my dream. Prescott can't just walk in and take over. If I give an inch, you'll take a mile. You're all I've got. I haven't had many women."

"You said you did."

"It was the early sixties. It was harder to get into a nice girl than the Yale Graduate School of English. I cherish you, Irene. I cherish what we have. I don't want to put it in jeopardy. Your body's special. I give you and only you satisfaction."

"I shouldn't be penalized for your past, George."

"And I fucking well shouldn't be penalized for yours!"

Irene turns her back on me and walks away. She's holding her ears. She's sobbing. "I wish I could be born again. In a small, sunny house—not a mansion. With brothers and sisters, and a real mother. And people who love me for what I am."

She slumps to the ground. I pull her to her feet. Her knees are russet from the clay court.

"I love you, Irene. You must know that."

"Do you want me to be happy?"

"Yes."

"Then let me see John."

"If he makes love to you, what've I got then? Where's mine? Sex is an intimate and sacred thing between a man and a woman."

"You're not interested."

"Only because you lie there like a banana. You don't have flair."

"I can't explain it, George. I just need John."

"You want a divorce?"

"I couldn't live without you, George. I'd kill myself."

"Then accept my judgment. The answer's no. You can't have him. I won't let you."

"You don't love me," Irene snaps. "You've never loved me."

Irene's face is as tight as a fist. She's wailing. Spittle drools out of the corner of her mouth. "I've never been happy, George. Never completely. Now I've found a way, I'm looking forward to life. LET ME BE HAPPY!"

"Shut up, goddammit!" I grab Irene by the arm. I squeeze it as hard as I can. Finally, she stops yelling. My finger marks are still on her skin. Her voice is weak. "It's like the greyhound and the hare. The greyhound chases the hare for sport. But the hare's running for its life."

Hands on my hips, staring at the sky to try to keep from crying, I hear myself say: "See him. But don't humiliate me, Irene. No sex, OK?"

"No sex," she says.

Irene sits down exhausted on the green tennis bench. I take a broom lying beside the roller and brush off the baseline.

After a few minutes, Irene comes over and kisses me.

"Watch out, Irene. You're stepping on the line."

"I love you, George," she says. "You'll see. This will be better for us all."

I'm hard. I've been honed in fire. I can take anything. I reach into the pile of Irene's billets-doux.

January 4, 1970

Irene my dearest,

This thought from Rimbaud: "Love must be reinvented."

We are alchemists. To us, nothing is base. For us, nothing is impossible. There must be no boundaries. I dream of nothing else but being inside you. When will we burn this last bridge of isolation between us?

J.

That pisses me off!

Bolder than James Bond—I open the door to the basement.

Cooler than Charles Manson—I climb the stairs to the second-floor landing.

Stealthier than Jack the Ripper—I tiptoe down the hall.

Faster than Superman—I lock Irene's bedroom.

Sneaker than Iago—I pocket the key.

The night belongs to me. I'm the birthday boy. I'm special.

"How old's Nana?"

Mom's eyes dart across to me, then back to George, Jr. "Over twenty-one," she says.

"I'm four and a half."

"Why don't you go play with your sister in the garden, and let Daddy and Nana talk?"

"I got to piss, Nana."

Mother scowls at George, Jr.

"He's showing off, Mom."

"He got it from somewhere, George. At least I brought you up to show respect. You had beautiful manners."

"Irene does a very good job with the kids."

"You can take this progressive stuff so far. Last week when I talked to Tandy on the phone—it's nice to be allowed to speak to my grandchildren once in awhile—she said her v-a-g-i-n-a was sore. How would you like somebody yelling *that* in your ear?"

"Let's drop the subject, Mom."

"OK, George," Mom says. "Have it your way. I've only been a mother for thirty-four years. I don't know anything."

Mom lifts George, Jr., onto her lap. She smooths down his hair. "From now on, sweetie, we call it 'tinkle' or 'number one' or 'making water.'"

"Mom, do you realize that until I was twenty-three I was so nervous about making a noise in the bathroom I'd get down on my knees and pee in the side of the bowl?"

"Don't tell me that kind of thing, George. You disgust me."

"That's not the worst. Once, when I was doubling with Angie and the girls were in the next room, I took off my pants and peed down my leg so's not to make a sound."

"I got to piss," George, Jr., says.

"I'm sick to my stomach, George. I hope you're happy."

Suddenly Mother stiffens in her chair. Her eyes shut. For a split second, I think it's another angina attack. "Get a rag, George," she whispers. "Quick."

Mother yanks George, Jr., off her knee. "You're a naughty, naughty boy," she says, slapping his bottom. George, Jr., runs out of the room screaming for Irene.

I sponge off her dress. "You didn't have to hit him. He said he had to go . . ."

"Urine stains. I've only worn this dress twice."

Mother holds out her skirt while I work. She stares out the window. Irene and Jenny Prescott swing the jump rope for Tandy. George, Jr., comes running out on the lawn. He clings to Irene's leg. She picks him up and hugs him until he smiles.

"You know, George, I don't think the kids love me." Tears well up in Mom's eyes. She wipes them on her sleeve.

"You're their Nana. Of course they love you."

"They never say, 'I love you'. They never paint me a picture at school. They didn't send me a birthday card."

"Mom, don't be silly. Your birthday's next week."

"You know the mails, George. Today's Saturday. My birthday's on Tuesday. If they haven't sent the card by now, it'll never get there."

"Mom, you're outrageous."

Mom stands up and straightens her skirt. She shakes her finger at me. "George, when I get home, I'm looking that word up and it better not mean what I think it does."

Tandy has kicked off her covers. Her nightdress folds over the top of her buttocks. Her little vagina is smooth and soft.

"Do you think she knows I'm her father?"

"They can't focus for three months," Irene says.

"She knows."

"I wish the nurses would clear away some of these flowers." Irene hands me the baby.

Tandy's skin is more delicate than anything I've ever felt. She smells fresher than honeysuckle. "You're a pretty little thing, you are. You're going to break a few hearts, Big Eyes."

Pushing up on her elbows, Irene reaches for her purse. She takes out a small tin and opens it. "What's that?"

"Tranquilizers."

"You've just had a healthy, happy six-pound girl. No complications."

"I've been taking them for months."

"That's dope. You could get hooked."

"They were in the medicine cabinet."

"I never saw them."

"They were there, George."

"Pregnant women who take LSD or mainline can do permanent brain damage to their child."

Tandy squirms in her blanket. Her eyes peek open.

"Dissolves right into the bloodstream. Shoots into the placenta. Down the cortical nerve. Bang into the brain. The kid's ruined for life. I read it in the *Times*."

Irene reaches for a glass of water.

I take the glass away. "Please, honey."

"The doctor prescribed them."

"They should at least consult the husband. You've got the constitution of a horse."

Tandy starts to cry. I cradle her. "Daddy's going to take good care of you, my beauty." She stops crying. Her hand jerks up toward my face. "You know, dear, I think she likes me."

"I breast-fed her for the first time today," Irene says, lying back in bed and toying with the plastic hospital I.D. on her left wrist. "They hand you this body. It's a stranger. You feel like saying, 'Wait a minute! We haven't been properly introduced!'"

George, Jr., sleeps with the Indian headdress I gave him by his pillow. I kiss him awake.

"Daddy," he smiles rubbing his eyes, and raising his right hand to his chest in the Iroquois greeting.

I put my finger to my lips. "Quiet, like a good camper."

"Let's play council fire."

"We're going on a scouting party, George. We may be away many days."

"Wow!"

"Get dressed."

"Will I earn feathers?"

"If you do as you're told, there'll be many feathers."

He sits up in bed, legs crossed, staring at me.

"C'mon, son, I'm going to wake your sister. What are you waiting for?"

"The prayer. No Indian starts an adventure without the prayer. Remember?"

My knees crack as I sit cross-legged on the floor. George, Jr., joins me. I hold out both arms. He grabs them by the elbow. With bowed heads, we say—

> *"Wah con don dey do*
> *Wah con din ah tey*
> *Wah con don dey do*
> *Wah con din ah tey."*

"When you were an Indian at Camp Caribou, Dad, what did that mean?"

" 'Father, a needy one stands before you. I who sing am he.' "

"We had to strap his hands," the nurse says. "He was yanking out the intravenous tubes. He may not look at you, but he's listening. He can hear."

The blanket is pulled up to Dad's chin. His face is as stark as a puppet's. His skin is sallow and stubbled. His jaw grinds slowly as he mumbles to himself.

"He's been having a busy time," the nurse says. "Tell-

ing Sam Goldwyn to stay off the set. Asking for the unit
costs. You just make a noise back at them. They're
happy. He even sang a snatch of something before you
arrived. At least, I think he was singing."

"Two days ago he was fine."

"I get a lot of famous people in this wing. I was in
show business. They know I'll take care."

"Would you take the straps off so I can hold his
hand?"

"He's a naughty boy," the nurse says, walking to the
bed. "Make sure he doesn't touch the bandages on his
wrist."

The nurse smooths Dad's pillow and wipes his forehead
with a damp cloth.

"He's going to be OK, isn't he?"

She reaches under the sheet and unbuckles the strap.
"The husband and I nearly busted a gut at *Crazy Sunday*.
We never missed one of Mr. Melish's pictures—even the
early Tyrone Power's. He was a household word. Weren't
you, Mr. Melish?"

The nurse puts Dad's hand on top of the sheets.
"You'll have to speak loud," she says to me.

Dad's hand is freckled and leathery. His grip is weak.
When I squeeze, there is only a flicker of response, as if
he were signaling from miles away.

"Dad, can you hear me?"

"I'm a great man," he says.

"Pop, it's your hotshot son. It's Georgie." His eyes
flutter open. "The temperature's down. We'll have you
out of here in no time."

He draws me close to his face. His fingers poke at his
chapped lower lip. "It'll cost more than *Doctor Dolittle*.
I couldn't have done the Gibbon property ten years ago.
The expulsion of Tarquin. Hadrian's Villa. The rape of
the Sabine women," he whispers. "Nowadays, you can
show anything. Anything."

Arms akimbo, Irene says: "It's my body. I can do what I want with it."

"You must be out of your fucking mind!"

"I'm not property."

"I allowed you to see Prescott. I made it happen. You owe your 'love' to me. Your liberation belongs to me. What have I got?"

"Keep your voice down, George. The children."

"Listen, the kids aren't stupid. They sense things. You want to traumatize them, too?"

"Don't be ridiculous, George."

"Ridiculous? Have you noticed your own son lately? What do you think peeing on my mother or hitting that Dempster girl at the Halloween party represents? I'll tell you. George, Jr., feels betrayed by the most important woman in his life. You've confused him with your antics, Irene. He won't sleep with his teddy bear anymore, he wants the cowboy doll between the sheets. He's the playground patsy. Why do you think I take him for nature walks and fill him full of Indian lore? To toughen him up, that's why. If you don't straighten up, Irene, I'm telling you this—you're going to have a screaming faggot for a son. The kids in the neighborhood'll start referring to our house as Vaseline Villa."

"I'm very discreet around the children. I'm there when they need me. They like John, too."

"I'm not taking sloppy seconds. I've never been second in anything."

"Dr. Freiman says it's inevitable. He says in this day and age . . ."

"That man's no psychiatrist, he's an orgy master. If it happens, I'll tell you one thing. It's bye-bye and amen. What's good for the goose is good for the gander."

"You promised you wouldn't carry on, George."

"Don't talk to me about *promises*. I kept my promises
—the big ones. I married you, didn't I? I came through
when the chips were down."

Tandy smiles drowsily as she sits up. "It's cold," she says
and hugs me close. I lift her out of bed. Tandy's little legs
squeeze my rib cage. I can feel her shivering. A child
needs its father's warmth.

"Tandy can't come with us," George, Jr. says. "She's
scared. She can't keep a secret."

"I can too come!"

"Don't worry, honey. Daddy won't leave you behind."

"Is Mom coming?" Tandy says.

"She's too weak," says George, Jr. "Anyway, who'd
take care of Uncle Fred?"

"It wouldn't be fair, would it?"

"I've got my penknife, Dad. And the flashlight, and a
whistle. I'm ready."

"Daddy, will you read me a story?"

"We don't have time, dear."

"Uncle Fred always reads to me."

"Tell us about the campfire," says George, Jr. "About
being chief."

"If you get dressed, chop-chop, Tandy, I'll read you
one."

She hands me a book and points to a poem. "It's very
funny," she says, taking off her nightdress and scurrying
to the closet. "This lady falls asleep and a man comes up
and cuts off her petticoat up to her knees. Read where it
says how she started to shiver and shake."

Holding her polo shirt, Tandy waits until I begin.

> *"She began to wonder*
> *And then to cry,*

> *'Mercy on me*
> *This is not I.*
>
> *But if it be I*
> *As I hope it be*
> *I have a little dog at home*
> *And he will know me.*
> *If it be I*
> *He'll wag his little tail*
> *If it be not I*
> *He'll bark and he'll wail.'* "

"Dad can make a fire from bark. He showed me."

"That's from a tree, George. This is another kind—a noise."

"Uncle Fred doesn't read as good as you," says Tandy.

> *"Home went the little woman*
> *All in the dark*   L
> *Up jumped the little dog*
> *And began to bark.*
> *He began to bark*
> *And she began to cry,*
> *'Mercy on me*
> *This is not I!'* "

"Dad's dead," Mom sobs over the phone. "What did I do to deserve this?"

I leave George, Jr., and Tandy to finish dressing.

I take a glass from their bathroom and tiptoe back down the hall to the master bedroom. I put the glass to the door.

All I can hear is the sea.

We press close to the cage. Tandy's holding George, Jr.'s hand. Their backs brush against my knees.

"Why couldn't Mommy come to the zoo?"

"She's playing tennis with Uncle John."

"Baboons are funny," laughs George, Jr. "Look at their red behinds, Daddy. That one's sticking his finger up!"

The attendant, standing on a platform beside the cage, adjusts the microphone strapped around his neck. He has a long cane he uses as a pointer. "The strongest male has the largest female following. The weakest has only two or three wives."

"Why don't you have more than one wife, Daddy?" Tandy says.

"Your mother's a wonderful woman. I wouldn't want anyone else."

The crowd edges over to the side of the cage to hear the attendant. Tandy and George, Jr., move with them. "The rank and file must pay their respects to the chief. They don't dare protest if the chief chooses to enjoy one of their wives."

"What's a chief?" says Tandy.

"An Indian," says George, Jr.

"The chief baboon is the head baboon. He's the strongest. Baboons are very fierce, and the chief organizes the group. They follow him."

"Daddy's the chief," says Tandy.

The attendant smiles at George, Jr. "The chief—or pasha as he is called—must grow old. He becomes too weak to maintain his position. Another baboon appears to fight and dethrone him."

"Time to get going, kids. Mommy'll miss us. It's late."

"No, Daddy," says Tandy. She starts to cry.

"Mister, why are their fannies red?"

The attendant undoes his microphone and holds it down under George, Jr.'s chin. He asks him to repeat the question so that the others around him can hear, George, Jr., holds onto my leg and turns away.

"Notice the flaming red hindquarters," says the attendant, stepping back on the platform and pointing to the dogfaced baboon at the front of the cage. "This is how the female lets the male know she's interested and that she wants to have babies. Her sexual parts swell up."

Tandy laughs. George, Jr., mimics her, and then pulls up the back of her pinafore. "Tandy's not red."

"She's too young for babies."

"Was Mommy red when I was born?" Tandy says.

"No, dear."

"Tandy'll get red. Red and ugly."

"These are monkeys. With humans it's different. Sometime I'll tell you about it. It's beautiful."

The attendant points to the chief's partner, who has slipped away from him to the other side of the cage where a male baboon is stroking her. "If the pasha catches her playing around, she has no other choice than to get mad at her seducer. The baboon is famous for its rages. One of the few animals who, instead of running away, faces and fights the intruder."

As if on cue, the pasha rises from his slumber and peeks over the rock ledge looking for his wife. The female baboon sees him and immediately turns her hindquarters toward him. At the same time, she scratches at the baboon near her, baring her teeth, slamming her hands on the rock. The pasha leaps off the rock and chases away the other baboon.

The audience applauds the sight. Even the attendant is laughing. "Once, when the pasha was chasing away some younger male," he says, "his partner mated with two others in the space of forty seconds."

Tandy giggles.

"What's so funny?"

"I don't know. It just is."

"Don't be silly."

"Sorry, Daddy."

"Let's go. I want to go home."

I pull the car into the garage. The kids jump out of the back seat. Through the air vent, I can hear Prescott's voice.

"Go see Mommy." The kids scamper up through the basement.

"Are my eyes still shining?" Prescott says. I can't hear Irene's answer.

I follow the kids upstairs. Tandy is sitting on Prescott's knee at the kitchen table. Irene is baking cookies. George, Jr., is explaining to her about the zoo attendant with the microphone.

"I'll be right back."

"Chocolate chip's your favorite, Daddy," Tandy says. "If you don't hurry, there'll be nothing left."

I go upstairs. My forehead is damp. My heart is loud in my chest. I walk into the bedroom. My attaché case is on the desk where I left it. Irene's nightdress is neatly folded at the foot of the bed. The pillows are smooth, the coverlet without a wrinkle. Everything seems in order.

I step beside the bed. With my eyes shut, I lift up the covers. I shove my hand deep inside the sheets.

Then, I feel the wet.

"No calls, Jackie."

"They need a decision on the Carl Reiner pilot. You can't put it off."

"Quit nagging me, for chrissake. You're as bad as my wife. Am I the boss or not? Do I give the orders around here, or don't I?"

"It's top priority," Jackie says. "It looks bad, George. I can't make the decisions."

I slam my door. I lock it. I go back to my desk. The script's open to the title page. I start to read.

It's no good. My eyes won't focus. Everything seems so stupid now. I pull open the bottom drawer. My week's work tumbles out. *Tough Titties*. Read it. *A Bird in the Bush*. Read it. *Lick My Boots*. Read it. Fourteen books in one week. I'm bored with conventional positions. I'm even bored with my own fucking. The books are no kinkier than the movies: they're all the same. Man on top of woman. Woman on top of man. We need new orifices. We need new organs. There must be more ways to receive sensation.

I pick up the phone. I dial the number I've doodled on the title page of the script. "Dr. Freiman, please."

"Speaking."

"This is George Melish. I believe you've heard about me. I'm Irene Melish's husband. Otherwise known as the Hunchback of Notre Dame."

"Oh yes, Mr. Melish."

"It's about a matter of anxiety, doctor. That *inevitable* adultery, doctor. I'd like—I believe this is the proper idiom—to have a consultation with you."

"We shouldn't break the rules," Dr. Freiman says.

I can't stop laughing. My eyes are tearing. "Rules?"

"While I've got you on the phone, Mr. Melish, there's a matter of five hundred and twenty-three dollars for your wife's last two months."

"I'm not paying until you take back what you said about my libido."

Shoelaces knotted, coat buttoned, Tandy stops at the door and goes back to her bed. She sits at the edge and holds out her hand toward the pillow. "There's nothing to be afraid of, Peter. You'll have many fathers. Don't cry. It's better than just one. Mommy'll never leave you. Come out and play. Mommy's got her own things to do."

"Peter's her friend," George, Jr. says.

I walk over and give Tandy a hug. "Tandy, dear, there's nothing there."

"Peter, say hello to Daddy. Even if he doesn't see you much, he loves you."

"We're going on an exciting trip. First to New York. Then, who knows where? Maybe we'll go to Greece. I know Greece. They have beautiful villages high in the mountains. The sun shines all the time. The only noise is the jingle of goat bells on the mountainside. Figs, olives, pomegranates, pears grow all around on the trees. We'll cook for ourselves. Nobody'll find us."

"Great," says George, Jr.

"Peter can come, can't he?"

"Stop this silliness, Tandy. There's no Peter. He's not real."

"You don't love him?"

"Darling, you can't love what isn't there."

"I'm not going unless Peter goes."

"Don't you want to take a trip with your father? Think of all the fun we'll have."

"Peter goes everywhere I go."

"What do you see in Peter?"

"He's my friend. He watches out for me when I'm sleeping. He plays with me. He loves me."

"That's my job, honey."

Tandy starts to cry. She turns her back to me. "Uncle Fred loves Peter. They sing songs together."

"All right, bring Peter."

Tandy smiles and wipes away her tears. "Give him a kiss, Daddy. He loves you, too."

I purse my lips. "Not up there," says Tandy. "Over here by my hand, where he's standing." I kneel down and kiss the air.

Holding their hands, I lead George, Jr., and Tandy down the stairs.

"Be quiet," I whisper. "Mom's asleep."

"Be quiet, Peter," Tandy says. "Mom's asleep."

On the way to Sally's, George, Jr., picks up a rock from the road. "Could you make a fire from this, Pop?"

"Only at war councils."

"Were you brave?"

"It was the test of a chief's warrior spirit. I was chief of the Blue Team, the Iroquois. 'Tonight, we hold our war council. In the week that follows, let our hearts be strong and our minds alert. Let it bind us together in one soul and one cause just as our brave ancestors planned the defence of their Iroquois nation long ago.' The Iroquois were the fiercest Indian warriors. So were the Blues."

"Did you have a secret?"

"I had a knack for keeping a spark alive. For building the flame in my cedar nest. You had to know when to strike the rock, and how hard. Each blow of the knife had to be calculated. Brute force wasn't the answer. You had to be tricky, and patient. When a spark caught in the nest, you had to nurse it gently—cradling it in the palms of your hands, blowing at it—until it became a flame."

"Who taught you, Dad?"

"I was Order of the Arrow. You had to learn self-preservation. That's what we're going to practice from now on."

"Was it exciting?"

"It was unforgettable. The cedar sizzled and popped as the flames licked between the logs. 'Oh, Firemaker—

bring forth this sacred flame, so that we may have warmth as great as our courage, so that we may have light as brilliant as the honor of our victory. Oh, Firemaker—light now the war council fire.' We'd plan our tactics. Divide into groups. Make sure each man knew his assignment. At the end of the evening, the braves would be whipped up into a frenzy. They'd link arms around the campfire. The last words—chanted by me while the others bowed their heads—were always the same: 'Good, better, best. Never let it rest. Till your good is better and your better is best.' We never lost a camp war."

"What are you doing with that hatchet, George?"

"You've got your secrets. I've got mine."

"Put that down, George."

"It's too late to start worrying about your hubby, my little cherry rose. I could kill myself, couldn't I? You see that now. One good rap on the head and my skull would split up the middle. Don't think I haven't thought about it. I even picked the place: JFK's grave. The light from the Eternal Flame glinting off the axhead buried in my cranium as I lie slumped beside the newly cut flowers. 'Ask not what your country can do for you, but what you can do for your country.' He knew the meaning of sacrifice."

"George, don't even talk like that. You scare me." Irene puts her arms around me. I poke her just below the armpits until she lets go.

"You'd be high and dry, Sadie Thompson. Then you'd know the meaning of guilt. Then you'd understand the suffering you brought down on our house."

"You always said sex was the only way to express love."

"Between married people."

"Love is love, George."

"Prescott's a killer. He's a fucking home-wrecker. He's an evil, selfish, jealous bastard. I should kill him, and then myself."

"Stop waving that thing."

"In some states, they'd let me off scot-free."

"There's nothing wrong with what we did."

"He'll be like Harvey, the invisible rabbit. He'll always be with us. I can take legal action."

"You can't prove anything."

I heave the hatchet at the workbench ten feet away. It sticks in the wood. "You forget I can use this thing, Scarlett O'Hara. But I'm not going to kill him, or me. Why waste what I've earned? Why give Prescott a quick death? I'm going to haunt you two like a bad smell."

"I still love you, George. I'm still here. I haven't abandoned you."

"You betrayed me."

"I can love you better because I'm happier."

"You lied to me."

"I didn't lie to you, George."

"You didn't tell me."

"You didn't ask."

"I was waiting for you to confess."

"Confess what?"

"You cheap, two-bit trick! You poxy whore!"

Irene rummages in the pockets of her jumper for a handkerchief. "You have everything, George Melish. Work. A name. Travel. What can I do in this country without a degree? I sit on the bus when I go into town and look at the ads. 'Don't Be a Drop-out.' I'm not poor. I'm not in a ghetto. In England, there are ways for a person of my class to get around these things. But what can I do here?"

"You and Prescott could set up a suburban call-girl syndicate."

Irene starts to walk away. I grab her and pull her back in front of me. "I'm not finished."

"We're not getting anywhere."

"Do you want a divorce, is that it? What if we split?"

"I'd kill myself."

"And leave the children without a mother!"

"Maybe they'd be happier with a nicer woman."

"You bitch!"

"You'd forget about me in a few years, George. You'd have another chance."

"I love you, Irene. I want to live with you. It's him I hate."

"John's a sweet man. Put yourself in his position."

"I don't want to talk about John. Right now my cock is so big it's aching. I'd like to jam it in you so deep you couldn't sit for a week."

"Why don't you?" Irene says, sliding her hand over my crotch. "I'm not wearing underwear."

"He likes it that way, does he?"

"George, please."

"Is his pecker bigger than mine? Does he do anything to you that I don't? Did he tongue you? Is he better than me?"

"Do you want to make love or not? The children are taking a nap."

"I wouldn't touch your scuzzy cunt. It's leprous snatch. I was the first. I knew the water when it was pure. Now it stinks of other people's leavings."

Irene's lips are trembling. "Sometimes I think you like hurting me."

"Don't panhandle for sympathy, baby. I don't have one tear for you."

"I feel so . . . useless."

"Useless? You're a mother. A wife. You're the cornerstone."

"Why go on?"

My hands are clutching her shoulders. I hold her straight in front of me. I make her look me in the eyes. "Everytime we take a plane trip I say a prayer before takeoff. Didn't know that, did you? 'O, dear God, please watch over Irene and me so that we may fulfill the promise and blessing of life.' The greatest sin is in pooping out on life. I hate a quitter."

"That's easy for you to say. You've gotten somewhere."

"It didn't come easy. Ever since I was a little kid I've been improving myself. Nothing is a waste of time, if it makes you a better person."

"That's what I was trying to tell you about John and me."

"Adultery is no improvement. We could've had a perfect marriage. But you have to work for your dreams. 'Tuchis afen tish,' Dad used to say. Put your ass on the table. John knows I'm right. After all, he was in the best secret society there was. Every society sent its men into the world with the same goal: to make the most of themselves."

"Not Skull and Bones."

"Are you telling me? 'Bones' was the mother of them all. We based our whole ritual on theirs: the study program, the truth sessions, the critical papers, the seminars. I spent my senior year at Yale rebuilding my personality. It was the most painful experience of my life. But I graduated a better man."

"That's not how John explained it."

"He told you?"

"Yes."

"You're lying. I can't trust anything you say anymore."

"Three-three-three. That's the secret number, isn't it?"

"Nothing's sacred to that old son of a bitch. What else did he say?"

"He swore me to secrecy."

"Who does he think he is? The Sheriff of Dodge City? I'm your husband, remember. I'm the only one you swear oaths to."

I yank the hatchet out of the bench. It splinters the wood and leaves a gash. "Tell me."

"He laughed about your seriousness. He said you were really fooled."

"Oh did he?"

"Their Holy Book . . ."

"Nietzsche's *Thus Spake Zarathustra,* right?"

"Tristram Shandy," Irene says. "The idea was to violate every canon, to turn Yale upside down. It was like Hell-Fire caves. All scatology and pornography."

"Bullshit, Irene. That's another lie."

"They were nude a lot of the time."

"There was hard work, excellence, pain. The bastard wanted to snow you. He wanted to get you hot. He'd shtup a snake."

"Don't get mad at me, George. Tell him."

"He was giving you a little bacchic blarney, waiting to dip his wick. You fell for it. How naive can you get?"

"I remember John saying to me: 'There's nothing we didn't practice. Nothing we didn't do. We blasphemed in the eyes of God and got away with it.' "

"That buttoned down WASP weewee couldn't offend a nun."

"Why should he lie to me?" Irene says.

"He lied to *me.*"

"That's not right, George."

"Don't talk to me about what's right!"

"He's always had a nice word for you. If you'd just talk to him."

I slump back on the workbench. "I know his game. He'll play Grandfather. He'll say I'm being hysterical. He'll say to look at it from an adult point of view. It just so happens that Sally thinks I'm one of the most impressive adults she's ever met."

"Darling, please don't cry." Irene pats away my tears with her handkerchief. "I hate to see you unhappy."

"All I ever wanted was to be good. To lead a good life."

"You *are* good."

"You don't know the meaning of the word." I slap the blunt end of the hatchet in my palm. "It's not fair."

The phone rings upstairs. "Don't answer it, Irene. I don't want to talk to anybody from the office."

"It's probably John. We were supposed to go for a walk an hour ago. I'm never late."

"Let the bird-dog stew."

"Please, George." Irene's eyes beg me to let her go.

I whirl around, swinging the hatchet at the line of jars above the workbench. Honey and glass ooze onto the wood.

"What are you doing?" Irene runs after me, but she can't catch me. I vault up the flagstone path and then bushwhack up the side of the hill toward the hive, pulling myself up by the roots of the pine trees. I stop and turn back toward the house forty feet below. Irene is standing staring up at me. The Hudson sparkles in the midday sun. The phone is still ringing.

"Be careful, George," Irene calls.

I raised the hatchet above my head with one hand. The other is cupped over my mouth. I give the Iroquois war cry. Then, I plunge back up the trail, my head giddy at the thought of my first coup.

"I don't want to go to Aunt Sally's," says George, Jr., pulling at my coat until I stop walking.

"We won't be long. Think of it as a watering hole."

"Mommy said Aunt Sally's a witch."

"Your mother was being melodramatic."

"She said Aunt Sally made Uncle John disappear."

"Aunt Sally's a lovely lady. She's a very generous person."

"All she gives us is Tootsie Rolls," George, Jr., says. "What does she give you?"

"When you're older, you'll like her better. She's full of life. You can do worse than marry a woman like that."

"I'm not getting married," says Tandy.

"Why not?"

"I don't believe in it. Neither does Peter. That's why we're living together."

"Keep Peter out of this!"

Sally strolls me onto the patio. The wind blows out her full-length skirt. It slaps against my leg. We lean with our elbows on the railing, watching John and Irene play cards by the fire. "If you're going to work hand in glove with my husband, you've got to know the power behind the throne."

I sip my brandy.

"I'm really very old-fashioned," Sally says. "I believe in elegance and artifice."

Sally inhales the sweet night air. "You know who my hero is? My patron saint?"

"A poet, most likely. Donne. Maybe Blake."

"Look at the amulet," she says, nodding toward her chest. "Don't be shy. Pick it up and have a gander."

My fingers graze her chest. Her skin is tight. "Your grandmother?"

"Her name was Sabatier. They called her La Presidente —La Grande Horizontale. The greatest men of France vied for her attention. She parlayed her body like a Wall Street wizard. By the time she was thirty, she'd made her fortune and her name. Artists imagined her boudoir as a bed floating on water, propelled by swans and attended by mermaids. Even as a little girl, I wanted to be a courtesan."

"You're special."

"It's lost on the Sneden's Landing crowd. Shocks them. But your generation is different. You live out your fantasies."

Sally shakes the hair out of her eyes. "My father was a horror. Always ridiculing. He was a musician. We moved in Bohemian circles."

"As a kid, I thought Bohemia was a suburb of Prague."

Sally gives a throaty laugh. Still smiling, she stares up at the stars. The muscles tighten around her throat. "I took my first lover—a dentist—when I was eighteen. I was a freshman at Sadie Lou. I wasn't his main mistress. He liked foreign exchange students with long legs. But I had something they didn't: hunger."

"You're not the type to play second fiddle."

"I was beautiful. I had my eye on the ball. I understood his kink. I could do him favors. In the three years until I graduated, I never did one thing that wasn't calculated for effect."

"But a dentist isn't big-time."

"He did the teeth of all the Broadway hotshots: Moss Hart, George S. Kaufman, Harold Clurman, Elia Kazan. I met them all. They were prepared to pave my way. Then I decided to get married."

"In all that time, didn't you want somebody to confide in, to keep you company?"

"A courtesan stays aloof. She doesn't want to be 'an item' in the columns, she wants power. Men only want what they can't possess, isn't that right, George? A courtesan never gives passion, she inspires it."

Prescott looks up from his cards and waves at us.

"You're going to be a great boost to my John," Sally says.

"I hope I can be useful."

"It's very satisfying to help someone succeed, don't you think?" She holds up a cigarette.

"Yes."

Sally cups her hands over the flame of my lighter. She draws the smoke deep inside her, and then exhales, watching the smoke rings dissolve in the darkness. "ABC reaches thousands of homes a day," she says. "The decisions you make control the minds of millions."

"I never thought of it like that."

"You should."

Irene comes out to the porch. "What about a walk by the river?"

"In a minute, honey."

Irene goes back to the fireplace.

"She's consideration itself, your wife. A real lady."

"She's wonderful."

"That's one of the things that convinced me you'd be good for John. You see, I can tell you're loyal. And careful."

Sally takes my arm.

Inside, John is holding Irene's evening coat, waiting for us.

Sally drops her cigarette and stamps out the ember. She kicks it off the patio. We start to walk in.

"The problem with courtesans, Sally, is that they're always lying. They never live for the truth."

Sally squeezes my arm close to her ribs.

"The one thing about lying," she says, smiling a silent hello to John and Irene. "It keeps your teeth white."

The moon chokes me up the way Rita does when she walks down the spiral staircase in *Cover Girl*. She's in her wedding dress and on the arm of her husband-to-be, but when she reaches the foot of the stairs, she runs away. At the bar, she finds Gene Kelly, her true love. Then, like now, I feel the tingle. I start to breathe deeply. Everything's possible. I'm going to be happy. I'm going to be joyful. I'm going to live. Tears sneak into the corners of my eyes. I picture myself standing legs apart like Yul Brynner in *The King and I*. I can handle anything, even my memories. I'm veiled in my own glow. I'm lucky. I'm large. My cock feels as gnarled and long as a shillelagh.

I ask Irene if she wants to walk up the hill to watch the sunset. The dishes can wait. "No," she says in a teary voice. Her eyes retreat from me. Another secret memory stirred, another wound.

Tandy says she'll go.

We walk silently hand in hand. Tandy snatches honeysuckle from the hedges. Will I ever know a lover's look again? That fierce attention?

With the back of her head pressed against my stomach, Tandy watches the sun dip below the horizon. When the glow has left the sky, Tandy turns to me, folding my arms in hers. "It's a miracle," she smiles.

Maddy sits, hunched, at the kitchen table. She grips her spoon like a toothbrush. She scoops mashed potatoes into her mouth. Her left hand is in a cast.

"How's my girl?" I kiss her leathery forehead.

"I'll be with them angels soon enough."

"Mom home?"

"Nope," says Maddy, sipping her glass of beer. "Your mother's livin' on 'magination since he died. She's not her ole self. I sure do miss him. I had two husbands, don'tcha know? The second was a no-account, but I loved the first one. He was a railwayman. When he died, I moved right out of Denver. Got me to Los Angeles. That's when I started workin' for your father. Nearly forty years now. Today I says, 'Mrs. Melish, you still got looks and money —do somethin' with yourself. You gotta crack eggs to make omelettes.' She just got ornery with old Maddy. So I shuts up. From now on, I don't say nothin'.'"

Maddy motions me close. She holds my chin in her hand. She draws my face close to hers. "You got them bags under your eyes, George. You need your sleep."

"I've been working hard, Maddy. Worrying."

"A boy your age don't have no worries."

"I got promoted. Didn't Mom tell you? They pay me fifty-five thousand dollars a year."

"Don't that beat all! Make it while you can, George. Save your money. Don't go throwin' it away. That Sue Kelley, she'da spent your money. Irene's got a head on her shoulders, that girl."

I take a seat, my knees brush against the wicker laundry basket under the table. "Is there anything I can buy you?"

Maddy chuckles. "At my age, ain't no use wantin'. Your father—bless his heart—left me a thousand dollars. That'll pay for puttin' me under. I eats. I does my work. I watches the TV. I gets tired walkin' outside. The machines go too dern fast. Always honkin'. It's a mess, don'tcha know?"

"But you're happy?"

"You people always been nice to Maddy."

"You raised us. You made us happy."

"Always took care of Maddy."

Maddy goes silent. We sit staring into space. Maddy fingers her rosary. She mumbles prayers to herself as if I were invisible across the table. After a few minutes, I stand up: "One weekend, we'll have you out to see the kids. They're big now. We've been meaning to ask you."

"Mrs. Melish say you got a beautiful house. I seen pictures."

"I'll drive in and pick you up. Irene'll make coffee cake and ham sandwiches with Swiss cheese. The way you like. I've wanted you to come out. But Irene and I haven't been feeling well."

"You busy, George. Take care of business. When you have time."

"Don't tell Mom I dropped by, OK?"

Maddy gives me a wink. "You call Maddy. I don't want to go when it's rainin'. Streets slippery as fish, don'tcha know?"

"I'll call you. I promise."

With her hand pressing the table, Maddy pushes herself to her feet. She takes a few quick steps to get her balance. She hobbles to the front door and undoes the lock. "I took a fall yesterday. Doctor says I have to have my hand like this for six weeks. I coulda broken my hip. God was watchin' out for me."

Maddy kisses my cheek. "Keep doin' good, boy."

"I will."

Her head juts out from behind the door. "Teresa, the Puerto Rican girl who does my hair, saw Mr. Melish in a dream last week. He was thirty-five. He had a full head of hair. She say when you get to heaven, you're young again."

"I love you, Maddy."

"Now, ain't that wonderful? Thirty-five forever."

She shuts the door. The chain lock slides back into

place. I hear her heavy-soled shoes scuffle on the linole-
um. Then, the whispering starts again.

I drop the hive on Prescott's doorstep. With my foot on
the edge of the box for balance, I lean into my job. The
hatchet crunches the wood, splintering it until the box is a
sticky, pulverized mess.

Bees swarm into the air, bouncing against the front
door in their buzzing confusion. The queen bee still cow-
ers in a chunk of honeycomb stuck to a piece of shattered frame. I decapitate her with a flick of my wrist. I
stuff her carcass through Prescott's mail slot.

"Get off my property," Prescott says from behind the
door.

"Get off mine."

"I want to talk to you, George. But not this way."

"I've got welts up and down my arms, John. The bees
are using me for target practice. But I can't feel the
sting."

"Believe me, it was not an easy decision. We agonized.
There was dignity."

"Walter Wanger shot the balls off his wife's lover in the
MGM car park. I'll show you dignity. I'll show you fair
play. Come out here!"

"You're hysterical, George."

"No, I'm not. I'm temporarily insane."

"Let's not split hairs."

"You got your satisfaction. I want mine. I'm pacing off
five yards. One yard for every year of loyal service to
ABC. I won't hide anything from you, John. I won't
sneak behind your back. I'll treat you with respect, not
like a mailroom clerk. If I miss, we'll bury the hatchet. If
I find my target, you'll be tomorrow's headline. You'll

make the "Late Night News." You'll be a star. You gave me my break, John. I want to do the same for you."

"I think, in the end, this will be good for all of us, George."

"Back off, jack-off. I'm wise to the rise in your Levi's."

I rip off my St. Christopher medal and throw it in the pile of torn wood. "Watch out, Prescott. I'm coming in!"

I rap the silver knocker three times.

Sally opens the door. She's dressed in a blue velvet pantsuit. Her eyelids are glossy with a matching eye shadow. She's black-penciled beneath her eyes, as boldly as a brass rubbing.

"Welcome," she says, smiling. Then, seeing the kids, she adds. "This is even better."

"Don't I get a birthday kiss?"

Sally comes close to me, stretching her arms slowly inside my sports jacket. Her fingernails trace a pattern up and down the back of my Ohrbach's permanently pressed fifty percent polyester shirt. As we stand cheek to cheek, my eyes strafe the new, framed sampler hung above Sally's desk in the hall: "HE WHO COMES HITHER SHALL NOT BE TURNED AWAY."

"What'd you do to your eyes, Sally? They look like the CBS logo."

"More dramatic, don't you think? Contrast is better for the screen."

Jenny walks out of the living room holding a sungun: a wooden T-bar with seven blazing lights attached. A man follows just behind her.

Tandy and George, Jr., hide their heads inside my coat.

Sally kisses me, then stands back to take a look at the birthday boy.

"What's going on, Sally?"

"I've been helping Jenny with her homework," she says.

The man moves closer. He kneels. He's aiming a camera at my face.

Prescott takes the hatchet out of my hand and lays it on top of the desk. "Sit down," he says, pointing to the chair beside it.

"I'll stand."

"Have it your way," he says quietly.

I stare at him.

"Well?" Prescott says, taking the seat.

"You started it. Now cure it."

"What?"

"This hate I feel."

"You're smarter than me, George. I don't have the right words. I fell in love. It grew slowly, over a long period of time. Nothing complicated. Very simple. Soft. Irene listened and laughed. She made me feel emotions I'd almost forgotten. She became important to me. She still is."

Prescott runs his hands through his full head of gray hair. "There are just no words, George," he says with a shrug.

"I have words."

"I don't believe you hate me, George. We've been through too much together. You're an educated man."

"Let me tell you what hate is. I own the copyright."

Prescott looks away. He takes a deep breath. I wait for his eyes to turn back to mine.

"Hate is like dry ice stuck in your chest: a fuming, lethal coldness. Hate is your eyes stinging, but no tears. You feel robbed, stripped to the bone, naked. Your body aches, but you can't locate the bruises."

"Like something to drink?" Prescott says. "A cup of tea? Some warm milk?"

"I'm a star turn. I don't want to spend the rest of my days staggering through life like a blind man in a brothel."

"Irene never once said she didn't love you. She's devoted to you, George."

"The sounds you make surprise you. Your actions disgust you. 'This is not me,' you say to yourself. Heart heavy, lungs choking, brain whirling—everything inside you wants an answer. You hate because you can't go back, and you hate because you can't see a way of going forward. The pain won't let you forget the dream's lost."

Prescott leans forward, hands on knees. "But was the dream realistic?"

"It's not for you to say!"

I catch a glimpse of myself in the hall mirror. Unshaven, I look older. A bee sting has swollen the right side of my upper lip. I'm as puffed and hideous as a KO'd fighter.

"It needn't be this way, George," Prescott says, shifting his weight in the chair to get up.

I poke his shoulder with my forefinger. He sits back.

"I hate Irene for making our marriage commonplace. I hate Irene for giving into her emotions. I hate Irene for killing the ideal of our love. I hate Irene for making me feel hate. I hate Irene because I can't live without her!"

My legs wobble. Suddenly, I feel tired.

The floor smells of polish.

Prescott's arms come around my back and under my shoulders. "I'm taking you home," he says, hauling me to my feet.

"I want Maddy. Take me to Maddy."

"Did you say 'mad'?" Jenny says, resting the lights against the wall and pointing the stick-mike closer.

"No."

"Speak up, Uncle George. This is rented equipment. It's not the best."

Sally steers the kids toward the kitchen. "They can play a part in this gala, too. They'll love my fudge."

"Your mother and I have very serious business to transact."

Jenny is braless. Her breasts hang low on her chest, pancaked by her yellow tank-top sweater. The brown coronas around her nipples are just visible through the cloth. "We're all life actors," she says. "Just do your thing."

"Jenny, please. My life's too complicated for fun and games."

"That's a Sony AVC-3400 video camera," Jenny says, twirling her frizzy hair and drawing it under her nose to smell. "We're only one-thirtieth of a second behind life."

The man inches nearer.

"Will you stop it!"

"His name's Chaim. He's from Israel."

"Does he understand English?"

"Don't make such a fuss, darling," Sally says, coming back into the hall. "Underground television's the latest thing. Chaim's a genius. I've seen his other films. He calls them 'realies.' Nothing's made up. No fiction. Our life is art."

"Warhol saw his work and flipped."

"Jenny, I know you're interested in movies. I encouraged you, remember? But believe me—this is amateur night. 'Underground' is the wrong name for this monkey business. It's more like an 'undertow'—it'll drag you away from serious study. You'll be swamped by manifestos. You'll forget the public: then you're really sunk. You'll end up a piece of meat in some switch-hitting hippie's chance sandwich."

"That's a beautiful riff, Uncle George."

Dressed in a Levi jacket with a Star of David tangled in his hairy chest, the Jewish cowboy stalks me with the camera into the living room.

"Get that creep out of here, Sally!"

Sally stands with her hand on Chaim's tie-dyed shoulder. "Jenny's just married him," she says. "It's the only way Chaim could get American working papers."

"I don't believe it. Not my Jenny?"

"We're calling this 'realie' *Celebration*," Sally says. "Their marriage. Your birthday. A day in my life. Chaim uses a Schwitters collage technique. Let things fall where they may. What happens, happens. Like life."

Jenny slides next to me on the sofa. "Did you get the grimace?"

Chaim nods.

Jenny kisses my cheek. "Don't worry, Uncle George. We don't live together. Chaim's got a girl. Sometimes he takes us both to parties. He introduces me as his wife and her as his mistress. It's a goof."

"Why do you kids turn everything into a joke?"

Chaim motions for Jenny to take the camera. She steps away from the sofa to get us both in focus.

"There are 525 scan-lines—as you know—in a cathode ray tube," Chaim says. "Jenny's taking your picture now, and the electron gun in the video monitor set up in Sally's room is banging out your image, zigzagging down in a split second. We can play you back on a video tape recorder. You are as real on television as you are in person. The same. Scientifically speaking—on screen or off —you are just a combination of electrons. Dig it? There's democracy in matter, Mr. Melish. So smile and stay cool."

"Fags," Mother says.

I hold her chair. She pulls it closer to the table. She smiles thank-you.

"There are dozens of faggot escorts I could've brought to dinner tonight. Real juicy ones. It's terrible when your husband dies. Sol was a real man, even at the end of his life. I'm not too old, but I won't be a fairy godmother. I still have something to give to a virile man. But who are they? Where are they hiding?"

Irene brings the consommé.

"You look well, Mom."

"Looks are deceiving."

"Are you sleeping better?"

"One, two hours a night. If that."

"Have you tried reading?"

"The doctor says it's bad for my eyes. Sight is one of the few pleasures I have left."

"What about pills?"

"They're no good. I've tried every kind. Nothing helps."

"You mean you lie there awake for eight hours? That must be torture."

"It is," Mom says, tasting the soup.

Sally lights a cigarette and tosses her head back. Her streaked hair falls dramatically over her shoulders. She looks straight into the camera.

"Even before he took my husband's job, I wanted to fuck George rigid. But I don't want my Georgie to get the wrong idea."

Sally touches my hand. I can't pull away.

"Not here," I mouth.

The camera doesn't see me.

"As you heard when I called him this evening, George asked if I loved him. Typical bourgeois habit. I'm in it for a laugh and a lay. I never make the unpardonable sin of feeling emotion. Fucking is like peeing. It's relieving yourself. Nobody wants any heavies. I've had many ex-tramaritals before George, but none that I fancied more. Thanks to my help, George is a very powerful man. He's going to hire me as a scriptwriter for one of his soap operas, but he doesn't know it. Well, now he does. My husband, John, had an *affaire* with George's wife. I knew it. It didn't bother me. But John flubbed the dub. He cared for this girl. One day, George appeared in the hall, and they argued. I only heard about it later because I was over in Nyack scoring a very successful banker who's also a notorious sex fiend. Fifty-seven and a body like a sprinter. Evidently, it was a tremendous fight. There were screams. Things were thrown. It was very melodramatic and messy. After that, John started to feel guilty. He was tormented. That got my goat. All these years he'd been true blue, if you don't count *Playboy* bunnies and hat-check girls. Let's say, true light blue. Suddenly, he's brooding like a ten-year-old. He won't eat. There are telephone calls in the middle of the night. And tears. Once, when he was straddling me, John even started to sob. It was a disgusting spectacle. Truly. I finally had to ask him to leave the house. There was no squabbling. I had him dead to rights. Afterward, when he'd moved to the ABC offices on the West Coast, I found her corre-spondence. I burned it. She signed in Italian. Can you be-lieve it? *'Je ne regrette rien,'* that's my motto. When John was in the hot center of TV he never helped my career. I didn't want my twilight years with all that chest-beating. So, here I am: 'over twenty-one' and full of fun. Anthony Burgess wrote his first novel at forty. Shaw was the same age when he wrote his first play. Alfred Wallis started painting at seventy. I'm a life-gambler. The world awaits me."

"This is the revolution," Jenny says, her hand sweeping between her mother and the camera. "Biofeedback—video without voyeurism."

Chaim moves the camera closer.

"We want people to tape their own stories and replay themselves. This is technological healing. People become their own heroes. Behavior can be analyzed and changed. Life is fed back to them. That's why we wanted to tape a VIP from an escapist Establishment channel. This could be a significant document. We could get a booking on educational television." Jenny's belly button peeks over the top of her blue jeans. "What do you have to say to that, Uncle George?"

I shake my head. I'm not talking.

The camera whirrs. Nobody says a word. Chaim motions with his free hand for someone to fill the dead air.

"I'm a materialist," Sally smiles. "My life is measurable. If I've had a bad week, it's because I ate three expensive but bad meals, wrote fifteen promising pages which finally displeased me, so I tore them up, and got laid three times. If it's a good week, my point count is high for the victories, low for the defeats."

Chaim gives Sally the thumbs-up sign.

I can feel Irene's warmth in bed beside me, but, in the darkness, I can't see her face. Her body brushes mine. I lean over to kiss her. "Want to?"

She kisses me sweetly. She says nothing. I nibble her cheek. "You turn me on."

My lips feel a moistness. With my fingers, I trace the wetness from Irene's eyes across her temples to her damp hair.

I lie back on my pillow. I stare at the ceiling. "What's wrong now?"

"Nothing."

"Has the word 'adultress' once come to my lips? I'm trying to imagine it never happened."

"It did happen."

"No it didn't."

"You didn't have to carry on like that, George. John's a sensitive man. After all, he made ABC possible."

"He couldn't cut it. He didn't have the drive, or the instincts."

"Imagine if you opened the door and there was a raving maniac waving a hatchet at you."

"Better a hole in the head than a hole in the heart."

"What's that supposed to mean?"

"Forget it."

Irene sighs.

We lie quietly for a few minutes. "Irene? You OK?"

"Fine," she says, her voice quavering.

"What's wrong?"

"John was supposed to call at three. I called his house four times. Each time Sally answered, so I hung up. I think she's suspicious."

"I called you three times from the office."

"He couldn't call Monday because you were in bed recovering from the bees. And now it's Wednesday and I still haven't heard. He never left it this long. How could he do this to me?"

"If that bastard doesn't call, I'll make him call."

"Stay out of this."

I rub my hand along the silky curve of her thigh. "I'm here, Irene. I love you. I want you. Let's pitch some woo."

"I can't, George. It hurts down there. I have this terrible irritation."

"You can be on top."

"I went to the doctor today. He said I had 'an inflammation of the napkin area.' They call it 'thrush.' "

"I could've told you that. It's the Seven-Year-Itch."

"You can't always give all the time, George," Mom says, folding her napkin and patting it beside her plate. "You've got to get."

"It's my job."

"You find these writers. You discover performers. You're always doing something for somebody else. They make fortunes. What's her name—you know, the Flying Nun—she'd still be behind the counter at Gimbels. And what about Dick Cavett? He gave an interview in the *Times* two weeks ago. Not one mention of you. It's George Melish they should be writing about. You're too nice, George. That's your problem."

"It's my job."

Mom lifts her handbag from beside the chair and takes out her compact. She scrutinizes her lips, then the pouches beneath her eyes. "You know George was a good actor," she says, turning to Irene. "Sol had him screentested. He could've been big. Al Pacino. Dustin Hoffman. Robert Redford. They're George's age and they don't have half his personality."

"Can we change the subject, Mom?"

"Next week, I want to take you both to dinner. My treat."

"That's very sweet of you," Irene says. "But you really don't have to."

"Would you call the Four Seasons, George, and make the reservation?" Mom says. "I'm an unknown in this town, now."

Irene stands up and starts to clear away the plates.

"How do you make that quiche so light?"

"It's like sex, Vera. Practice makes perfect."

The doorbell rings. It's the chauffeur for Mom.

"May I use your bathroom?" Mom says, dabbing Binaca on her tongue. She stands up and walks into the hall.

"I'm worried about your mother, George. She's still in bad shape. It's almost a year now. You should really spend more time with her."

"Was that necessary, Irene?"

"She doesn't live that far from the office. You could meet for lunch. Or drinks."

"Do you have to wash our dirty laundry in public?"

"George, you're wandering off the point."

"Not as far as you wandered."

"I refuse to talk about it."

"You don't have to. Don't think I don't notice. The way you wrap your legs around me. How you move your body. What you let me do when the 'thrush' isn't nesting. That's new. You didn't learn those tricks from me. You're as ruthless as the Duchess of Windsor and her Scissor Grip."

"I thought you liked it."

"That's not the point."

"I'm not the one who mentions You-Know-Who."

"I disgust myself."

Mom walks into the dining room. "It was a lovely evening," she says. I hold her mink coat as she slips into it.

"God bless you both," Mom says, kissing us. "I'm sorry Sol wasn't here to enjoy it. But I'm sure you understand."

"What time is it?"

"Let's give him a love zap, Mom," Jenny says, moving close. "We're wasting tape."

"It's almost eleven-twenty," Sally says, sliding beside

me and putting her arm around my neck in a playful hammerlock. "Relax, honey," she whispers. Her breasts press against me.

"In two minutes, I'm thirty-six."

"What's going through your mind?" Jenny says. "Tell the camera."

"No."

Jenny's knees nudge mine. "You're perspiring," she says.

"My father died at seventy-two."

The three men sing "Happy Birthday," sounding out the name on the invoice they hold in front of them as they reach "Happy Birthday, George Melish, Happy Birthday To You." They hand me the cake in a brown box. "Yale Cake Service" is printed in blue across the top. I close the door.

"Last year it was a hamper from Abercrombie," Angie says. "Vera's coming down in the world."

I put the box on the living room table. I open it. A chocolate layer cake.

"When I was a kid, I used to have this fantasy," Angie says, his legs dangling over the side of the sofa. "I used to dream of diving into the Winged Foot Country Club pool. Only it was filled with chocolate cake, not water. I had to eat my way out."

"That's funny."

Angie sits up. "How about a swim?"

Laughing, we strip off our shirts and pants. We spread a newspaper on the carpet and place the cake on it. Hunched on our hands and knees, we bend our heads into the cake. Angie starts from the north. I'm coming from the south.

The icing squishes like finger paint. Chocolate streaks my hair. Cake gets in my eyes. It clogs my nose. Then, still swallowing furiously, I look up. Angie's face is as blotched as a mudman's. I grab a chunk of cake and mash it against his chin.

Angie pulls my hair and yanks me on top of the cake. "Happy birthday, sweetie," he laughs. The cake flattens under my weight. I'm sweating. Crumbs stick to me like sand. I grab Angie's nipple. The Blue Louie makes him scream. He falls back paralyzed, momentarily, in pain. I roll on top of him, grinding the sugary cake into him. With my free hand, I grab the last wedge of cake. I shove it down his Jockey shorts. I hold my hand on his crotch and push.

He screams and wriggles. I hold tight. "Dirty fucker," Angie laughs.

"I love you too, sweetie."

Exhausted, we lie on our backs. With our fingers we dab the icing off our bodies and eat it.

"I know about orgies. I'm no Johnny-come-lately. I've just been to one."

"Who said anything about orgies?" Jenny says.

"I'm hip. I've seen all the films: *Events, Deep Throat, Trash.* You're trying to get me hot. You want a cheapo, B.O. success. I know you kids better than you think. I keep up. It's my job. When you make a film that's good, I'll know about it. You'll tell me. It's a buyer's market. And I've got money to spend."

I take out my wallet. I wave it at the camera.

"Uncle George, the vein in your neck's bulging."

I catch a glimpse of myself in the gilt-edged mirror behind Sally's sofa. My hair is ruffled. I smooth it down.

"Feel those stomach muscles."

Jenny taps my gut. There's a hollow thud.

"That's the body of a young boy. If I took off my shirt, you could see my ribs."

Sally slips her arm through mine. "Come out on the patio."

I press my back to the sofa. "You're not getting me out there again. That place has a history."

"So do we, George. That's what we're trying to film. Our history."

"The youngest programming executive in television. The man who commissions over fifty new films a year. That's more than L. B. Mayer in his heyday. I have a fabulous history. But I'm not making it easy for these kids, Sally."

"We could reenact our first tempestuous meeting," Sally says, tilting her head and smiling softly. "It's very *Dolce Vita.*"

"Are you all right, Uncle George?"

"Everything's easier for you kids—even thinking. When a problem comes up, you throw the *I-Ching.* You drift away chanting your prescription mantra. You don't know the first thing about suffering. You think you're special because of the lines on your palm or the astrological chart you've made. You believe in 'vibes.' There's no work in any of it. No discipline. Vibes are as easy to fake as an orgasm."

Jenny leans calmly against the arm of the sofa. She brushes her hair out of her eyes. Her lips curl upward in a confident smile. "For three hours a day, I sit in the video lab rerunning pictures of myself. I'm my homework. I know my walk. My laugh. My disguises. My friends. I can play them back, speed them up. After a while, the Jenny on the screen is a character in somebody's else's film. I can be objective. By watching her, I've eliminated a lot of the things I don't like seeing in myself. Now, I'm a person I like looking at much better. I've improved."

"You know you're attractive. You wear these skimpy see-through numbers. You can see the outlines of your underwear inside your blue jeans—sometimes you even forget the underwear. You make a mockery of emotion. Have you ever known love?"

"I never use the word. It's so . . . Hollywood."

"A deep, enduring relationship?"

"I've found that it takes more than one man to make me happy."

"What you need is a good spanking."

"It's eleven-twenty-one, Uncle George," Jenny says.

"I have the whole 'underground' on my coffee table and in my record cabinet. You sold your secrets cheap. At least my generation kept theirs to themselves. You keep telling us to have a healthy attitude toward the body. Now, when I was a camper, we used to say, 'The body is the temple of the soul.' But when something's holy, there's a certain way to approach it."

"Who's talking about the body?"

"This documentary's typical. You want everything up front. Everything's blatant with you kids. Where's the subtlety? A symbol must conceal and reveal. A woman's a symbol, right? The Feminine Impulse. Fertility. Instinct. Intuition. Rita Hayworth, in other words."

Chaim puts his camera down. Jenny goes over and picks it up. "Rita Hayworth has pockmarks," Chaim says.

"Don't get fresh with me, young man."

"I saw her in person at the Plaza. She was here to promote that TV revival of her films."

"I was responsible for that. You never saw Rita in the raw. She left something to the imagination."

"Happy birthday!" Sally shouts. "All right, children!"

Tandy and George, Jr., step sideways through the dining room carrying a birthday cake. Chaim takes the cake from them and puts it on my lap. "The pits in her skin are hard to miss," he says.

"Try finding thirty-six blue candles in Sneden's Landing," Sally says. "Aren't you going to say something, George?"

"I'm leaving."

"I'm leaving," Dad says, slamming the bedroom door. "I've had it!"

I crouch in the shadows. A sleeve from Dad's pajamas hangs out of his suitcase.

"Kiss the children good-bye," Mom yells. "You gave up a treasure when you walked out on Vera Melish!"

The door slams. Minutes later, the elevator slides open, and closes with a bang.

I tiptoe to the window and peek behind the blind. The street lamps are still on. A wino covered in newspaper sprawls on a park bench. Dad walks to the corner. No cabs pass. He steps off the curb and looks up and down Fifth Avenue. He blows into his hands and rubs them together.

In the hall, Mom dials the telephone.

The phone rings. I pick it up quickly.

"I'm calling on a matter of principle," Sally says.

"All's fair in love and war, Sally. I told John either he cuts bait, or I turn over the letters to Elton Rule."

"No matter what Irene tells you, I'm leaving John, he's not leaving me."

"I feel so small," Irene says. She takes her red toothbrush and sticks it deep inside her mouth. I hold her head over the sink. She gags, and then vomits. I reach into her bathrobe and grab the rest of the Compazine. I flush them down the toilet.

Irene sits slumped and pink-eyed on the edge of the

bathtub. The neon light is too bright for her eyes. Her lids struggle to stay open. "I felt like a tightrope walker. I couldn't help myself, George. I was scared to death, but thrilled. I was up so high. It was as if John were waiting for me at the other end of the wire. He was willing me to greatness. There was nothing I couldn't do. Each step was exciting and graceful and dangerous. I felt so strong. I thought I could balance. We both knew that one false step could mean death. That's what was so heroic. And when I finally crossed the wire, when I was safe in his arms, he let me fall."

I blink back tears. "I want to give you happiness, goddammit! To me you're Rita Hayworth, Marilyn Monroe, the 'Mona Lisa.' You're everything. And you'd disappear from me like that. Without a note. Without an explanation. Dead on arrival."

"He's a coward," Irene says, her fists banging on the side of the tub. "He said he'd rather write than talk. Two hundred yards away. We were lovers. Now, we're pen pals. His letters are so distant and chatty. We weren't like that. We were passionate."

"You want me to be more romantic?"

"He treated me like a goddess."

"He didn't have to wipe up your barf."

"Sally's turning him against me. I know she is. I told him I'd adjust. 'Name the terms,' I said. 'No terms, no expectations.' I can't live without hope. He's scared of what might happen. He's thinking of taking a room at the Yale Club. He'll tell the receptionist to say he's not in. I'll never talk to him."

The tiles are cold under my feet. Irene rubs her bare shoulders to keep warm.

"Don't you see what you're doing to us, Irene?"

"I can't see anything when I'm like this, George. I'm dead inside."

Irene's hands tremble.

"You're not going to make me dead. You're not going to smother me. There's a life to enjoy. We're blessed. We have more than nine-tenths of the universe. I want to enjoy it."

Irene shakes her head. "Always tired. Always knowing that sooner or later I'll feel like this. Small. Helpless. Sick."

"Don't talk silly."

"You don't know what it's like to want to kill yourself."

"You're a bundle of energy. Look at all the things you do."

"Another thirty, maybe forty years of this bloody pain."

"Let's do something about it."

"I just wanted to go to sleep."

"You can work for me. A girl Friday kind of thing. You can help with casting."

"I just wanted to shut my eyes and fall into a smooth, long sleep."

Irene motions me away from the toilet bowl. Holding her hair behind her, she bends over it. She heaves. When she backs away, she has to lean on my shoulders for support.

"Bread and jam," she says. "Get some, darling."

"You've been blowing lunch for half an hour."

"Protein and sweets. That's the antidote."

I sit Irene back on the bed and cover her up. "Why didn't you tell me about this before we were married? That's what gets me mad. I wasn't prepared."

"You wouldn't have married me then, would you?" she says, patting her pillow.

Sally gets up and walks to the record player. "Before you go, George, I want you to hear this."

Jenny moves the stick-mike close to the loudspeaker.

"It comes out next week," Sally says. *"Variety's* already touting it for the charts."

I'd know that sound anywhere. The harmonica and electric guitar. The sidemen who sound like they're playing pots and pans. I introduced them to the nation. It's Astroflash Fred. He sings like a meths drinker: all slur and spittle.

> *I'm a lover*
> *And a thriller—*
> *The moment's filled now*
> *The past is killed now.*
> *I dig the flame,*
> *I crave the game.*
> *Call me Lover,*
> *That's my name.*

"I spawned that crackpot troubador! It's like an infection. Frank, Nat, Perry, Tony—in my day, all the singers sang about being faithful."

"Ssssh!" says Jenny, bopping in time with the music. "The second verse is a stone gas."

> *I drink deep now,*
> *Get good sleep now,*
> *Sighs are highs now,*
> *I dig lies now,*
> *I'm a thriller,*
> *A killer-diller,*
> *I'm a lover.*

"Well?" Sally says, putting the record back in its slip-cover.

"The man's ruthless. He's preaching a gospel of wanton lust. Even passion has responsibilities."

"Passion's only responsibility is to keep going," Sally says.

"Great beat," Jenny says. "Sexy."

"Don't you think it's good, George?"

"Sure it's good. That's what pisses me off."

Sally hands me the record. "Irene wrote it."

"I need this like a hole in the head," Mom says, sliding along the plastic covering of her sofa to the armrest and refusing to even look at the newspaper.

"Irene and I worded it carefully. The *New York Review of Books* is the Bendel of publications."

"The locks on my doors can be snapped as easy as celery. They get your name out of one of these ads. You answer the door. They look polite. And before you know it —voom—they've got a knife in one hand and their 'corporal' in the other. They push you on the bed. They're breathing heavy. They force you to strip. At my age, rape would be the last straw. It's hard enough living alone."

"How do you find Mr. Right if you won't look, Mom?"

"If God meant it to be, Mr. Right will find me."

"The whole idea about marriage is changing," Irene says. "Professors, lawyers, doctors all advertise in the paper. It's the done thing."

"There are a lot of widows in this town, and they're hustlers, to boot. They fight dirty. My name's blue-chip. I've worked for charities and the UN. Once they get hold of this, it'll be all over New York. No man'll call me. I'm not a tramp. I'm no *fille de joie*."

"Will you just look at what we wrote? Your name and address aren't even mentioned."

Mom puts on her bifocals and picks up the paper. We stand behind her while she reads:

VIVACIOUS, youngest-looking middle-aged widow, seeks kindred spirit to live sophisticated life. Likes theater, dancing, movies, long walks. Well-connected. Mensch, marriage, moolah a must. NYR, Box 222.

Mom puts the paper down. "They'll think I'm Jewish," she says. "After all those years of education, George, couldn't you express yourself with something better than Yiddish? 'Lean bon vivant,' for instance."

"There was a word limit."

"I'm also an avid reader. I belong to the Book-of-the-Month Club."

"You need something punchy to attract attention. This paper goes all over the world."

"You think film people read it?" Mom says, taking off her glasses.

"Everybody does."

Mom stares across at the mirror. With her hands at her temples, she pulls her skin tight around her eyes. Then, she feels the folds under her chin. "You think I should have a face-lift?"

Sally flicks lint off my lapel. "When you see the bedroom, George, you won't want to leave. You'll forget everything."

The record's dropped to the floor. Somehow, it's wedged under my heel.

Jenny goes to the magazine rack and holds up the plush red velvet and brown mahogany interior of Hugh Hefner's suite. "We got the idea out of 'Playboy Pads,'" she says. "Hefner's got a seven and a half foot revolving bed with an Ampex television camera—the forty thousand buck model—trained on it. There's an engineer on call twenty-four hours a day. A series of banked television screens can play back the 'beautiful moments,' as he calls them. He can plug in cassettes and remember his golden goodies."

"The kids can provide the same experience for seventeen hundred dollars with a Sony Video Rover," Sally says. "I'm not the type to be thirteenth at life's table."

"If Irene could see me, pictures would speak a thousand words. You could invite her up here tomorrow morning. She'd sit down. Then, she'd see me. She couldn't escape. She'd have to listen."

"Anything's possible with biofeedback," Jenny says. "We can bend time around. This'd be a great test to see how far we could make secondary experiences replace primary ones."

"I'd want to be photographed here on the sofa with the library shelves behind me. I'd knot my tie. My legs would be crossed. A cigarette would be burning casually in the ashtray. No middle-long shots. Just close-ups. I'd want this to be as straightforward and confidential as the Dristan ad. Irene must see I mean business."

"George, have you been listening to me?" Sally says. "I'm offering you my body."

Jenny hushes Sally. "The camera's your stage," she says, pointing to Chaim. "Use it."

"My mother always said I could've been an actor."

The door from Studio C wheezes shut. Irene and I walk back to the office. She carries the clipboard. The callback sheet, with her notations, is on the top.

"In my next incarnation, I want to be a rock star. I've got presence. All I need's a voice. They could dub it."

Irene yawns. "Long day," she says, glancing at the photographs of the ABC stars which hang along the corridor.

"It was like a meat market," Irene says. "Everybody's so nervous."

"They should be. A series about the adventures of a rock group is gold. Whoever we chose'll be on this wall soon enough. He'll be able to buy the place."

We pass the water-cooler. A young man in cowboy boots and a red and black checked lumber shirt bends over the spigot. He's holding back his blond hair to get a swig. His guitar case lies on the floor behind him. Over the front, painted in green, is : "C'mon Baby, Let The Good Times Roll."

We walk by. He doesn't look up.

"We saw that one, didn't we?"

"Yes," Irene says. "I talked to him when he left his pictures and demo record. He's originally from England. Near Wolverhampton. Used to be an art student."

"You're a very efficient girl Friday."

"He was very funny. Confident, but not pushy. Calls everybody 'Luv.' I asked him why he gave up painting. 'Chucked me out, luv, didn't they?' he said. 'The school got tired of my "Abyss" paintings.' I asked him to describe them. 'Painted the word "Abyss" in different Dayglo colors, luv.' 'But abyss is depression and darkness,' I said. 'That's the difference between a rocker and a lady,' he said, tipping his cap. 'Letting go for you is hell; for me, it's liberation.' "

"He's in the final ten, isn't he?"

"Yes."

"We're calling them back on Monday. What's his name?"

Irene checks the list. "Fred Lorber."

I'm lining up my croquet shot on the lawn when I see George, Jr., kick his yellow ball closer to the hoop.

"Put that back, George."

"I didn't do anything, Daddy," he says with a straight face.

Irene starts to laugh. Then Tandy gets the giggles.

"There's nothing funny about cheating. If you won't play seriously, we won't play. Give me the mallets."

"It's only a game, George," Irene says. "You and Tandy are five hoops ahead."

"My son cheated. That may be OK in your book, Hester Prynne, but it's not in mine. Somebody's got to set a good moral example in this household."

"Who's Hester?" Tandy says.

"Why don't you ask Uncle John? He knows all about the women in the neighborhood."

"Finish the game, George."

"By encouraging a cheater, you are also a cheater. It's time these kids learned about morals."

Irene glares at me. "George, you're being childish."

I belt the yellow ball into the bushes.

"Do you have any other words of wisdom to dispense on the playing fields of Sneden's Landing?" Irene says, picking up the remaining croquet balls.

"As a matter of fact, I do. Never argue with your mother, kids. She's typically English—nasty, British and short."

"You're part of my story, George," Sally says, kneeling beside me on the sofa. "I've already explained the events leading up to your entrance to the camera. That footage will be wasted."

The heat from the sungun is on the back of my neck. My armpits are drenched in sweat.

"Look at me," Sally says, lifting my chin out of my hands. "Are you listening?"

"If only Irene had kept in touch."

Sally sighs. Her hand leaves my knee. "The show must go on."

I take the cushion from the sofa and hold it over my face. Dots dance like amoebas inside my eyelids. The blackness calms me.

"What are you doing, now, George?"

"Collecting my thoughts."

Mom swivels around from her dressing table. Behind her, pictures of Dad are stuck to the mirror with black masking tape. Whimpering, she waves her hairbrush at me. "You haven't set foot in this apartment for six months."

"But, Mom, I'm here now."

"You're as selfish as the rest, George. You don't give a damn what happens to me."

"Mom, all I said was not to worry because there weren't any replies to the ad yet. We still have two weeks."

Mom stands up in her slip. She blows her nose. "I dedicated my life to you. Suffered Sol's sharp tongue. The language of that man! All for you. You wouldn't be where you are now, brother, if it weren't for me. Melish men are all alike. Me, Me, Me—the whole time."

Mom turns on the light to the closet. She steps inside. Her shoe rack flaps on the back of the door. Her hats are stored in see-through boxes on the shelves above her clothes. "I haven't got one decent thing to wear to this party. Not one. And who am I dressing for? Tell me that? Every time a man says something nice to me, I think he's a rapist. I can't look him in the eye. I think he's read the ad you placed in that sex paper."

The smell of camphor makes my nose itch. "I can always call and see if they'll take it out."

Mom pulls a turquoise Chanel suit off the hanger. "Don't threaten me," she says, holding the dress over her slip. "You like it?"

I nod yes.

"You're ungrateful, George. That's the fact of the matter."

"What are you talking about, Mom? I left work early. I made a special trip."

"Don't let me keep you." Mom turns off the lights. She walks out and sits down in her chair. "I had to tell you what I felt," she says, opening her jewel box and taking out her charm bracelet. "It'd be dishonest to keep it to myself."

Mom looks at me in the mirror while she brushes her hair. "Do you stay in contact with Dad?"

"He's been dead almost two years."

"That is not the point. If you really cared, you'd make the effort."

"If Houdini couldn't make contact with his mother, how am I supposed to do it?"

"Don't taunt me, George. My heart's not that good. I could keel over dead any minute. Then what? You wouldn't even stay in touch with your own mother. That's gratitude for you."

Chaim is crouching three feet in front of me. Sally and Jenny stand behind the camera.

"I want to begin this fireside chat with two brief points of information. One, the kids are fine. Two, the last time we talked—before you hung up—you accused me of having a 'star complex.' This is not true. I've never thought of myself as a star. Truthfully, I've always seen myself as a building—the George Melish, like the Osborne or the Empire State. You and the kids are part of Melish Enterprises. Not the luxury items, but the foundation of the whole structure. We're all of a piece. That's something to be proud of . . . of which to be proud. And grateful. I say this to remind you, Irene, that I am a tough businessman. And when I sign a production contract, you can be damn sure I'm going to get satisfaction and results. You can't simply walk off the job. We've struck a bargain. You should be penalized for reneging. But I want to negotiate a compromise. That's why I've come before you this evening. I want to meet face to face. I want Melish Enterprises to continue as usual. We're blue-chip. And right now I'm holding two sleepy little aces until you show your cards.

"I know you've been moonlighting. I've just heard 'I'm a Lover.' You were always facile with words. You've finally found a job: prophet in plastic. But ponder this: Is it better to be a lover or a mother? You can't be both. These songs are subliminal advertisements for anarchy. You're beaming rogue ideas into these kids who walk naked to protest President Nixon, who meditate in the raw squatting in the sandpits at Carl Schurz Park at the crack of dawn. I've watched them from the patio with my binoculars. They're oblivious to the eyes of strangers. These kids give up their families to live in communes. They fornicate like baboons with any genitalia that happens to be exposed. Their children are raised by whatever person is lying beside them at the moment. Do you really want that? You wouldn't even kiss my cock . . . excuse me . . . penis. For a long time, I couldn't take a business trip because you said you couldn't sleep alone. You: Irene Melish—mother of two, denizen of Ascot, Fortnum and Mason, Annabelle's. The kids claim, 'You are what you eat.' Why don't you admit you're *paté de foie gras,* and not Spanish fly.

"In the dark night of my soul, I've been reading the Bible. I quote—

> *"For love is strong as death;*
> *Jealousy is cruel as the grave.*

"My love is that strong, Irene. And so is your jealousy. You can't give me the heave-ho like Sue Kelley's cheeseboard. My job's not my girl friend. You are. I can't fuck my job. In the beginning, it was me that wanted to screw for fun, and you who wanted 'a ring by spring.' Don't think I haven't played around. I have. Don't think women aren't attracted to me. They are. I've threaded the eye of the Golden Doughnut many times. But in bed, I have to pretend I'm married. I can't enjoy it without marriage. You started that, Irene. Now finish it.

"You bitch!

"Sorry.

"You tit!

"There I go again. A slip of the tongue.

"Love isn't promiscuous. A relationship takes time. And I don't have time to start having *affaires*. You're coming back to me, Irene. I'm going to be your husband, like it or not!"

"Shit!" Chaim says, waving his hand. "Another tape clip."

"I'm cooking. I can feel it."

"You're fabulous," Jenny says, handing the new clip to Chaim. "You come across like Edward R. Murrow."

"I don't want to lose it."

My head is clear. I'm rising like a soufflé. I need constant heat. One breath of cold air could bring me down.

Sally tosses Big Fred's record on my lap. "Stanislavski says props help to generate emotion."

"You call this a prop?"

"Take it from the top," Chaim says, pointing at me.

"What do you mean, 'The moment's filled now'? Was I just a breath going over your body, Irene? Did I leave no memory? I can pop your prophecy like a pimple. Onehanded. Watch.

"It broke easily, didn't it? Like my heart. I offer this record up as a sacrifice to our marriage—an unholy wafer

I'm not swallowing—first halved, now halved again. Four pieces. One for Prescott the Perfect. One for Big Fred. One for me and my thirty-seventh year. One for nearly eleven years of marriage in the eyes of God. I didn't want marriage. I got to like it. I didn't want television. I got to like it. You can adapt to anything, Irene. You need a positive mental attitude."

"George, your hand's bleeding!"

I wave it at the camera. "The Blood of the Lamb!"

I jump up. My breath fogs the lens. "You mangy muff! Twat! Cunt! You forgot my birthday!"

A hand touches my forehead. It's soft and scented. "You fainted," Sally says.

"I had her against the ropes. My footwork was incredible. Each word was an uppercut. My gloves were stained with her blood."

"Not your gloves, dear. Your pants."

"What a feeling! Each syllable skin and bone."

"You were standing up, pointing at the camera. Then, the first thing we knew, you toppled. It took all three of us to get you in here."

I prop myself up on my elbows. "What's going on?"

"Your head hit the camera. Your eye started to swell. We thought bright light would irritate it."

"Turn on the lights."

"Relax, George," Sally says, kissing my ear.

"You brought me into the bedroom!"

"You were bleeding like a stuck pig, George. Do you know what a Mohawk carpet costs?"

"You took advantage of me!"

I sit up. I grope my way toward the bar of light shining from under what must be the bedroom door. "You've turned a nice evening into a farce, Sally."

I yank open the door.

Chaim is lying in prone position, pointing his camera at me like an M-16. "Out of my way, schmuck!"

Jenny aims the sungun low. She gives a wolf whistle.

I look down at the spotlight. Grabbing my crotch, I leap back into the bedroom. I slam the door. "Turn on those goddamn lights, Sally! Where are my pants?"

"Dacron dries easily," Sally says. "They should be ready in an hour."

"I don't have an hour."

Sally snaps on the light. She's standing in a scarlet kimono. Her legs are thin and tan. Her fingernails glisten. "Yes, you do," she says.

"I think I shocked your daughter."

"You did," Sally says, stepping closer. "She's never seen a man in garters."

Sally undoes her kimono. "Come here," she says.

"This is unfair. You've caught me with my pants down."

"Attention must be paid to this body," Sally says, opening her robe wide. "Describe me."

"Your Mound of Venus . . ."

"Golden, isn't it?"

"Your mammaries . . ."

"A meal, aren't they?"

"Sally, I want a meaningful relationship."

Her hand covers my mouth. She clicks off the light. "Nibble my nuggie," Sally whispers.

I lie underwater as immobile as a turtle. I can see Tandy wading toward me. I nip playfully at her ankles. She dives in, skittering around me.

We stay close to the bank where the water's warmest. Except for the splash of the waterfall, it's silent here in the woods, only three-quarters of a mile from Palisades

Road. George, Jr., rummages in the underbrush for arrow-heads. Tandy and I gaze at the waterfall that spills thir-ty feet over mossy ledges to this green, smooth basin. Let Irene and Prescott have their gin slings and Scrabble on hot summer days, the kids and I have our own special place.

"Everybody weighs the same in water, did you know that?"

"No," Tandy says, splashing me.

"Five pounds."

Tandy puts one hand under my back and one under my leg. She glides me along the water laughing at her new power. "I can save your life," she says. "Now, it's your turn."

I buoy her up with my knee. Her firm rear end passes over my hand. She wiggles. I can feel the cleft between her cheeks. Tandy turns to me. "Tushie," she smiles.

Tandy takes my hand and leads me carefully to the waterfall. We stand behind the spray, which dazzles in the sunlight.

"See," Tandy says, pointing in front of us. "A rain-bow."

I lift her up so she can touch it. She looks back at me. "You too."

I hold out my hand into the arc of color.

George, Jr., stands by the side of the pond with a rock in his hand. He's yelling for us to join him. We pretend not to hear.

"It's our rainbow," Tandy says, kissing me as I put her down.

The water rattles the shower curtain. Irene sticks her head out of the bathroom door. "Take a shower with me?"

I hold up the script. "Reading."

Irene tiptoes to the chair and slides over the arm onto my lap. "Do you think I have a nice body for the mother of two?"

"You're wet."

"How about a warm, soapy rubdown? An executive scrub."

"Look, darling, I got you the job. I'm home by five-thirty every night now. I've kept my part of the bargain."

"Don't hold today against me," Irene says, nestling her head under my chin so I can't see the page. "On my new schedule, I usually keep too busy to let memories mess me up. Today was a temporary setback. I just felt heavy inside."

"This is the pilot of the rock series. It's great."

"Am I forgiven?"

"The part was made for Lorber."

"You know I'm grateful, George. But I started thinking about all the things I could do and probably won't. I got sad."

"Take your shower." I pat her rump.

"Come with me." Irene grabs the script out of my hand.

"Don't be childish." I snatch it back.

Irene stands up. Her hand is on my shoulder. "I want to be a good wife, not a nuisance."

"Who said you were a nuisance?"

"That's what you think sometimes, isn't it?"

"Don't be provocative."

"I think I'll have a long soak," Irene says. "Before I go, is there anything you want?"

"Peace."

Sally's legs coil around me. Her heels scrape my backbone. "Eat me."

"Irene liked being cuddled."

Sally's hands are on my head. She pushes me farther down her body. "Eat."

"We're eating."

Tandy stands barefoot by my chair. She's in her pajamas. She holds a tennis racquet.

"When your mother comes out of the kitchen, she'll show you. Then to bed."

"That's a big guitar you've got there," Fred says.

"It's not a guitar," Tandy says, laughing and looking down.

I sit Tandy on my knee. "She's a great fan of yours. Doesn't miss a show."

Fred smiles. "You like my singing, luv?"

"You give Mommy goosebumps. I've seen them."

"You listen to your mother, luv. She knows what's best."

Irene comes in with the chocolate cake. On top of the icing is a miniature electric guitar.

Fred winks at Irene. "My favorite."

I raise the wineglass. "Well, here's to the second season."

"Twenty-six shows a year, twelve hours for one episode. That's hard work," Fred laughs. "I don't know if I should toast a treadmill."

"The minute you walked into Studio C, I had a flash. Confident, I said to myself, but not pushy. Sense of humor. This boy's going places."

"I've got other interests besides work," Fred says. "Plants, photography, poetry."

"I write poetry," Irene says.

"Poetry?"

"Sometimes," Irene says, turning toward me.

"What's iambic pentameter, honey?"

"I write to please myself, George."

"You don't know how many cold feet there were at ABC, Fred. I never doubted. When I have an instinct, I trust it."

"Me too," says Fred.

"They're all worry-warts down there. Worry slows you down. You lose time."

Irene crumples her napkin on the table and stands up.

"Show me the serve again, Mom?" Tandy slides off my lap. "Please?"

Irene takes the racquet and spins it in the palm of her hand. "You take the ball in your left hand. You toss the ball up. It should drop two inches inside the baseline. You find your point—that's the imaginary spot where the ball should be. You aim for that. You want to hit the ball when your arm's stretched out straight." Irene takes a demonstration swing. "The important thing is balance."

"You've got style," Fred says.

"I'm past it," Irene says. "I could've been good. I'm too old now. I've retired. But I know about competition tennis."

"I ask Irene to play. But she won't anymore. Scared of Big George's top spin."

Fred lifts his glass. "Let the good times roll."

We all drink to that.

I sink down between Sally's legs like a soldier taking cover.

"Tigerrrr!" Sally groans, grinding her pelvis into my face. "Claaaaaw me!"

Angie drops his pencil and stoops under the large table.

The Reading Room stinks of sweat and smoke. Students bend over their books trying not to notice the blonde sitting five chairs away from us.

I feel a tug on the cuff of my khakis. I look down. Angie on all fours. "Quivering quim!" he says, nodding in the direction of the open stacks. Nonchalantly, I leave my seat. I take my notepad with me. She'll never suspect. A few minutes later, Angie reconnoiters by the American Studies shelf. "What a snout full!" he says, rolling his eyes.

"She's a scag."

"Are you kidding, George? That's a pelt and a half."

"Nothing upstairs."

"I got a clear shot. She's sitting there with her legs open."

"I walked by her notes when she went out to get a drink of water. Her underlinings are terrible."

"We're in Muff City and you're talking literature. I'm telling you this girl can be approached. She's open for business."

"I like a girl with a head on her shoulders."

"I like a girl who gives head."

"That's the wrong come-on to a graduate student, Angie. A girl's most sensitive erogenous zone is her mind."

"George, underneath that plaid kilt is a Pulitzer Prize pussy."

"She's not my type."

"A girl just doesn't forget her drawers. It's a Freudian slip. Gap teeth and bare snatch are surefire signs. This cheese wants to get planked."

"I can't get it up."

"How many decent girls do we see around here? You've got to eat it while it's hot."

"I've got to hit the books."

"Four weeks to Winter Weekend," Angie says, grabbing my arm as I start to leave.

"I've got enough to keep me busy."

"So do I," Angie says, mugging like Groucho and flicking ash from an imaginary cigar. "Back to the Beaver Patrol."

Sally's arm slaps the bed like a wrestler breaking a fall.

She yanks me by the hair. My head jerks up. "Kill me," she whoops. "I can take it."

She shoves me back. Her thighs pinch my ears.

I can't breathe.

"Keep your nose out of my business," Irene says, closing the desk.

"You call this poetry?

> *"Stallion-strong,*
> *He loves me.*
> *Lean and long,*
> *He loves me not.*
> *Starlight eyes,*
> *He loves me.*
> *Sweet good-byes,*
> *He loves me not . . ."*

"That's my private property!"

"Are you seeing Prescott again?" I grab her arm and wrench it behind her back.

"Bully!"

"Is it Prescott?"

"No . . . I swear! . . . No."

Irene bites her lip. I inch her arm higher behind her back. "Who is it?"

"You're hurting me."

"My hammerlock's worse. I could break your neck."

"Fred," she says.

I shove her on the floor.

"Bastard!" Irene screams.

I stand above her. She's not crying. Neither am I. "I'm a gentleman, Irene. I've been raised to keep promises. I live an ordered life. I believe in duty. I'm loyal."

"Don't go on about loyalty, George. Ultimately loyalty is forgiveness."

"There's vomit in my throat. I feel dirty. I feel like I'll never be clean."

"I want something to look forward to."

"Sometimes even a gentleman has to think of himself."

"You had no right, George!"

"I had every right."

"My private property . . ."

"Here's some more." I pull my wedding ring off and throw it by her feet. "Add that to your list of recent acquisitions."

Outside, I take a deep breath and walk calmly to the car. She knows where to find me.

I dry my mouth on Sally's skin as I slide up her body. Her fingers dig into my back. "You renegade!" she pants. "You Brando bruiser!"

Finally, I find her mouth. I kiss her quiet.

She presses her chest tightly against me. "Rough me up," Sally says. She rolls me on my back. She straddles me.

Always had a knack. I could play a girl's body like a piano.

"I'm a woman," Sally says, guiding me inside her.

Why do I always call women "girls"?

"Maul me."

Sally rides me like a horse. Her knees grip my flanks. She leans back. She's posting on my cock. Irene hugged me close; Sally gyrates far away.

"This is a small place," Jackie says, pouring me a brandy. "But it's cheap. Anyway, I don't stay here much."

"Three weeks at The Westbury is all I can take. Check your mail slot. Call down for meals. Come home to a room with a paper seal across the toilet bowl to show it hasn't been used. The seal routine finally got me."

"You can stay with me if you want," Jackie says, handing me the brandy. "Until she calls."

"She knows where to find me."

Jackie kicks off her slippers. She sits cross-legged on her bed, combing her hair. "It's weird having you in my room. Seeing you with your shirt off. You have little titties. They're cute."

"How old are you?"

"Twenty-five."

"All my college friends in New York, and I end up spending the night on your floor."

"I'm better-looking than they are."

"You don't worry about things, do you?"

"Like what?"

"About being seen with a married man."

"How will they know?"

"My ring."

"You're not wearing one."

Jackie slips into bed. "When I was your age, most girls were scared of what people might think."

"My mother used to tell me about pleasing men," Jackie says, turning on her side.

"We never thought of anything but nookie."

"But I'm out for my own pleasure. I don't want words. I want sensations."

"Don't you want something permanent?"

Jackie laughs. "I want many men. Not indiscriminately—but as many as I genuinely feel something for. I want to be fantastic in bed. To come every time. To have incredible fun and not look back."

I drain the glass and spread out Jackie's sleeping bag. I turn off the light.

"Did you actually call up girls for dates?" Jackie says. "I find that so plaintively obvious."

"I'll tell you in the morning, when I'm feeling younger."

May I have this dance?
    May I hold your chair?
    May I have your telephone number?
    May I kiss you?
    May I touch you?
    May I make love to you?
    May I?

Sally bends forward on both hands like a defensive tackle digging in at the line of scrimmage.

Her breasts fall around my face. "C'mon," she wheezes. "C'mon."

I push harder.

"Take the bull by the horns, George."

"I left her because I love her, Maddy. It's three months now since we spoke."

"Shoot," Maddy says, sipping muscatel from a mayonnaise jar. "I heard tell of a lady whose husband got turned

into a toad by the Devil. This was one mean-lookin'
married toad. He was ugly. Now the lady, she was cryin'
and screamin'. She cursed that toad a blue streak. Paid it
no never mind. An angel of God appeared and he say,
'Don't be 'fraid, chile. Hold onto it, girl.' And this lady
believed. She grabbed that warty toad. Right away, it
turns into a hyena. But she don't let go. The hyena turns
hisself into a rattlesnake. She kept squeezin' that tail.
Derned if the snake don't become a piece of red-hot iron.
But she don't drop it. The pain was somethin' fierce. She
fainted dead away. When she woke up, there was her
husband lyin' by her side, fresh and friendly as a May
mornin'."

"Don't you think I did the right thing, Maddy?"

"Marriage just like that toad, George. You gotta hold
on to find out what you got."

"I'm coming."

"Not yet," Sally grunts, her body moist with sweat.

"Don't come if you don't want to," Mom says. "See if I
care. But spiritualists have helped bigger men than you,
Mr. She-Can't-Do-This-To-Me."

Sally's body trembles. She jolts up and down. "Wait for
me!"

One. Two. Three. Four. Five. Six. Seven. Eight. Nine.
Ten. Eleven. Twelve. Thirteen. Fourteen. Fifteen. Sixteen . . .

"Sixteen replies," Mom says. "And one pervert."

She hands me a letter.

Dear Box 222,

I'm a stud with hot blood. I'd like experi-
ments with experienced ladies. If you want
pleasure while waiting for a partner, I could be
a gold mine.

V. Angell.

"I'm coming," Sally moans. "Oh, God!"

"For God, for coun-try, and for Yale." Still singing, we
wave our handkerchiefs at a defeated Harvard across the
football field.

I hear myself snoring.

A breeze cools my aching body.

"Thirty-eight—twenty-four—thirty-six," a voice
whispers.

"Who is it?"

"Thirty-eight—D."

"Rita?"

"I saw everything. You were ruthless."

I can feel a nightgown beside me in the bed. "I'm not
opening my eyes, Rita. I won't be tempted."

"Don't you know when a girl's telling you she's in love?
I'm yours, George, to have and to hold."

I put the pillow over my head.

"You passed the test, George. You've tamed me." Rita

tries to poke her head under the pillow. I hold it tight around my ears.

"I've seen you soul-kissing, hugging, lying in bed with guys. You're a cocktease."

"George, that's just the movies."

"You've been married five times. You don't know the meaning of the word 'faithful.' "

"Those kids call themselves fans! They turned you against me. You never noticed the pockmarks. Nobody's perfect."

"You had your hairline lifted."

"If I tell you about the voice-overs, if I confess that, will you forgive me? Will you let me love you?"

"I want a noble love. A distinguished love. A unique, devoted love. Pure and unbetrayed. What about the voice-overs?"

"I was dubbed, George."

"You mean that perfect pitch, that sultry and intimate Lady-Is-a-Tramp sound, that comforting mental Muzak which keeps my nose happily at the grindstone isn't you?"

"JoAnn Greer in *Pal Joey*. Anita Ellis in *Gilda*. But the body, George, that was mine."

"You disgust me. Get thee behind me, Rita."

The window bangs shut. It's quiet again.

I open my eyes.

"Cold?" Sally says, standing over me and rubbing the shoulders of her nightgown. "You slept like a log."

"I was making progress. I was cleaning the attic."

"You really banged those bedsprings, Steve McQueen. I thought we'd busted the lapel-mike pinned to the sheet. But we're OK. The fidelity's great."

I sit up on the edge of the bed. I feel the stubble along my jawbone. "Fidelity's important."

"Laugh if you want," Mom says, fitting his picture back

in the Tiffany frame on her coffee table. "But James. C. D. B. Childress is a man of great powers. He's the reason I'm feeling so good. I swear by him."

"You sound like you're in love."

"He's an educated man," Mom says. "His last book, *Medium with a Message,* has been optioned by David Susskind."

"You're so girlish again."

Mother lounges on the sofa. "I'm telling you, George, it's like a happy ending. I walked in his door. And the first thing he said to me—it was uncanny—he said, 'You've been through a lot, Mrs. Melish. You've been hunting for answers and you haven't yet found them?' He really understood."

"And did he give you answers?"

Mom lowers her voice so Maddy can't hear from the kitchen. "He told me things about your father, George, that nobody but me could know."

"Like what?"

"He said Sol wanted his second pair of false teeth thrown out. Now, how did James know I kept that second set in the closet and hadn't been able to face getting rid of them? He said Dad wasn't angry with me trying to date other men. But now I can talk to Sol, I'm not worried about remarrying."

"Did you tell Dad about me?"

"James said Sol was sorry about Irene. You let her boss you around too much, he said, and you shouldn't lower yourself by begging her to come back." Mom stops and chuckles to herself. "Dad also said, 'Never run after a bus or a girl, there's always another one coming.' I'm glad heaven hasn't spoiled his sense of humor."

Mom stands up and comes behind my chair. She massages my shoulder blades. "He brings peace of mind, George. You really should see him. I asked your father why he had frightened me so in the early days after the funeral, shaking my bed like that, yelling at me so I couldn't sleep. Sol said he just wanted me to know he was there."

"It costs a fortune to go to this man."

"But he gets results. Last week, it was like a miracle, I asked Sol if his first wife—that little hustler—ever got to heaven. Sol said no, and anyway, I was the one. I was his love. He said he'd be waiting for me when I took my step."

"I go around talking to myself, explaining to myself. I have all these memories, Mom. But nothing fits. I feel this incredible anger. If I could just see Irene and talk to her."

"James works on a principle of love. That's how he makes contact with the other world. I was very nervous today. I wanted to know if Dad liked the clothes I'd bought. You know how Sol is about clothes."

"And what did he say?"

"James said, 'He likes your red dress.' "

"But Mom, you didn't buy a red dress."

"Sol means my blue."

"I'm seeing spots."

"That was my flash attachment," Sally says, counting the sixty seconds before opening the back of her Polaroid. "The kids got a lot of good sleeping footage. You looked cute with the pillow over your head."

"Can I have my pants now?"

"They're going to dub our voices over the slow-motion shots of your nightmare. The tossing and turning will look very Ken Russell."

"It wasn't a nightmare. Just growing pains."

The timer buzzes. Sally opens the camera. "This will be *Celebration*'s final image."

Sally gives me the picture. My head's in my hands. My

eyes are pink. My boxer shorts are crunched into my crotch. My legs are ashen.

"We wanted the most truthful shot we could get for the freeze-frame," Sally says. "The kids left it up to me."

"This picture's a lie."

I tear it up.

Sally kneels down to pick up the pieces. "That was very selfish of you, George."

"I'm going to simplify things from now on. I'm going to be a little selfish."

"And boring."

"The one thing about anger, Sally, it's never boring."

"All that stuff you were muttering about 'a noble and distinguished love.' I was lying awake, thinking about it. Maybe we could make it as partners, George. But I'd have to be happy in my career, too."

"That Polaroid developing fluid sticks to your fingers. It smells like formaldehyde."

"La Grande Horizontale could be true to a man who took care of her. I'm a real talent, George. All I need's a push."

"At Merton, if girls stayed after midnight when the gates closed, I'd help them over the west wall. The college put glass and grease on top of the wall. I'd throw my jacket or a blanket over it. I'd give them a push. My things always got ruined. Some way, I'd always get hurt."

Sally sits beside me and presses her bare feet against mine. "It wouldn't hurt to give me a berth on a soap opera."

"And when I gave Irene the girl Friday job, what did I get for my kindness?"

"I'm a professional, George. All I want's a chance to raise the level of mediocrity."

"I've always shown women every kindness. Bought them flowers. Taken them dancing. Remembered their birthdays. Kept my hands off when they balked. I'm tired of being pushed around."

Sally reaches under the bed and pulls out a large loose-leaf notebook. "Look at these notices. I can act, too. Don't think you're doing me a favor. You'd be damn lucky to get me in that fourth-rate collection of Actors Studio pouftas."

"I've really got other things on my mind."

Sally grabs my chin and makes me look her in the eye. "Is there another woman?"

"It's none of your business."

"That's why you were so distant tonight."

"I didn't say anything."

"You used me to get your rocks off."

"You've been the guiding light, Sally. You've helped me to see things."

"There's another woman, isn't there?"

"Maybe."

She squeezes both my hands. "George, my need is greater than hers."

"I have to think of myself."

"Is she as experienced in bed?"

"Technique isn't everything."

"Is she younger than me?"

"Dante's Beatrice was nine."

"I'm young at heart, George. I have a girl's craving."

"Petrarch's Laura was twelve."

"You're trying to humiliate me, is that it?"

"Inspiration has nothing to do with age. Edgar Allan Poe married a fourteen-year-old."

"So did Jerry Lee Lewis," Sally says, "and it ruined his career."

I stand up. Outside, the sky is an early-morning gray. "My hands have an odor. Your perfume is all over me. Who was it who said, 'No scent is a virgin'?"

"You're talking in riddles, George. Are you asking for your walking papers?"

"Just my pants."

There they are—my kids, my strangers.

They were so easy to bring into the world. A few sighs and squirts in the dark. And when they came out, shriveled and pink, I thought they looked like Irene. Then, later, I could see myself in them, especially Tandy, who has my nose and mouth. I had nothing to do with it, really. Neither did Irene. Nature's plan. Handsome, healthy, happy—after all, I'm one-tenth of one percent.

Lying here on the bed, their faces smudged with icing from my birthday cake, they look like Halloween trick-or-treaters. But they'll never go begging. With each genration, the idea of struggle gets farther away. They'll have money and manners and the charm that comes from being loved. They'll be vaguely grateful. I'll be a picture in their wallet. A card at Christmas. A summer job.

Let them wear Irene down—demanding, whining, asking questions only a father could answer. Soon, she'll be dowdy and bedraggled. I'll be fresh. I'll be beautified by memory.

They'll have to learn to share me with my projects. George, Jr., won't mind, he's got so many hobbies to occupy him. Tandy's the problem. She's the possessive type. She'll want more of me than one month a year spaced out in dribs and drabs. And she'll want me to herself, the little minx. She'll be prettier than Sue Kelley and tougher to tame.

"So, it's the cover girl, is it?" Sally says, barging into the bedroom and tossing me my pants. "Miss Suzy-Floozy, or whatever she's called."

I step into my dacron pants. The thighs are damp, but there's no trace of blood.

"I'm not just another pretty face," Sally says. "I'm a woman of promise and feeling."

I stare at the kids. They sleep curled up and content like cats.

"Don't give me the silent treatment, George. I heard. I know."

"I saw Sue Kelley a few days ago wheeling a baby carriage down Madison Avenue. When I dated her, strangers used to come up and congratulate me for my good taste. Sometimes on the dance floor, when we'd be twisting, I'd catch sight of faces watching us. People couldn't take their eyes away. 'Lucky dog,' they were thinking."

Sally peers down at the kids. Their chocolate fingerprints stain the bedspread. She hurries into the bathroom. "I'd be on call twenty-four hours a day, George. When I'm not on a script, I'd do your sewing—everything. That'd be part of our understanding."

"She used to have that emaciated-model look. But she's filled out. Her calves are like drumsticks."

Sally comes back with a washcloth and basin. "You've got to think of the children."

" 'I've been thinking of you, Sue,' I said. 'I clipped your wedding announcement in the *Times*. I found your number in the phone book. We always said we'd get together after we were married. I'm separated now.' "

Sally inspects the bedspread. "There's chocolate over everything."

"Sue smiled at me. A vacant smile, but welcoming. 'I've been remembering the old days,' I said. 'Do you still have my letters? I'd like to read them.' 'Letters?' she said. 'I burned them when I got married. My husband never knew.' "

"No respect for private property," Sally says, wiping the bedspread. "It's a disgrace."

" 'Call me tomorrow,' she said, patting my hand. 'It's great to see you again, Gordon.' "

"Who's Gordon?" Sally says, looking up from her scrubbing.

"That's what I'd like to know."

Tandy turns over in her sleep.

"How'd she get chocolate all over her dress and knees?" Sally says.

I take Sally's washcloth. "Keep out of this."

I pull back Tandy's dress and, gently, wipe the chocolate off her knees. "Better to love than be loved. Better to console than be consoled."

"You don't give a damn about other people."

"Call my secretary this afternoon. She'll take care of you."

Tandy's eyes blink open. She sits up and gives me a kiss.

"What's my name?"

Tandy puts her forehead against mine. We both shut our eyes, then open them. "Owl Eyes," she laughs.

"She loves her father." I turn around, but Sally's left the room.

"From now on, sweetheart, call me Pooper."

Sitting by the bedroom window, Sally watches us leave. George, Jr., is propped up in my left arm with his Indian headdress draped over my shoulder. Tandy closes the front door.

I don't want a Vargas girl or a *Playboy* bunny. They're mass-produced masturbation. Who needs dream-walkers carving up your cerebellum in their stiletto heels and garter belts? I'm beyond black rubber and bare buttocks. Tumescent titties and latex longing—you can't escape them. You've got to defeat them. Every ad, every pop painting, every billboard, every book jacket shoves boobs in your face. There's no end to the temptation that awaits the man alone. Cocktail waitresses aren't perky maids anymore, they're costumed to conquer—nipples like bullets, legs as lethal as laser beams. I've even eaten off tables sculpted in the shape of a woman's backside. I've thrown my hat on a coatrack replica of Marilyn Monroe. These objects shine. The surfaces are tempting. They arouse a man's sense of touch. They're exhausting. I'm a liberal guy, but the boundary between art and life must be maintained.

George, Jr., pulls my hair. "Where are we going?"

"Home."

"What about the adventure?" he says, punching my back.

"We're living to fight another day."

George, Jr., starts to cry, "Daddy . . ."

"His name's Pooper," Tandy says, taking my hand. "That's what Peter and I call him."

George, Jr., gives me the secret handshake. He promises not to squeal to Irene. He pulls the blanket over his head.

I tiptoe back into Tandy's room. She's sitting in her nightgown on a chair beside the bed. Her legs are crossed. She's wearing one of my old hats.

"C'mon, honey. No games. Time for bed."

Tandy leafs through the *Yale Alumni Magazine* she picked up in the garage as we snuck upstairs. "There'll be no good night kiss, Miss Tandy Melish, until you're in bed," she says, in her deepest voice.

"Pooper?"

"In that bed," Tandy says. "Make it snappy."

I play along and lie down. My falsetto voice squeaks. "My one and only."

Tandy giggles and then recovers her seriousness. "I'm a busy man. My name is George, it just so happens. I wrote this."

"My rainbow. My darling."

Tandy yawns and takes off my hat. She puts it on the bedpost. Tired of our game, she hands me the magazine and gets under the sheets. The cover story is "Co-education at Yale: The First Five Years." I flip quickly to the Class Notes. Tandy snuggles close. "Read it, Pooper," she says.

George Melish
Director of Programming
ABC
1330 Avenue of the Americas
New York City 10019

LITERATI. When it rains, it pours. I didn't know so many of you out there were trying to be creative. Bad news for all you fifties pud-pullers. Dr. F. ("Fritzy") FERNBAUER has come up with a debatable thesis in his book—blatantly called *Sex*. Says Fritzy, salting his medical prose with scare headlines like "Sex Manuals May Harm"—"Books showing positions for sexual intercourse not only fail to help improve sex-life—they do harm. By focusing the attention as the neurotic does on the act itself in its external manifestations . . . it may well urge people toward that objectification and that exertion of the will on sex which belongs in the brothel." As one husband who's enjoyed the fruits of matrimony over the years, I object strongly to being termed "neurotic" because, like all men wanting to please their partners, I consulted Dr. Eustace Chesser and Dr. E. van Loewen. Fritzy's book is tailor-made to the Sexy Seventies.

THUMPER TAFT's exhaustive study of Vietnam, *Waist-deep in the Big Muddy* is certainly an indictment. I've dipped into it, and there's a very long, touching account of the late SANDY VAN MEGS, who was instrumental in designing the Scrambler grenade which, in a freak accident, killed him. "Thumper," who was king of the "Happy Hour" at Zeta in his day, has some unhappy things to say about technology, but I'm glad to report he doesn't rough up the TV boys. We did play a part in stopping the war that "Thumper" and his crew started.

On the lighter side, VICTOR ANGELL has left the photography racket to join BILLY WADS-WORTH at BBD&O. This doesn't mean "Angie" has cut out the cheesecake. He and "Wads" have put out their answer to the Pirelli calendar—*Boys in the Buff.* Angie is Mr. August. I wish we'd all stayed as trim and had such fun.

Also a note from Professor FIELDING WILLIS accompanying his *After the Ball Was Over: A Pictorial History of the Yale-Dartmouth Bladderball Contests.* "I never expected to be in print before you," Fielding writes. Well, F.W., while I'm not writing books myself, a lot of my projects have been made from them and I reach a larger audience than Shakespeare.

I turn toward Tandy. "Shakespeare was the greatest writer in the world."

She's fast asleep.

Carefully, I unlock Irene's door. She and Fred are nuzzled together like pigs in a pen. I think of Tandy's innocent sleep. She lies as pale and perfect as a madonna. Tucking her in, I could feel the glow around her body. How can Irene claim I don't appreciate women?

Dr. Chesser was wrong. It was never Love Without Fear; it was always Fear Without Love.

The engine purrs. I let it warm up, leaning my head on the neck rest, closing my eyes.

The smell of Sally's body has vanished from my fingertips. Irene's face fades out of memory. I feel a geyser of effervescent words stirring inside me. A new generation awaits its teacher. There's a whole vocabulary of romance to be rediscovered, debased endearments to be purified. Tenderness will be reborn.

Top down, sweet air making my head swim—I honk my horn like a newlywed as I streak down the empty road. I rename the car "Galahad."

On the George Washington Bridge, I glance downtown. The visibility is perfect. The peaks of the skyscrapers dazzle in the morning sun.

I can be the Knight of Faith—ardent, strong, strenuous, pure. I can wage war without fighting a battle. The heart can't recover what is lost, it can only shift tactics. This is the Siege Perilous.

At a stoplight on Ninety-sixth Street and Columbus Avenue, a placard in a storefront window catches my eye.

HATHA YOGA—

DO THE DEED,
SAVE YOUR SEED.

"For he who keeps or takes back his seed
into his body, what can he have to fear of death?"
                                        —*Upanishads*

I take a picture of Tandy out of my wallet and pin it to the inside of the car's sun visor.

A beautiful brunette in an evening dress hurries into her apartment on Central Park West, checking her wristwatch as she pushes open the door. I know what that chippie's been up to. But I don't imagine her nude. I don't see myself straddling her from behind with my mammoth tool. There's not even a palpitation in my heart or an itch in my groin. When you're faithful, you see other women in a different way.

I turn on the radio. Another golden oldie, only today I feel as young and invincible as when I first heard it.

I sing along with Bobby Helms.

> *"You are my special angel.*
> *Sent from up above . . ."*

How sweet it is! It'll be like the old days. The thrill of small pleasures—holding hands, leg occasionally brushing leg, the smell of perspiration and perfume. It'll be true nobility—suffering without reward. I'll plow my new electricity back into work. I'll be a dynamo—

> *"The Lord sent down his angel*
> *To guide my way to love . . ."*

I feel full. I feel alive and blessed.

> *"You are my special angel*
> *Through eternity . . ."*

This is what was missing when Irene asked me to marry her—background music.

> *"You are my special angel,*
> *Heaven sent you to me."*

I turn south toward the office. I pull the visor down. Tandy's face smiles on me. Let Irene have her divorce. I have her daughter.

FAWCETT CREST
BESTSELLERS

CENTENNIAL *James A. Michener*	V2639	$2.75
AFTER THE LAST RACE *Dean R. Koontz*	Q2650	$1.50
THE ROMANOV SUCCESSION		
Brian Garfield	X2651	$1.75
LADY *Thomas Tryon*	C2592	$1.95
GOD AND MR. GOMEZ *Jack Smith*	X2593	$1.75
GLORY AND THE LIGHTNING		
Taylor Caldwell	C2562	$1.95
"HEY GOD, WHAT SHOULD I DO NOW?"		
Jess & Jacqueline Lair	X2548	$1.75
YEAR OF THE GOLDEN APE		
Colin Forbes	Q2563	$1.50
BED/TIME/STORY *Jill Robinson*	X2540	$1.75
THE ART OF HANGING LOOSE IN		
AN UPTIGHT WORLD *Dr. Ken Olson*	X2533	$1.75
THE PROPERTY OF A GENTLEMAN		
Catherine Gaskin	X2542	$1.75
BREAKHEART PASS *Alistair MacLean*	Q2431	$1.50
THE LAUNCHING OF BARBARA FABRIKANT		
Louise Blecher Rose	X2523	$1.75
TWO-MINUTE WARNING		
George La Fountaine	Q2529	$1.50
THE HOUSE OF A THOUSAND LANTERNS		
Victoria Holt	X2472	$1.75
A LONG WAY, BABY *Grace Lichtenstein*	Q2474	$1.50
THE MILLIONAIRE'S DAUGHTER		
Dorothy Eden	Q2446	$1.50
VOYAGE OF THE DAMNED		
Gordon Thomas & Max Morgan Witts	X2449	$1.75
CASHELMARA *Susan Howatch*	C2432	$1.95
THE SNARE OF THE HUNTER		
Helen MacInnes	Q2387	$1.50
THE TURQUOISE MASK *Phyllis A. Whitney*	Q2365	$1.50
TUESDAY THE RABBI SAW RED		
Harry Kemelman	Q2336	$1.50

FAWCETT

Wherever Paperbacks Are Sold

If your bookdealer is sold out, send cover price plus 35¢ each for postage and handling to Mail Order Department, Fawcett Publications, Inc., P.O. Box 1014, Greenwich, Connecticut 06830. Please order by number and title. Catalog available on request.